My Heart Belongs

in the

Superstition
MOUNTAINS

My Heart Belongs

in the Superstition MOUNTAINS

*Carmela's
Quandary*

SUSAN PAGE DAVIS

BARBOUR BOOKS
An Imprint of Barbour Publishing, Inc.

© 2017 by Susan Page Davis

ISBN 978-1-68322-007-7

Adobe Digital Edition (.epub) 978-1-68322-295-8
Kindle and MobiPocket Edition (.prc) 978-1-68322-296-5

This book is a work of fiction. Names, characters, places, and incidents are either products of the author's imagination or used fictitiously. Any similarity to actual people, organizations, and/or events is purely coincidental.

All scripture quotations are taken from the King James Version of the Bible.

Series Design: Kirk DouPonce, DogEared Design
Model Image: Susan Fox/ Trevillion Images

For more information about Susan Page Davis, please access the author's website at the following Internet address: www.susanpagedavis.com

Published by Barbour Books, an imprint of Barbour Publishing, Inc., P.O. Box 719, Uhrichsville, OH 44683, www.barbourbooks.com

Our mission is to publish and distribute inspirational products offering exceptional value and biblical encouragement to the masses.

 Member of the
Evangelical Christian
Publishers Association

Printed in the United States of America.

Chapter One

April 28, 1861
Tucson, New Mexico Territory

You get out there, and I mean now." Uncle Silas glared at Carmela, his white eyebrows nearly meeting over his thin nose.

"I don't think I can do it." Her voice broke.

"Of course you can. You had it word-perfect last night."

Her breath came in shallow gasps. She brushed back a strand of hair with a hot, moist hand. Carmela was frightened. Ma and Pa would never have made her do anything like this. But they were gone now, and Uncle Silas was in charge.

She peeked around the doorjamb. The large room was filled with noisy people, all except for the clear space at the front, where she was supposed to go and stand.

"It's all men," she choked.

"No, it's not."

She peeked again and spotted a few women with their hair piled on top of their heads or hanging down in braids. A few ranchers and merchants had brought their wives, but by far the majority of the people packed in were men.

One woman seated between two men in the front row wore a

bright yellow dress with a plunging neckline. The stage driver had told her uncle that Tucson was home to about eight hundred people, and more than half of them were Mexicans. But this territory was part of the United States now, so more and more Americans were moving in. She wondered if every single American in Tucson had turned out for this performance.

"I'll go out and introduce you again," Uncle Silas said. "Then you'd better come out."

His menacing voice made Carmela shudder. She supposed she would have to do it. He had said they would earn some money tonight and that it was a way for her to repay him for coming all the way from Massachusetts to fetch her.

The army captain and his wife who had housed her for nearly two months at Fort Yuma after her parents died were complete strangers, and yet they had been kinder than Uncle Silas when he arrived to take her home.

He strode out before the crowd that had jammed into the biggest saloon in Tucson—the largest space they had available indoors.

"Ladies and gents," he said, holding up a hand. The assembly quieted. "I think you will understand my niece's reticence. It is only a few weeks since she was rescued from her ordeal among the savages, and she has not met a crowd this large or been expected to tell her story to half so many people." He always said that, although it was a lie. Carmela's parents had died nearly three years ago.

"I ask you to hold your applause and remain quiet," Uncle Silas went on, "not only so that you can hear her soft voice but so that you don't frighten her. Remember, she is not used to loud noise. After what she went through, yelling and clapping might sound to her like an approaching battle. I have assured her you mean her no harm, so please give her your attention but restrain your enthusiasm. Without further ado, Miss Carmela Wade."

She pulled in a deep breath and stepped into the doorway. A smattering of controlled applause greeted her. She walked slowly across to stand beside Uncle Silas. The room grew very quiet. She could hear their breathing. A hundred or more eager faces gazed at her, hungrily taking in every detail of her simple dress, leather leggings, and braided hair, but especially the ugly black and blue designs on her face. She could see pity in their eyes. A few women's faces convulsed as though the sight of her revolted them.

Uncle Silas put his hand on her back and pressed against the layers of her clothing.

"H–hello," she said.

A great sigh went up from the audience.

"Go on, my dear," Uncle Silas murmured.

She shot him a quick glance. *My dear?* She didn't think he considered her dear, unless it was for the money he hoped she would earn tonight.

He nodded and smiled encouragingly. She looked away, toward the woman in the daring yellow dress. Her black-rimmed blue eyes surveyed Carmela eagerly.

"I. . ." Carmela choked in another breath, trying to remember the new, more elaborate script he had given her to memorize. "I was with my parents, going across. . .to California. We had been with some others, but they went off on a different road. My father said we could make it the rest of the way ourselves. We were nearly there. . .he said. I don't know how far we had to go."

The people had relaxed on the benches and chairs, as though settling in for a good tale. She hoped she could remember it all. At the same time, she wanted to scrub it from her mind and run out the back way.

Lies, all of it.

Carmela didn't think she would mind speaking to crowds so much if what she said to them were true. She hated being the center of attention, with the bright lanterns shining in her eyes and the people staring at her, then opening her mouth to lie.

The people smelled. The fumes of liquor assaulted her, and the whole place reeked of sweat. This rough border town was full of men—rugged, rude, and in some cases half-drunk. She spotted another woman, brightly dressed, with raven hair and dark eyes. Her gown was of shiny red material, with black lace at the throat and wrists. She was wedged in between two men, and both of them were staring at her.

The pressure from Uncle Silas's hand on her back increased. He was poking his fingertips into her spine.

Carmela opened her mouth and continued the story, all of it false, about her family's trek across the desert, being separated from their traveling companions, and being ambushed at night by a pack of howling savages. As long as she kept speaking, Uncle Silas left her alone.

Her chest hurt with each breath, but once she got into the next part, about life in the Indian tribe, it was easier. She pretended she was telling a story and that no one really believed it was true. She told about the plants she had helped gather for food and how the woman in whose tent she slept gave her only small portions to eat and whipped her if she did not work fast enough. She hated accusing someone of evil they didn't actually do—but the Indian woman wasn't real, so perhaps it wasn't too vile of her.

"One day a small group of soldiers came to the village." The audience was silent, waiting for her next words. She tried to remember the story she had memorized. She didn't like this part. "As always when strangers came to the camp, the savages hid me. But it was too late. One of the soldiers had seen me."

The crowd listened eagerly as she recounted the tale of her rescue. Her voice choked as she told of her joy at being returned, tempered by the sorrow of knowing her parents had been murdered by the vicious Indians. Her face felt hot, and she wanted to bathe it in cool water. And she wished she could scrub off the horrid ink markings Uncle Silas had so painstakingly drawn on her chin and jaw. At first she hadn't believed they would get away with this, or why Uncle Silas would want to. But it had been more than two years since he arranged her first speaking engagement, and she knew he wouldn't let her stop now that her speeches were a paying enterprise.

When she finished her recital and said, "Thank you," tears streamed down her cheeks. The people applauded enthusiastically. Some of the women, and a few of the brawny men, wiped their eyes. Her uncle came to stand by her and held up both hands. The room seemed to shrink and press in on her.

"Thank you, kind people," Uncle Silas said. "I've heard my niece tell the story of her ordeal many times, but it still moves me."

He allowed questions for about fifteen minutes, and Carmela had to respond to them. This part frightened her, because she had no idea what they would ask. For the most part, people wanted more details about the ambush and her time in captivity. She tried to make it sound as realistic as she could, but she had to invent some details about the work the imaginary Indians had forced her to do and the living arrangements she supposedly had with a Mojave family.

"What did you use to tan the deerskins?" one man called out.

"I—I don't know." She glanced at Uncle Silas.

"Most likely it was brains," he said. "Isn't that what the savages usually do?"

Brains? Really? Whose brains? Carmela thought she would be sick. Uncle Silas would probably make her learn all the details about that next.

"Did the redskins hurt you bad?" the woman in yellow asked.

Uncle Silas said firmly, "My niece suffered wounds as well as many indignities and humiliations. We ask that you not press her too closely for details. There are things she needs to forget."

Carmela knew her cheeks were flaming.

Finally it was over. She turned and walked quickly out the back door of the saloon. Her uncle had told her to stay with him through the final applause, but she couldn't stand to be in there another minute.

The cool night air helped some, but her lungs still felt squeezed. She flopped down on the wooden steps in the shadow of the building and sobbed. How could Uncle Silas say such things about her and make her say them, too? It wasn't true, any of it, but she couldn't deny it. If she didn't say her piece word-perfect and reply to the people's questions with the answers he had formulated, she would pay dearly for it later.

Her tears came faster, and she put her head down, burying her face in her skirt, and wept.

Hesitant footsteps jerked her upright.

"Are you all right, miss?"

He was a boy, not much older than she was, standing in the alley between the saloon and the mercantile next door. His pale hair gleamed in the moonlight, almost white, and curly.

She sniffed and wiped her face with her sleeve. "Yes, thank you."

"Are you sure?" He stepped closer. "You're her, aren't you?"

"Wh–what?"

"You're that girl that the Indians stole. I saw the handbills, but my brother wouldn't give me a dime to go and listen to you."

Fresh tears bathed Carmela's face. "I'm glad he didn't."

"Why? Don't you want people to come to the show?"

She shook her head vehemently. "I wish there wasn't any show."

"Do you not like speaking to people?"

"It's awful."

"Why did you do it, then?"

"I have to," Carmela blurted, before she thought of the consequences.

The boy frowned and peered closely at her. "Here." He thrust a crumpled handkerchief into her hand.

She hauled in a ragged breath. "Thanks."

"My name's Will."

She wiped her face and looked up at him. "I'm Carmela."

"Can I help you somehow?"

She shook her head. "No one can help."

"Why not?"

Carmela looked over her shoulder at the closed door behind her. She was forbidden to speak to anyone about her circumstances, but she would explode if something didn't change. Uncle Silas had told her that he was now her legal guardian. Unless a miracle happened, she would have to answer to him until she was twenty-one—another seven years.

"My parents are dead, and my uncle—he's in charge of me. I have to do what he says."

"Even if you don't want to?"

She sobbed and clutched the handkerchief to her mouth. She gave a quick nod.

Will stood before her, shifting from one foot to another. "Look, I'm going to get my brother. Wait here. He can do something."

"No, don't do that. He couldn't possibly—"

"He's a deputy marshal."

Carmela stared at him. Could a deputy marshal get her out of this mess? She doubted it. Uncle Silas avoided lawmen whenever possible. She had a vague idea that what she and her uncle were doing was illegal. "I don't think that's a good idea."

"You wait."

Will turned and ran up the alley then dashed around the corner of the building. As he ran, the door behind Carmela opened. She knew without looking that Uncle Silas stood in the doorway. She could smell his hair pomade and feel his displeasure.

"There you are. Come on. We have to get our things. We have a stagecoach to catch. We'll do this again in the next sizable town."

Carmela's heart sank. He had made her tell the story in every town they stopped at on this never-ending journey. The white-haired boy and his brother could do nothing.

Freeland McKay ducked as the drunken man swung at him. He let the cowboy windmill around and gave him a push toward the saloon door. The man sprawled over one of the poker tables. The four men who had been sitting around it grabbed their drinks and stood hastily, moving toward a corner of the room.

As Freeland stepped over and cuffed the drunk's hands behind his back, the man moaned and began to struggle.

"Take it easy, Burle," Freeland said. "I've got a nice quiet place for you to take a nap. Let's go." He hauled the man to his feet and marched him toward the swinging doors.

"Thanks, Deputy," the bartender called.

"Anytime."

The prisoner stumbled as he lurched onto the sidewalk outside, and Freeland grabbed his arm to steady him. "This way."

"Free! I need you."

He turned toward the voice. His kid brother, Will, charged across the street and bounded onto the boardwalk. "Come quick!"

"What is it?" Freeland held firmly to the prisoner's forearm.

"The girl at the Green Bottle—the one who spoke tonight. She's crying." Will gulped in a quick breath.

"Crying? What about?"

"I'm not sure, but she said her uncle makes her do stuff she doesn't like."

Freeland frowned at him. "What kind of stuff?"

"Make speeches, mostly. At least I think so."

"Did he strike her?"

"I don't know. Don't think so. But I told her you could help."

"You want me to go talk to a girl who's crying? And nobody's hurt or anything?"

"Well. . ." The boy eyed him anxiously in the lamplight spilling from the saloon door behind Freeland. "She was awful upset."

"Was anyone else upset?"

"I didn't see anyone else."

"Hey, take these things off me," the prisoner yelled, jerking away from Freeland.

"Burle, take it easy," Freeland said.

Instead, the hefty man lurched down the sidewalk and fell flat on his face. A string of profanity issued from his mouth.

"Will, I need to get this man over to the jail," Freeland said. "Once I've got him locked up, maybe I can go with you and see what this business is all about."

"But she might be gone. He'll make her go inside. Please, you have to come now."

Freeland stopped and glared at his brother. "I can't. This is serious business. You run ahead and open the jail door."

Will opened his mouth as if to argue but then turned and raced down the boardwalk. Burle had risen and lumbered down into the street, and Freeland went after him.

"Come on, fella. This way."

Ten minutes later, the drunk was sleeping on the cot in the jail's one cell, with the handcuffs removed and the door securely locked. Will waited impatiently near Freeland's desk.

"All right," Freeland said. "Show me where you found this girl."

Will raced ahead and across the street, dodging around the people streaming from *la Botella Verde*. Freeland quickened his pace and followed him around to the back of the building. Will had pulled up short at the rear entrance.

"She was right here," he panted. "She was sitting on the steps, crying her eyes out."

No weeping girl sat there now. Freeland sighed and tried the back door, but it was locked. He knocked briskly, and a moment later the door opened.

"Oh hi, Marshal," said Stanley Dittmer, who had booked the performance and hoped to build a theater in town soon. He was dressed in his best clothes, as though the saloon were a fine concert hall. "Can I help you?"

"Where's the girl who spoke tonight?"

"She and her uncle left ten minutes ago. They were going on toward California tonight."

"They already left?" Will's voice cracked.

"That's right, sonny."

"Are they taking the stage?" Freeland asked.

Dittmer nodded. The Butterfield would be pulling out about now, westbound. "You might catch 'em if it's important."

Will whirled and dashed down the street toward the next corner. The adobe that served as a stagecoach stop wasn't far away.

"Thanks." Freeland followed his brother with long strides. When he turned the corner, he could see that the yard in front of the stage stop was empty. Will had pulled up short at the edge of the street. A lantern shone inside the small house where the station agent lived. Its light spilled out a window, illuminating Will's doleful face.

"They already left."

"I'll speak to Isaac." Freeland had frequent business with the station agent, and he had no qualms about knocking on the door. The news was as he'd feared, and he returned to his brother.

"The stage pulled out as soon as they were on it. We're too late."

"She needed help." Will kicked a pebble across the street.

Freeland laid a hand on his shoulder. "I'm sorry. If it had been something serious, Mr. Dittmer would have helped them before they went."

"It was serious. She was crying. If you had just hurried a little faster—"

Freeland sighed. "I can't be everywhere at once."

"Maybe you could—"

"I'm not riding after the stage, Will. My job is here, and there's nothing we can do for her now."

"That's what she said. Nobody could do anything. But I told her you could."

"You shouldn't have told her that. You had no idea what the problem was. Maybe she was missing her folks. Didn't I hear that Indians killed her parents?"

"I guess so. But I don't think that was it."

Freeland stopped at the corner. He didn't like to think of all the possible wrongs that could have been done to the poor girl, but he couldn't ride out of town and pull her off a stagecoach when he had no evidence of a crime. "I've got to go back to the jail and stay there tonight. You get on home or Ma will be worried about you."

Will shoved his hands into his pockets and trudged away, his shoulders drooping. Freeland gazed after him for a moment, wishing he really could have done something for the girl—and for his little brother. Fifteen was a hard age for a boy with a big imagination, especially when there were so few damsels in distress to rescue.

Freeland liked his job. Sometimes he did get to help people. The worst thing about it was that he couldn't always right the wrongs. Tonight he had chosen to detain a man who was endangering people and property, rather than try to help a girl who was weeping in an alley. He ran through it in his mind once more, but he didn't see how he could have done both. But had he chosen right? He headed for the jail, sending up a silent prayer for a girl he had never met.

On the boardwalk outside the building, he paused. A young man was racing down the boardwalk.

"Marshal!"

"What is it, Len?" Freeland asked.

"Mr. Stiles said...to come and tell you..." The young man panted. He was a helper at one of the saloons.

"Is there trouble at the Double Cactus?"

Len shook his head and caught his breath. "A fella rode in from Maricopa. Said we're at war."

"What?" Freeland stared at him. "With who? Mexico?"

"No, the Union. Southerners fired on a fort in South Carolina."

"When?"

Len shrugged. "Dunno. A couple weeks ago maybe."

"Well, if that don't beat all. Thanks. And let me know if you hear anything out of Albuquerque or further east."

War again. This one had been brewing for a while, he supposed, but he'd hoped it wouldn't come to this. And would it matter way out here? South Carolina was a world away. Freeland sighed and plodded toward the jail to check on his prisoner.

Chapter Two

May 1866
Tucson, Arizona Territory

armela scanned the audience during the introduction. She hadn't been in the Southwest since before the war. Tucson was part of the New Mexico Territory then. Now it was part of the new Arizona Territory. The town had grown considerably, but the architecture still followed Mexican tradition, as mud was the building material that was cheapest and most readily available. La Botella Verde was gone, though plenty of saloons still lined the main street, and the new theater took pride of place.

She remembered a boy who had tried to comfort her in the alley out back of the old saloon. The towheaded lad hadn't been able to do anything for her, but she had not forgotten his tender heart. Many times over the years she had thought of Will and his assurance that his brother, the deputy marshal, could help her. Would he still be living in Tucson? She searched for a man with curly blond hair, knowing her heart would recognize him should she see him again. But no one in the audience fit the mental picture she cherished—the young paladin who had cared about her distress.

"It's been more than ten years since my niece was rescued by cavalrymen," Uncle Silas was saying. Carmela hoped none of them did the arithmetic too closely. They had last been here five years ago, just two years after her parents had died. Her uncle had adjusted the timeline after they hurried eastward at the outbreak of the war. He said people would be more sympathetic if they thought she'd been captured at a young age.

"She has been able to readjust to her life in our world, but her memories are still fresh, and she will tell you about the privations and brutal mistreatment she suffered under the hands of the heathen."

Carmela gritted her teeth. As she grew older, Uncle Silas embellished her life story more and more. He seemed to think the people wanted to hear about violence and abuse, while Carmela preferred to talk about how the tribes made their clothing, the plants they used for medicine, and the way they crafted their household goods. That was boring, Uncle Silas insisted, though she must know those things in order to sound authentic. But the crowds wanted to know how badly the savages had treated her, and if she expected people to pay good money, she would have to give them what they wanted.

She made it through the performance once more, and the audience seemed enthusiastic in their applause and kind words to her, but she couldn't shake off an uneasiness that had shadowed her since they rode the stagecoach into Arizona. When she was here five years ago, she had been young and naive. Now she scarcely believed they got away with the lies. People traveled more, and here in the Southwest were many people who had contact with the Indian tribes. How could they not know she told falsehoods? Her fear was that she would slip up and someone knowledgeable would expose her.

They stayed overnight in Tucson this time. They would take a stage in the morning, heading north for Prescott, the territorial capital in the wilderness.

They would have to share the coach with whatever passengers and freight the driver took on. Since the beginning of the war, the Butterfield Overland had suspended its regular runs through the Gadsden Purchase. But communication was needed between towns like Tucson, Yuma, Prescott, and Albuquerque, and so several men had jumped to open new lines. Service was reported to be sporadic, and the vehicles weren't as easy riding as the trains in the East or the Concord coaches Carmela had become familiar with. But Uncle Silas was sure they would make a lot of money in Prescott, where Carmela had never before appeared.

♥

At their early breakfast, Uncle Silas ate heartily but had no kind words for Carmela.

"You've got to put more feeling into it." He frowned as he reached for another biscuit.

"I'm sorry." Carmela immediately regretted the words. Why must she apologize for lying without enthusiasm? She cut a bite of pancake with her fork and put it in her mouth, which gave her an excuse not to talk.

"People want to see the fear and sorrow in your eyes when you tell about your mistreatment."

This was a perpetual complaint of his, but she shrank from sensationalizing her supposed treatment by the natives. She swallowed and said, "I didn't hear anyone complain."

"It was a full house," he noted. "I don't expect they get a lot of entertainment in these parts, since they're under the Reconstruction government. I shall be surprised if Arizona becomes a state anytime soon."

Carmela had heard tales of the Confederates' short-lived formation of their own Arizona Territory in these southlands, one reason the federal government had chosen to build the new capital farther north. That and the minerals that had been discovered up there. The valley around Prescott reportedly swarmed with miners. Since she didn't presume to know much about politics, Carmela seldom expressed her opinions on anything. If she did, Uncle Silas would correct her.

When they finished eating, her uncle grudgingly paid two Mexican boys a half dime apiece to carry their baggage to the stage stop, a nondescript adobe on a side street. Behind it was a large corral with several horses eating their feed from a trough. Any grass inside the fence was long gone.

Their "coach" waited in the yard—a modified farm wagon with benches fastened down on each side of the bed and a rolled-up canvas top.

"Morning!" The station agent, a lanky, windblown man in his forties, greeted them. "Heading for Prescott."

"That's right." Uncle Silas had paid him the day before for their passage.

The driver was greasing the wheel hubs, and the shotgun rider frowned at Carmela's trunk. He packed their suitcases close behind the driver's seat and tied them down. Four horses were hitched to the wagon. They languidly swung their tails to keep the flies moving. To Carmela, they didn't look very enthusiastic about pulling the loaded coach twenty or thirty miles in the desert sun.

The agent gave her a hand up. She climbed on the little stool he provided, grasping his hand, and awkwardly stepped into the wagon bed. She sat down on one of the side benches, behind the driver's seat. As was customary, Uncle Silas would sit beside her so that no strangers could get too close to Carmela. Ordinarily, she would cover the lower part of her face with a fascinator or a shawl, but the heat was already intense and would probably be unbearable by noon. No shawls today.

Carmela disliked travel on principle. Locomotives were noisy and smoky, and as often as not she ended a rail trip with holes in her skirt from flying cinders. But they were comparatively swift, and she could open or close the windows and take a berth for the night on some trains. In this wagon, she would be exposed to the elements, and there were no berths.

Other passengers were boarding—two men who appeared to be ranchers and a bearded fellow with a canvas carryall, a bulging burlap sack, and a bundle of mining tools. They sat in a row opposite Carmela and gazed without apology at her tattooed face. She instinctively put a gloved hand over her chin, though she knew she couldn't sit that way all day. When people saw her chin, they always stared, but she had to wear the hated tattoos. It was all part of her story. She couldn't spend the entire trip covering them. Slowly, she lowered her hand but avoided making eye contact with any of the men.

Uncle Silas stayed on the ground to make sure the luggage was all loaded and secured. Her trunk of stage costumes was loaded last, partly blocking the tailgate, where people had to get in and out. The shotgun rider and station agent hefted it in, muttering to each other. Uncle Silas scowled at them. After all, he had paid a premium for the extra luggage.

He climbed in at last, and Carmela passed him his cushion before he sat down next to her. She had bought small seat cushions on the advice of a woman in Albuquerque, where she had performed more than a week ago, and she was glad to have them now. The plain wooden benches would jounce and pound them mercilessly. This wagon didn't even have the leather thorough braces that Concord coaches had, to let the passengers sway gently on the coaches' frames instead of bouncing continually.

To her surprise, when she had thought they were nearly ready to leave, a man wearing a badge entered the yard. A second man walked beside him, chained to his left wrist. The lawman looked young for one of his career. He had a pleasant face, if a bit careworn.

Carmela caught her breath and stared at him. She was nearly twenty now, and this man looked a few years older than her, perhaps as old as twenty-five. He couldn't be Will, her champion. Or could he? She knew she ought not to stare, but she was sure she saw a bit of pale hair, bleached almost white by the Arizona sun, peeping out from beneath the broad brim of his hat.

He spoke to the station agent then had the prisoner climb up before him. Awkwardly, they both scrambled into the wagon bed then squeezed around Carmela's trunk and the pick and shovel. They sat down with the marshal next to Uncle Silas and the prisoner on the end. The three men opposite turned their attention to the new arrivals, allowing Carmela a moment's peace. She was glad the lawman wasn't seated opposite her. Staring back would be far too big a temptation.

He and the prisoner adjusted their positions, settling in for the long ride, and she exhaled heavily. He was not Will, she was sure. But she remembered he had said his brother was a deputy marshal—one who could help her. Was this man Will's brother? And could he still hold the same job after the chaos brought on by the war?

She had hardly noticed his prisoner, having only a fleeting impression of hard eyes and scruffy beard. But his warder, the lawman—now, there was a handsome man.

Uncle Silas leaned toward her and whispered, "We need to go over the bit about when the tribe was in its winter camp, but I guess we'll have to wait until our next hotel. I didn't figure on so much company on this part of the trip."

Carmela nodded but said nothing.

One of the men across from them said, "Morning." He grinned, exposing a gap in his tobacco-stained teeth.

Carmela smiled back and nodded. Despite their rude stares, she was glad for the men's presence. They would keep Uncle Silas from discussing the finer points of her recitals during the trip.

♥

"All right if we board first?" Freeland asked Dwight Herder, the stagecoach driver, after their first stop. They had paused for fifteen minutes at a way station and were about to resume their northward journey. The two ranchers had left them, but they were adding two more miners and a freighter going north on business.

The driver scratched his chin through his graying beard. "Prob'ly a good idea. Get the prisoner settled before the other passengers load."

Freeland nodded to the felon handcuffed to his wrist. "Get in. Sit toward the front of the wagon." He extended his left arm so that Rudy Dix could navigate the climb without too much trouble. While he didn't like being handcuffed to his prisoner, Freeland considered it prudent while traveling.

The tight quarters of a stagecoach for the journey invited close scrutiny. At least if he had Dix in a corner between the side and front end of the wagon, he would have more control over the man's interaction with other passengers.

Of necessity, he followed Dix closely and sat beside him on the left-hand bench. He hoped no more passengers arrived. They already had six, besides him and Dix. The miners and the freighter were the usual variety in these parts. He hadn't gotten a good look at the couple earlier, but when they had disembarked at the way station, he had noticed the markings on the young woman's face. The man was older and well dressed. Freeland wondered about them.

The two climbed in and took the seats they had occupied before, now directly opposite him and Dix. Perhaps he would learn more about her.

He was glad the canvas was rolled up, so the air wouldn't be so close in the stage. Before they'd left Tucson, he had insisted that the prisoner wash himself thoroughly and had provided him with clean clothing. A man who had been cooped up in a cell for a month wasn't the most pleasant company under ordinary circumstances, but squeezed into a stagecoach with half a dozen other people, it could get right distasteful.

"I liked it better on the other end," Dix said.

Freeland scowled at him. "Hush. You're fine right where you're sitting." He had let the prisoner stroll about for a few minutes at the stop, knowing he would be confined for a long, long time when their journey ended. But Dix was known as a violent man, one who would resort to any means he could to escape justice. Freeland felt safer when they were sitting in the wagon and nobody was moving around.

The other four men took their seats, and Freeland hoped that was the lot of them. He tried not to stare at the young woman across the way. The man beside her didn't appear to do anything to assure her comfort—quite the opposite. She was the one who took charge of the seat cushions and offered him a clean handkerchief from her handbag.

Her father, perhaps? He looked to be forty-five or fifty, and his thinning hair was oiled with something that smelled more pungent than the girl's scent. He studied their fellow passengers with a sharp eye.

All of the men stared at the young woman, and Freeland let his gaze drift back to her. His stomach knotted at the sight of the dark geometrical markings on her chin. Tribal tattoos, but the girl was definitely white. He'd heard of a few Indian captives who had been tattooed, and one stood out in his mind. Was this the girl who had come to Tucson five years ago and spoken about her captivity? If so, she would be the same girl his brother had begged him to help.

He had almost forgotten about that girl, until he'd seen handbills around town advertising her "return appearance" this week. It had to be her. He had meant to go around to the theater last night and see if he could meet her, but the goings-on at the saloons and the newly opened dance hall had kept him busy. So this was the maiden Will had wanted him to rescue.

If he stared at her eyes and ignored the tattoos, he could imagine her face without the disfiguring ink. She had grown into a beauty. Her brown eyes retreated behind down-swept lashes. Beneath her hat, her glossy brown hair caught a glint of sunlight. No wonder Will had been so taken by her. She seemed poised, and Freeland was pretty sure she was not still in need of rescuing.

The coach swayed as the driver and shotgun messenger climbed to the box. With a slight jerk, they set off.

The older man leaned toward the young woman and spoke to her in low tones. Freeland seemed to recall Will saying that her uncle traveled with her. He must be her guardian. He figured they were nearly forty miles out of Tucson, and this was desolate territory into which he was taking her. Did it pull up unpleasant memories for her?

As they rolled along, traveling into barren land populated only sparsely by Indians, Dix relaxed and closed his eyes, leaning back in the corner of the seat. Freeland, however, became more alert. The sooner they reached Prescott, where Dix would be tried for his crimes, the better.

Chapter Three

$\mathscr{A}$t the third way station, they stopped long enough for all of them to eat a hasty meal. It wasn't much—beans, cornpone, and fried bacon, but it filled their stomachs.

To Freeland's relief, all of the passengers except the young woman and her guardian were leaving them. The tenders switched out the canvas-covered wagon for a sturdier rig. He puzzled over its shape and then realized it looked like the ambulance wagons used during the war. The owner must have found a bargain somewhere.

Freeland felt easier with fewer fellow passengers. Dix had behaved himself so far, not causing any trouble beyond the ordinary discomforts Freeland experienced when shackled to a felon. The seats were more comfortable, and they had a solid roof over their heads. They sat as before, two facing two. The sun was high, and the temperature had risen to where it would be unpleasant if they were jammed too tightly together.

The older man spoke up as soon as they were underway again. "I'm Silas Holden, and this is my niece, Carmela Wade. It seems we are to enjoy each other's company a bit farther, gentlemen."

Freeland nodded. "I'm Deputy Marshal McKay, and this is Dix. Heading for the capital."

"Ah." Holden eyed the short chain that linked them and said no more.

After a nod of acknowledgment, Miss Wade gazed out her window, looking ahead and to the side of the trail. Freeland let his thoughts wander. He'd be home in less than a week. He hoped so. A lot could go wrong while he was away.

About an hour had passed when the young woman spoke. "Those mountains are striking. Is there a name for them?"

Freeland leaned past Dix and looked. Off in the distance, several stark mountains seemed to jut up suddenly from the harsh land. He had ridden out there a couple of times, chasing thieves who thought they might be a good place to hide.

"Folks call those the Superstitions, ma'am."

Her eyes flickered. "What a charming name. May I ask how it came about?"

Freeland shrugged. "Because of the Indian tales, I suppose. The Apache say there's a hole in those mountains that leads to the underworld. The wind that blows all the time through here and causes sandstorms comes from there, if you believe it."

"How interesting."

Encouraged, Freeland went on. "The Pima have a legend, too. They say there was a great flood. One of their shamans was saved from drowning by making a hollow ball out of spruce gum. He and his wife stayed in it during the flood and landed on top of Superstition Mountain—the big one there."

Miss Wade's delicate eyebrows arched. "A native Noah?"

"Something like. They say that after they climbed out of the gum ball, they were the parents of all the Pima who live here now." There was a lot more to the tale, but Freeland couldn't see spinning it out all afternoon.

Miss Wade smiled. "Thank you for telling me." She adjusted her hat and settled against the back of the seat. Freeland didn't suppose anyone could sleep in this heat, what with creaking and bouncing over the desert, but soon she appeared to be doing just that. Her guardian slouched as well, letting his hat slip down over his brow, and Dix leaned back in the corner. He was soon breathing regularly, except for an occasional snort.

Freeland stayed alert. Dix was the sort of man who would feign sleep and take advantage as soon as you quit paying attention.

A bugle blast jerked him to alertness three hours later. Some of the drivers carried horns and sounded them to announce their arrival.

"We must be getting to the station," Miss Wade said.

"It's about time," Holden replied. They had barely spoken during the journey, and Freeland supposed his presence and Dix's had muzzled them.

They drove up to the low adobe building, but no one waited in the yard. No tenders came out with fresh horses. The driver, Dwight Herder, climbed down and opened the door.

"Folks, I don't know what's going on here, but something doesn't feel right. The station agent usually meets us and has a fresh team ready. I suggest you all stay in the stage while Tom and I check on things."

Beside Freeland, Dix stirred and yawned. "Got troubles, have we?" He extended his arms to stretch his muscles, and Freeland's left arm went with them. Holden stared at the handcuffs. Miss Wade turned her face toward the window.

Dwight shut the door, and the passengers all looked at each other.

"I hope nothing's wrong," Miss Wade said.

Holden leaned past her to peer out the window. "Just relax. I'm sure everything's fine."

"Will we be in Prescott by nightfall?" she asked.

Holden hesitated, so Freeland said, "No ma'am."

Dix sat up straighter. "We going up Black Canyon?"

Freeland shook his head. "Wickenburg way. It's a little longer, but it's easier and more traveled. We won't be there much before dawn, but I expect we'll get our supper at one of the way stations." *Barring any serious trouble*, he thought. Their driver was right—something felt out of kilter here.

"So, we'll reach the capital tomorrow?" Miss Wade persisted.

"Yes ma'am; that's the plan. Most likely not long after noon," Freeland said. He'd made this trip before, and the schedule was loose of necessity.

Through the window, Freeland saw Dwight walking back to the coach. He opened the door.

"Well, folks, the station seems to be deserted. Now that's not good. If outlaws or hostile Indians are active in the area, it may be a while before we can get to the next stop." He eyed Freeland keenly, and Freeland nodded.

Silas Holden scowled at the driver. "We're going on with these horses? Shouldn't we hole up here and wait for someone else to come through?"

"No sir," the driver said. "I don't recommend that. Tom and I are bound to keep moving if we can. Besides, the next stage won't come along for two days."

"Are there any horses here?" Freeland asked.

"Nary a one, so we can't replace our team. This one's tuckered out. We're going to water them and give them a half hour of rest, and then we'll go on. I'm sorry there's no meal waitin' for you, but the necessary is out back. Just keep your eyes open, folks. Tom and I think we're alone here, but we could be wrong."

The shotgun rider stood guard outside the outhouse while each of them took a turn inside. Miss Wade emerged with her cheeks flaming. Freeland had to accompany Dix inside, which was no treat. When they came out, they found Miss Wade and her uncle near the well.

"The driver brought us a tin basin, so we could wash up," Miss Wade said. "And the well water is sweet. That in the bucket is fresh."

"Thank you, ma'am," Freeland said. Somehow, he and Dix worked around the handcuffs to wash their hands. Freeland lifted the dipper to drink, and Dix managed with his left hand.

They waited uneasily in the shade of the station building, exchanging only a few words and watching the road. The shotgun rider climbed to the roof for a vantage point but came down after a few minutes, saying he would bake to a crisp if he stayed up there.

Finally, the driver hitched the team up again. Freeland wished he had the free use of both hands and could help him. The crusty man fastened the last line, took his hat off, and wiped his brow on his sleeve.

"All right, folks. Let's get out of here."

They boarded and settled into the same seats they had held before, with Miss Wade and Holden facing Freeland and Dix. Freeland's stomach felt hollow, and he hoped it wouldn't rumble loud enough for the other passengers to hear. He ought to have put some jerky in his carryall.

Dwight set the horses off at a slow jog. "It will take us twice as long at this pace," Holden said after a mile or so.

"Maybe so," Freeland conceded. The driver was no doubt saving the horses in case he needed a burst of speed.

"This man going to prison?" Holden nodded toward Dix.

"His trial is in Prescott."

Holden nodded. "They need to build railroads out here. Railroads and telegraph wires."

"I expect that will take a while," Freeland said, gazing out at the empty desert. Now that the war was over, there was no money to build things like railroads. The West needed time to recover.

"I had to write months ahead to schedule my niece's performances in the major towns, and we'll have to set up additional ones along the way if we hope to pay our expenses."

Little more was said over the next two hours, but at last the driver halted the team without blowing a blast on his horn.

Smelling smoke, Freeland put his head out the window. The remains of a building smoldered in the twilight.

The driver jerked the door open. "Looks bad, Marshal."

"They've burnt the station?" Freeland asked.

"Looks that way. We'll take a look-see. You folks wait."

Freeland nodded and touched the butt of his revolver.

"Maybe you should get loose of me," Dix said.

Freeland didn't even glance his way. "You'd like that, wouldn't you?" Dix chuckled.

Freeland watched intently as Dwight Herder and Tom, the shot-gun rider, cautiously approached the ruin. When Tom leaned over something on the ground, Miss Wade caught her breath. At the same instant, Freeland realized what Tom had found.

Miss Wade turned away from the window, her gloved hand at her lips. A few minutes later, the driver came to the coach.

"Two men dead. There's one fellow who's still alive. One of the tenders here. He said they were attacked by a large band of Apache."

Miss Wade gasped and looked not to her uncle but to Freeland, her eyes wide and her lips trembling.

"What do you want to do?" Freeland asked.

"We have to go on."

"Should have stayed at that last place," Holden said.

"I say we go on." The driver looked hard at Holden. "If we wait here, we're targets."

Freeland wondered if the stage was carrying a payroll in its treasure box. Keeping a somewhat arbitrary schedule didn't seem enough for Dwight's urgency. But surely they would have a military escort if they were carrying valuables. Whatever his reasons, the driver seemed determined to get them to safety. That was probably best for the girl.

"What about the horses?" Freeland asked.

"We'll have to rest them again. Four hours, at least. I suggest you all try to sleep."

"If you can find a secure place for me to handcuff my prisoner, I'll help you bury the dead," Freeland said.

"Fair enough, and I thank you." Herder turned away.

Holden looked at the rest. "Well, I'm getting out. I'm certainly not sitting in this box for four hours while the horses graze."

He climbed down. "Come on, Carmela." He handed his niece out of the coach.

"Well?" Dix demanded.

"We wait until the driver finds a place for you."

"Oh, come on, McKay! Where am I going to run to?"

"I don't know, but I don't want to find out."

They sat another five minutes, until the driver returned. "There's a couple of wheels off a wagon you could cuff him to. I doubt he could drag them far."

Freeland tugged Dix's arm with the handcuffs. "Come on."

They walked behind the burned-out station, to where the driver had found the wheels. Freeland eyed them dubiously and took out the key with misgivings.

"Where we going to be working?" he asked.

"Yonder, I reckon." Dwight pointed near the corral fence, half of which had been destroyed by the fire.

With his help, Freeland positioned the wheels and ran one handcuff through the spokes of both. He fastened Dix's wrists together and left him there, cursing.

Freeland and Dwight met up with the shotgun rider near the coach. He had unharnessed the team and picketed them.

"We found a few supplies," Tom said. "Most of it's ruined or stolen, but they must have dropped some. I asked Miss Wade if she and her uncle can put together something for us to eat when we're finished."

They had also found a usable shovel in the rubble. Freeland, Herder, and Tom took turns digging as darkness fell. They had just finished burying the two dead men when Mr. Holden came toward them.

"The last one's died, I'm afraid."

Herder sighed. "I don't suppose you'd take a turn with the shovel, Mr. Holden?"

"I fear my heart wouldn't stand it." Holden walked away.

"I'll do it," Freeland said.

Tom picked up the shovel. "You had the last turn. You two go fetch him over here. And make sure he's really dead. I don't trust that dandy's judgment."

He was dead all right. Freeland took a letter from the man's pocket. If it was from family, he might be able to get word to them that their son had died.

At last it was done. They walked back to the stagecoach. Someone had started a small fire between it and the corral. Apparently Holden had found enough fuel for Miss Wade to cook some bacon and a passable cornmeal mush, which she prepared in a blackened pot.

Dwight brought a lantern from the stagecoach, lit it, and hung it on the side of the coach to give them more light while they ate.

Freeland watched the young woman with interest as she used a paddle to dip out a portion of mush onto a tin plate. She was quiet and competent, wasting no motions. Was this her natural attitude, or had she learned this serene efficiency in her time with the Indians?

She brought him a serving. "I'm sorry we have no flatware, Mr. McKay."

"I'll manage. Thank you." He looked toward where Dix was man-acled to the wheels. "Do you have some for the prisoner?"

"My uncle took him some earlier, though he didn't wish to."

Freeland smiled at that. The skin on his lips cracked. "I'm glad he took it, not you."

"I would have, if he'd refused."

"You have a kind heart, Miss Wade."

It wasn't the tastiest meal Freeland had ever had, but it filled his belly. It felt good to be free of the prisoner.

"Might as well rest," Herder said. He lay down on the grass beyond the blackened fire line and closed his eyes.

Freeland walked out of the circle of lantern light, over to where he'd left Dix. The prisoner appeared to be sleeping, and the handcuffs were still doing their job. It seemed a good time to catch a few winks, but Freeland ambled around the grounds instead, watching the horizon. Tom was also watchful, while Holden sprawled in the grass and Miss Wade had taken refuge in the stage. Freeland put out the lantern to save fuel and resumed walking.

On his fitful rounds, he stopped once to talk to Tom.

"What do you figure our chances are, really?"

Tom squinted toward the black bulk that was the distant mountains. "Depends on if the next station's been hit. We can't go much farther than that with these horses. We'll have to stop there—or somewhere—longer if we can't get fresh animals."

Freeland nodded.

"I don't like it," Tom said.

"None of us do."

Tom spat in the grass. "I'm glad you're along, Marshal."

"I'll be right there with you if you need me."

Tom nodded then eyed him keenly. "Just between you, me, and the hitchin' post, we're carrying gold. The stage line took pains to keep it quiet, but that treasure box is about full."

Freeland was silent for a moment, considering that information. "You couldn't get an escort?"

"Nope, nary a man."

"You're sure nobody knows about it?"

"Can't never be sure. Someone might've heard us requesting a detachment. But the Apache don't know. They wasn't who we was worried about when we set out."

"Trust God we don't have to deal with them."

"Besides that, I allow Mr. Holden's carrying a lot of cash. They had a big audience last night."

"You're right. Let's hope those Apache have moved on." Freeland walked toward the roadway, thinking and scanning the horizon all around, where the dark earth met the edge of the star-strewn sky. The treasure box was no doubt bolted to the floor of the driver's boot, which made it harder to steal. If they did fall into an Indian attack, he would try to save the people first, not the treasure, that was certain. But he might not have the chance to save either.

Two hours later, Tom roused the sleepers. While he and Dwight hitched the team, Freeland once more cuffed himself to Dix and took him to the coach. Miss Wade and her uncle were already inside.

They rode in silence, with the horses walking most of the way. The night wore on as the coach creaked and rattled over the road.

Miss Wade sank low on the seat, and her eyelids drooped. Such a pity her face was so disfigured. Freeland's mind wandered back five years. What had made her cry that night? She seemed fine now. He wished he could tell Will he had seen her. He dozed fitfully, even though he didn't mean to.

A distant shout came from outside, jerking him awake, and gunfire erupted. Dwight yelled to his team and popped his whip. Dix sat up, blinking.

"What in tarnation?"

Miss Wade's huge eyes glittered in the gray before dawn. "We're under attack!"

Carmela tensed, gripping the handle of her purse with one hand and a leather strap hanging near the door with the other. The coach rocked and jerked as the tired horses lumbered along. Gunfire cracked right over her head, and she assumed Tom, the shotgun messenger, was returning the interlopers' fire.

The deputy marshal drew his sidearm and leaned over to see out his window, pulling his prisoner across the seat with him. Uncle Silas braced himself and pulled out his wallet. He withdrew a sheaf of paper money and shoved it down his boot top, leaving only a few bills in the wallet, which he then stuck back into his inner coat pocket. She didn't have to ask why. They had been robbed once before after a performance, and Uncle Silas lost his entire wallet full of money. Now he carried the bulk of their proceeds in a money belt at his waist and enough for immediate expenses in his wallet. Even so, he wouldn't want to lose more than was necessary. He would give the outlaws only enough to convince them he wasn't holding back.

Carmela's right hand went instinctively to the hem of the fitted jacket that matched her traveling dress. The rolled up bills she had sewn into it before they left New England three months ago were secure. If the worst happened, they would not be utterly destitute.

The prisoner's shrewd gaze was on her, and she jerked her hand away. She must be more careful.

"Indians or outlaws?" Uncle Silas asked grimly.

"I'm thinking outlaws," McKay replied.

Carmela wondered on what he based his conclusion. Was it the sound of the guns or the lack of wild war whoops?

The shooting continued around and above them. What would they do if the outlaws shot the horses? Her hand ached from clinging to the leather strap.

"Giddup!" The whip popped again, but the coach was slowing.

Crack!

McKay had fired his revolver out the window, and the sound exploded inside the coach. She clapped her hands to her ears and sent up a silent prayer for mercy.

The stage slowed even further, and a heavy thump sounded on the roof above her. She looked to Uncle Silas in alarm. He had produced a tiny gun from somewhere within his clothing, a derringer he had purchased in Boston during their wartime travels.

"Steady, my dear," he said. "I'm sure—" His eyes flew wide open, and his mouth rounded into a silent exclamation. He dropped the gun and clamped his hand to his side.

"Uncle Silas!" Carmela leaned over and pulled back the folds of his coat. Blood seeped between his fingers. "No, no! Uncle Silas!"

She looked across at the deputy marshal, who was hurriedly reloading his revolver.

"My uncle is shot."

"I'm sorry, ma'am." He sounded tired.

Carmela raised her chin and looked out the window. The coach was no longer moving.

Chapter Four

*T*hrow yer guns out!"

Carmela flinched. McKay looked over at her and then outside.

"Hurry up," came the gravelly voice.

The deputy hesitated but then tossed his revolver out. Carmela could scarcely believe he had given up so easily.

The door was yanked open. It flew back and banged the side of the coach.

"Git out." A man holding a revolver squinted in at them, his eyes dark orbs above the bandanna covering the lower part of his face. Just behind him stood a second man with his rifle trained on Deputy McKay.

McKay climbed slowly down the step and waited while Dix followed him.

"Well, well," the first robber said when he saw the handcuffs. "You got another peashooter, Deppity?"

"No," McKay said.

"Then just git you over there."

The large man leaned into the coach, his bulk throwing the interior into deeper shadow. "Lookee here. Get out, lady."

"My uncle is hurt," she protested, determined to stay with Uncle Silas.

"I said git out."

"I can't."

"Sure you can." He grabbed her ankle and yanked her toward the door.

Carmela gasped and grabbed the sides of the opening. "Unhand me, you brute!"

"Take it easy, J. J.," the second outlaw said. He was standing back but pointing his rifle toward her.

The one called J. J. let go of her but stared at the expanse of leg he had revealed. Carmela glared at him and pulled her skirt down as she sat in the doorway of the coach.

"How dare you?" She made her voice as scathing as possible.

"Git out," J. J. repeated.

Resigned to obey, Carmela eased out the rest of the way and climbed down unsteadily. The sooner they gave these thugs what they wanted, the sooner she would be able to help Uncle Silas.

Deputy McKay, who stood with Dix, the two of them with hands in the air, shot her a sympathetic look. Her head started to whirl when she realized a third robber was holding the pair at gunpoint, and Tom, their shotgun rider, lay lifeless on the ground. She turned to look for Mr. Herder. He was up on the driver's box, his empty hands skyward. Another masked man held the lead horses' heads, and a fifth one was climbing up beside the driver.

She looked again toward McKay. Would any of them survive this? She suspected Tom was dead, and Uncle Silas had a serious wound, perhaps mortal if they didn't get him aid soon. The deputy didn't return her gaze. He was too busy watching the road agents, maybe counting their weapons and figuring their chances at zero. At least, that was Carmela's impression. Five armed men versus a disarmed driver, a young woman, and two able-bodied men chained together. Deputy McKay must be frustrated beyond belief. If he weren't shackled, he might be able to do something, but she couldn't count on him.

She resigned herself to losing her belongings.

"Stand over there," J. J. said.

She walked over on shaky legs and took up her stance beside McKay.

"You all right?" he murmured.

She nodded. He was talking about physical wounds, not insults.

J. J. pulled a sugar sack from his pocket and opened its mouth. "Drop your money in here."

"I got nothin'," Dix said.

McKay worked his free hand into his pocket and brought out a couple of silver dollars. He dropped them into the sack.

"Got a watch?" J. J. asked.

McKay shook his head.

"Your turn." The outlaw moved in front of Carmela, holding out the small sack. She opened her handbag and put the three dollars and change she had carried in it into his bag without making eye contact.

"Jewelry?"

She hesitated then reached up with trembling hands to unclasp the chain of her necklace. It wasn't very valuable, just a piece of pretty turquoise she had bought in Tucson. She found it hard to breathe, let alone undo the tricky hook. Would they leave when they had it, so that she could rush to Uncle Silas and tend his wound?

"Hey," the robber on the stage cried, and a gun went off. Two more reports followed. Her hands still on the clasp at the back of her neck, Carmela was shoved rudely to the ground. She landed in the dusty red clay and lay still for a moment, her heart racing and her ears ringing.

Sounds of a door slamming, harness creaking, and hoofbeats reached her.

"Throw him off," a man yelled.

She sat up and stared toward the stagecoach. It was moving swiftly away, in the direction they had been heading. She supposed one of the outlaws was now on the box, because the driver lay in a heap a few yards from her, where the coach had stood a moment ago. Three horsemen raced after it, one of them leading a riderless horse.

"Mr. McKay!" She shoved herself to her feet and whirled toward him, but Dix was bending over the inert form of the deputy.

"Is he shot?" she asked.

Dix flicked a glance at her. "He's right bad, miss."

The outlaws must have shot him, Carmela surmised. Either he or the driver had made a move of resistance. McKay had probably tried to distract the other robbers when the driver pulled a hidden gun, and was shot for his pains. There was no one left to help her.

"My uncle!" She hoisted her skirts and ran after the coach, terror driving her. "Stop!"

They were too far away, and she knew they wouldn't stop for her anyway. She stood gasping as the sun rose in splendor. Rivulets of sweat rolled off her forehead and mingled with her tears.

Slowly, she turned and walked back toward Dix. He was patting the deputy's pockets.

"Help me with him, missy."

"What can I do?" She approached cautiously, dashing a tear from her cheek.

Dix straightened with something in his hand. Carmela stared at it. A derringer, just like Uncle Silas's. She looked into his flinty eyes, and a flash of understanding passed between them. Dix had scooped up Uncle Silas's gun when it fell to the floor of the coach and McKay was distracted, either by the outlaws outside or his reloading.

She swallowed hard. "Did you shoot him?"

"No ma'am, not me. In fact, I don't think he's shot at all."

How could that be? But if it was true, maybe Dix wouldn't shoot her either.

"You've got two good hands, missy. The deppity's got the key to this bracelet in his pocket. Get it out now."

His voice was smooth, almost slimy.

She shuddered.

"Why should I?"

"Because I can't do nothin' chained to him. He's dead weight."

Still she hesitated.

"And because I'll kill you if you don't. Now, come closer."

She clamped her teeth together. "You back off."

He laughed and then moved back as far as he could from McKay, his cuffed arm extended.

"I won't bother you if you do what I say. Go on." He waved the derringer a little, indicating for her to approach.

Carmela dropped to her knees beside the deputy. Her heart leaped when she saw his chest rise and fall.

"He's breathing."

"Course he is. He'll be all right in a while. But I'll be gone."

She began to take hope. If Dix ran off, who cared? She would stay here with McKay, and when he came to, they could figure out what to do. So what if his prisoner escaped? They would both be alive.

She patted McKay's pockets gingerly and felt the key in one. She reached in with two fingers, found a loop of string, and pulled it out with the dangling key.

Dix grinned. "Atta girl! And now, if you'll be so kind, unlock this side first."

Carmela wasn't sure this was wise. What if Dix broke his word? He could grab her as soon as he was free and do whatever he wanted with her. Handcuffed to McKay, he couldn't move very far.

"Now!" Dix aimed the derringer at her face.

If he killed her, he would eventually get himself unshackled, Carmela knew. Even if she first threw the key out of his reach, he could drag the deputy's body to it. She could run away with it, but where to?

Kneeling beside him, she fumbled with the key, trying not to touch Dix's hand. The bracelet clicked open, and she sat back on her heels as he pulled it off his wrist.

"What's that?" Dix raised his head and peered into the distance.

"What?"

Before she could rise and look where he was gazing, Dix bent and slid the empty bracelet over her own wrist. She caught her breath and tried to jump away, but he clicked it shut. He stood back and chortled, holding up the key.

"Well now, ma'am, you have yourself a pleasant mornin'." He swept off his hat and made a courtly bow, then turned away.

"What? Wait!"

"Sorry." He turned backward as he walked away from her. "I got a horse to catch."

Carmela stood and strained against the handcuffs and McKay's weight. In the distance, she could make out a saddled horse with its head down, looking for something to browse between the scattered cacti.

"Please," she called. "Don't leave me here like this. If he doesn't wake up, I could die."

"Someone will come out looking for us when the stage doesn't show up on the other end of the line," Dix said. "Adios." He walked toward the loose horse.

Carmela could do nothing but watch him. Her heart hammered, and fractured prayers began to form in her mind. *Heavenly Father, help us! Don't let him leave me here!*

Maybe that was the wrong prayer. Maybe she should be glad Dix was leaving.

The horse snorted and jerked its head up, eyeing the approaching man suspiciously. Dix paused and held out a hand toward it. The horse turned and trotted over a rise and out of sight. Dix plodded after it.

Carmela exhaled and looked around. The body of the driver lay about ten yards from her, and the shotgun messenger a little farther. From where she stood, she couldn't see any movement of breathing. McKay, on the other hand, let out a soft moan.

She knelt and studied his face. His lips were dry, and he took shallow, steady breaths.

"Mr. McKay? Deputy?"

His eyes remained closed.

She couldn't see any blood on him. Was Dix right, and he hadn't been shot? Then why was he lying here senseless? She pushed back his pale hair and ran her fingers cautiously over his scalp. On the left side of his head—the side that had been nearest the prisoner—he had a large, tender bump. She didn't want to hurt him further, but she probed it gently and took her hand away. No blood.

"That lowdown skunk."

She settled down to sit more comfortably. They could be here awhile. The sun had risen fully above the horizon now, so that way was east. They'd been headed mostly north, and somewhat west, toward Wickenburg. How long before the stage line's people there started a search?

Her stomach growled, and she rubbed it with her free hand. Twenty-four hours ago, they had been eating breakfast in Tucson. Would she ever see food again? She pushed back a lock of hair that had come loose from her updo. All of her extra clothing was gone, with the stagecoach and Uncle Silas. The small hat she had worn on the stagecoach wouldn't protect her from the sun.

She peered all about. Nothing moved. The vast panorama she had enjoyed earlier from her window now seemed harsh. She couldn't see anything edible, though an Indian might be able to find nourishment in some of the cactus blades or fruits. Even those were out of reach. With McKay at the end of her right arm, she was like a horse picketed in one place.

The authorities would want to know what happened, she told herself. She went back over the recent events in her mind. The ambush, the horses slowing down and stopping, the noises on the roof. Tom, the shotgun messenger, had been shot first. A stray bullet had come through the coach door and struck her uncle. Where was he now? As she reviewed things, she realized that the one outlaw who might have seen Uncle Silas was probably the one who had been shot in the final skirmish. The others had tossed him inside the coach and driven off with it. They might not even know they had Uncle Silas in there, too. What would they do with him when they discovered him?

For some reason, driver Dwight Herder had tried to make another play against the robbers, and they had shot him. That was when she was pushed to the ground. Who had shoved her? She was standing closest to the deputy. She looked down at his placid face. Had he meant to push her out of harm's way when the firing resumed? That noble gesture had cost him dearly, she decided. That must have been when Dix managed to get hold of a rock and hit him with it. He didn't shoot him, though he had the derringer. He didn't want to take any chances of being left attached to a dead man. He probably didn't want to use his only bullet up either. Things had turned out rather well for Dix, she decided.

Carmela shivered. Maybe she was the one who would wind up shackled to a dead man. She certainly hoped not. She wished she had some water to splash in McKay's face, or at least to wet his lips. Panic started to rise inside her, and she shoved it down. *Lord, let him live! And show me how to help him.* Losing her head certainly would not help.

She looked again toward where Dix had disappeared and thought about the horses. One of the road agents had driven the stagecoach when they fled. Why? Did they want the baggage? If they searched Uncle Silas's body, they would find his money belt. But were there other valuables on the stage that she didn't know about? A chest full of gold or silver coin would be too heavy to carry away on horseback. Maybe that was why the driver had tried to make one last stand.

That loose horse. . .it must belong to the outlaw who had been shot. It ran off, and they hadn't bothered to catch it, though they had led one horse away, probably the new stagecoach driver's mount.

The sun beat down on her. Carmela rolled from kneeling to a sitting position and arranged her skirt. When Mr. McKay woke, maybe he would know how to get the handcuffs off. If not, this could get downright embarrassing.

His breathing continued, slow and steady. Maybe he had slipped from unconsciousness into natural sleep. She touched his shoulder.

"Deputy McKay, can you hear me?" She shook his shoulder. "Please wake up."

No response. With a sigh, she drew her knees up, tucked her skirt and petticoats around her, and laid her free arm across her knees as a pillow for her head. She let her right hand rest on the ground, next to

McKay's shackled left hand.

The breeze from the Superstition Mountains might be what saved them. At least they wouldn't bake outright in the heat of the day. She closed her eyes and resumed her silent prayers. All she had now was the faith her parents had taught her so many years ago, and now it seemed very small. Giving in to exhaustion, she lay down on the ground next to McKay, being careful not to touch him.

♥

The sun stood high in the sky when she awoke. She lifted her hands, and the hot metal of the handcuffs seared her skin. She gasped and laid a fold of her skirt over the cuffs.

McKay appeared to be still sleeping. His face was sunburned, and she touched her own. Her skin tingled and burned beneath her fingertips. She leaned over and adjusted his hat so that it shaded most of his face.

She sat up and lowered her head to her knees again, in an attempt to shield herself from the sun's rays. Off and on, she whispered a sentence or two of prayer. How long could they survive the heat and the burning sun?

The breeze touched her, but it was not enough to offset the heat. Her right foot felt numb. Carmela sighed and shifted her legs. A few tattered clouds hung far in the west. She didn't suppose they would bring rain. She dozed off again.

Sometime later, she awoke. She jerked her head upright, aware of an ache in her neck. At the same moment, she heard hoofbeats.

She shrank instinctively, hoping to appear small. Would this mean rescue or terror? She hoped Dix hadn't caught the horse and come back. Unless, of course, he intended to unshackle them and help them get to civilization. With the escaped prisoner, a pack of robbers, and a band of marauding Indians in the area, she couldn't hold much hope for anything good.

She held her breath, peering toward the sound. It came from the direction of the craggy mountains, not along the rough road they had traveled. Perhaps she should play dead.

Too late. A brown-and-white horse was walking toward her, and on its back sat a rider. Carmela caught her breath and stared at him. An Indian, probably an Apache. He wore his hair loose, with a strip of cloth knotted about his brow, and he sat straight on the horse's back. He was magnificent. Carmela couldn't look away. He halted his mount just yards from her and sat for a moment, studying her.

The man swung his leg over the horse's withers and hopped down, landing lightly on his feet. He walked closer to her. Carmela trembled as he stood over her. He took her chin in his hand and frowned at her face.

She had nearly forgotten her tattoos. Could he tell at a glance they were fraudulent?

He spoke in low tones, a guttural language of which she understood not one syllable. She stared up at him hopelessly and shrugged, giving her head a little shake. He lifted her right hand and examined the handcuffs then keenly eyed the deputy. McKay was still out cold, and the badge on his chest glimmered in the sun.

The Indian spoke again and drew his knife, a long, cruel-looking blade.

Carmela gasped. "Please don't!"

Their eyes met, and the warrior gazed calmly at her for a long moment.

"Please." She hated the quake in her voice. "Please do not kill us. Some robbers left us here. I didn't do anything, really. A bad man put the handcuffs on me." She looked into his dark eyes, wondering if he understood.

He pulled McKay's arm up by the chain, and with his knife, made a slash in the air above the deputy's wrist.

Carmela's throat felt as though a boulder had taken up residence in it. This Indian would cut off Mr. McKay's hand in order to free her. And then what? Would he take her with him on his big paint horse?

She shook her head. "No, no! Please, don't do that. Don't hurt him. He's a good man. He wouldn't mean you any harm, I'm sure."

She pulled their chained hands to the ground and covered McKay's with her own. She looked straight into the Indian's eyes. "No."

He frowned and straightened then walked to his horse. She didn't believe for an instant that he would just ride off. She watched but couldn't tell what he was doing. Rummaging at something tied to his saddle, perhaps, which in itself surprised her. Didn't all Indians ride bareback?

He came back with soundless steps, carrying a leather bag about as large as a five-pound sugar sack. He thrust it into her hands. Its plumpness and the give when she squeezed it told her it was full of liquid. A water skin. She had seen them on their wagon train so many years ago, when her parents were alive.

The warrior pushed it gently toward her and nodded firmly. He walked back to the horse, leaped astride, and trotted off down the trail.

Carmela sat still, watching until she could no longer see him or the horse. Heat waves wriggled above the ground where he had passed. She listened until every whisper of hoofbeats faded. Tears flowed down her cheeks.

"Thank you," she whispered. She fumbled with the skin and found a plug. It wasn't a cork, but perhaps some dried cactus or yucca stem. She held the skin carefully and opened it then took a drink. The water tasted heavenly. She swished the second sip around to moisten her dry mouth.

McKay. She poured a little water into her free left hand and carefully dribbled it over his lips. He stirred and moved his mouth. She gave him a little more. He didn't awaken, but she was encouraged. Maybe a little more sleep was all he needed.

She plugged the opening in the water flask and set it down between them then lay down on the ground with her arm over her head.

Had she made a huge mistake and doomed them both to die? She couldn't think it would have been better to let the Apache mutilate McKay and leave him bleeding to death in order to save herself. They had a small amount of water now, perhaps a quart. She would make it last. She refused to think what she would do if McKay didn't wake up.

Chapter Five

Freeland woke, aware of the hard ground and pain in his head worse than when he'd tried to clean out Bill Halpern's saloon and one of the Mexican rowdies clobbered him with a tequila bottle.

He struggled to sit up, his left hand hindered by those confounded handcuffs. The skin on his face and the back of his hands burned. He blinked in the blinding sun.

Someone spoke. A woman. He scrunched his eyes tight shut, which hurt, and then opened them cautiously. One impression overcame all the others. He was no longer cuffed to Dix. It was that girl, the one with the tribal tattoos. Miss Wade.

"What happened?" His own voice sent a searing echo through his skull. He reached up to cover the place that hurt worst, hauling her arm along by the chain.

"We were attacked," she said.

"I know that." He started to nod and thought better of it. Best sit still while he lightly explored the bump that had risen just back of his temple. "Where's Dix?"

"He went off to try to catch the horse the outlaws left behind." She shook her head slightly. "How much do you remember?"

"Not much after the heist and us putting stuff in their sack."

"It was right after that," she said. "They started shooting again."

"Dwight." Freeland lifted his chin and looked around. "They got him, didn't they?"

Miss Wade nodded. "Him and the shotgun rider both. They're lying over there." She pointed with her free hand. "I thought you were shot, too."

"Something hit me," he hazarded.

"I'm guessing it was that Dix fellow. He'd got my uncle's derringer, and he made me take your key and set him free. Then he tricked me." She cleared her throat. "I'm sorry to say he tricked me and hitched me to you with the handcuffs. I'm sorry. I should have been more alert. But my uncle..."

Her uncle. The older, dandified man. Freeland wiped his hand across his eyes. The sun hung in the sky, more west than east. Four o'clock, maybe, and they'd been attacked just before dawn. He'd been out for hours. He studied her troubled face.

"Your uncle was shot when we were still in the stage."

"Yes."

He looked around again. "Is he dead?"

"I don't know. The bandits drove off with the stagecoach." She picked up a squishy leather bag and held it out. "Here. You must be thirsty. Have a drink of this water."

He took it and stared at her. "Where did this come from?"

She hesitated. "It was the oddest thing. An Indian came riding down out of those Superstition Mountains and gave it to me."

Freeland frowned. "An Indian?"

She nodded. "I don't know who he was or where he was going. But he left us that."

"That *is* odd. Did he say anything?"

"Not that I could understand."

"He wasn't one of the people you lived with before?"

After a moment's silence, she said, "No. He took out a knife, and I may be mistaken, but I thought he was going to cut your hand off to get me free of you."

Freeland stared at her. "I slept through that?"

"I'm afraid so. I begged him to leave you be, and he gave me the water skin and rode off."

"Well, I never." Freeland fumbled with the plug and tipped up the skin, letting sweet water run into his mouth. Not cold but so refreshing. He lowered it and put the plug back in. "Thank you. For everything. It seems I owe you my life." He couldn't imagine living without his right hand, if he survived something like that. More likely he'd have bled out on the sand. Whoever found poor Tom and Dwight would have found him, too, with his hand severed. They'd probably think Dix did it to get away from him.

"So Dix hightailed it?"

"That's right. Left us here to die of thirst."

"And your uncle?"

"He was still in the stagecoach. I had told one of them he was in there, that he needed me, but. . .I think he was the one who got shot in that last fray. They tossed him in the stage and drove off with him and Uncle Silas both."

"Could be they had a surprise when they got to their hideout and found out they had an extra passenger."

"Yes." She gazed off toward the trail. "He was carrying a lot of money. If he doesn't die from his wound, they'll probably kill him for that." Tears rolled down her cheeks.

"Someone will come looking for us," Freeland said. "When they do, I'll contact the marshal, and we'll get up a posse to go after them. Maybe it won't be too late for your uncle."

"Maybe." She didn't sound hopeful.

He looked down at the water skin that rested on the ground between them. He picked it up and studied the fringe at the bottom and the beaded strap sewn to one side.

"This looks like Apache work."

"Probably so," she said.

"You don't speak their lingo?"

She shook her head.

"Well, I'd say we're lucky to be alive, on several counts. First the road agents, then Dix, and then the Indian."

"So, what do we do now?"

He looked around. "We head for the next station and hope someone's there. Going back won't do any good."

"How far?"

"I'm guessing ten or fifteen miles." He glanced at her and then away. "I don't suppose you know where the key is, or you'd have unlocked us."

"Dix took it."

"Right. This could be embarrassing, but, uh. . .well, we'll have to take care of some business."

"Business?"

"Aren't you uncomfortable?"

"Oh." Her face was already sunburned, but it deepened even redder. "I. . .yes."

He nodded. "Figured as much. We'll have to find a place where we can each be on opposite sides of something—a rock or a bush, maybe. And I promise I won't look."

After a moment's silence, she said softly, "Can you wait until it's dark?"

"I don't think so."

She sighed. "Me either."

❤

Carmela trudged along beside McKay, determined not to slow him down. He looked awful, with his burned face and peeling lips. She supposed she didn't look much better. They'd been walking for an hour since tending to business.

She'd hated to leave the dead men lying exposed, but Mr. MacKay had pointed out that they had no shovel to bury them with and nothing with which to cover them.

"We can send men from the next town to recover the bodies," he had said. He took the driver and shotgun rider's personal effects.

Carmela shuddered, remembering.

"You all right?" he asked.

"Yes."

With the sunset came a cooler breeze. The western sky they faced held ribbons of pink where the clouds caught the dying rays of the sun. They deepened and spread as she watched.

"The Lord gave us something pretty to look at," she said.

He followed her gaze. "He sure did."

The bits of pink and vermillion in the sky darkened to purple. Carmela walked on. Her throat was parched, but she would not ask for more water. She knew he was trying to conserve it until they found a stream or some other source. A cactus wren winged above them, zooming down to her chosen cholla. From her previous travels and her study of books and pamphlets of desert flora, Carmela knew that was one plant not to be touched. Though it looked like a harmless shrub, its piercing spines would leave painful wounds. The little bird had its nest there, and the cactus protected it from predators.

When the last of the beautiful colors had been replaced by twilight, she could barely make out the rough trail. She shivered. The cooler temperature she had longed for had come. Now her burned skin was shocked by it.

"It'll get cold before mornin'," McKay said.

"I expect so."

They walked onward in silence for a long time. Because of the handcuffs, Carmela couldn't even hug herself or rub her arms. Her dark blue cotton traveling dress had absorbed the heat all day, making her perspire and fear sunstroke, but it had kept the direct sun off most of her skin. Now it offered little warmth, but neither of them had additional clothes they could layer over what they wore. The deputy was shivering, too.

"We should rest," he said at last. He looked around, and she stood beside him, waiting for him to make a decision. Darkness had fallen, but because of the bright moon, past half-full, and the canopy of glittering stars, they could make out the shapes of rocks and bushes.

"There." He lifted his hand toward a small tree that grew several yards off the trail.

She trudged with him toward it and sank down at the base of the tree. He sank to the ground beside her. Carmela leaned against the bole and sighed.

"What sort of tree is this?"

"They call it velvet mesquite."

"Of course. The Indians eat the pods."

"Yes. Squirrels and other animals do, too."

She nodded. "I'd forgotten."

He offered her a drink from the water skin, and then they sat in silence for a few minutes. Carmela sensed him watching her. She would feel flattered if it weren't for her disfigured face. People always stared at her out of curiosity.

"So, you are the captive girl. The one who spoke in Tucson."

"Yes. Carmela Wade."

He nodded. "I'm Freeland McKay. You can call me Freeland if you like."

She wasn't sure whether she wanted to or not. "Is it a family name?"

"No. My mother heard it somewhere and liked it."

"I see."

"So, where were you captured?"

"I'm not exactly sure. The tribe moved around a lot. I was. . .recovered west of Yuma." Even as she said the familiar lines, she hated herself. *Liar.* But Uncle Silas had come there to retrieve her and take her home with him, so perhaps it wasn't quite a lie to say she'd been recovered. "My. . .my parents died in the Sand Hills area. At least that is what the authorities told me. I was quite young, and I didn't keep track at the time."

"Of course. They weren't Apache though."

She said nothing. She and Uncle Silas had gone round and round over what tribe she had supposedly lived with. In fact, in the early days she had stated on more than one occasion, at his insistence, that she had been captured by a band of Apache and enslaved by their tribe. Then her uncle had decided it would behoove them to say she'd been with a smaller and lesser known tribe. And McKay knew she didn't understand the Apache language. She felt trapped. And wicked.

She said nothing.

Finally he spoke again. "Think you can sleep?"

"Maybe."

They settled down, and Carmela stared up at the stars. She usually slept on her side, but she couldn't do that without either facing him or dragging his arm over her if she faced away from him.

If they spent much time this way, forced into an intimacy neither of them wanted, he would learn the truth. She was sure of it. She wanted to pour it out now and expunge the guilt of lying to him. But she had lied to thousands of people. If he learned that, would he arrest her?

Lying was not a crime, she supposed, unless you were under oath in court. But defrauding people, that was certainly against the law, and she had a strong conviction that she and Uncle Silas had defrauded many, many people. Everyone who paid money to hear her story had been cheated.

McKay stirred and shifted a bit without touching her, but the chain tugged a little at her wrist. So he was awake, too.

"Why was Mr. Dix arrested?" she asked softly.

He lifted his head and peered at her in the shadows.

"He killed a woman."

Startled, Carmela turned toward him and pushed herself up on her elbow. "A woman? His wife?"

"No. A girl at the dance hall in Tucson."

She thought about that for a minute. "And you caught him yourself?"

"Yes. He'd left his horse at the livery, and I caught up with him there. Somebody ran and got me as soon as it happened, so I got to him before he could ride out."

Though she was exhausted, Carmela found it impossible to sleep. Scenes moved through her mind like a play performance—Dix killing the dancing girl, McKay chasing him down and arresting him, then back to the mysterious Indian who had given her the water, and beyond that to the attack on the stagecoach. She closed her eyes and begged God to let her stop remembering so she could sleep, but still she remembered.

After perhaps an hour, McKay said, "You awake?"

"Yes."

"We should move on. Maybe we can make it to the next station before morning. It'll be hot again then."

She rolled to her knees. McKay put a hand beneath her elbow and boosted her to her feet.

"Do you think we'll be able to get out of these handcuffs there?" she asked.

"I surely hope so. Are they hurting you?"

"It's chafed my wrist a little, but that's mostly because of my sunburn, I think."

"Yeah, I got a little of that myself."

He didn't ask about her feet, and Carmela wasn't about to reveal how sore they were. She had thought these were good sturdy shoes when she bought them and would last her for years, but they certainly weren't made for a twenty-mile hike across the desert. She clenched her teeth and set out at a slow but steady walk.

Chapter Six

They were moving slow—too slow to suit Freeland, but he couldn't ask Carmela to increase the pace. The poor girl had been through enough already. Still, he doubted they were making more than a couple of miles an hour. He hated the discomfort and embarrassment the handcuffs caused her, but he couldn't think of a way to get them off without a key or tools. If he still had his gun, he'd shoot through the chain, but that possibility had galloped off with the outlaws.

They'd been slogging along for more than an hour when the wind freshened and he thought he caught a different smell in the air. He stopped, and Carmela paused, too, not speaking, but looking warily up at him.

He swiveled his head, looking hard for something different.

"There." He pointed to the left of the trail. "I can't hear it, but I think there's water over there. See all the bushes?"

"I think so."

"They may be treetops. I'm hoping they're down in a streambed."

She matched his stride without question. Freeland liked that about her. Though she made her living as a speaker, Carmela seemed to be a woman of few words when she had a choice.

In the darkness, it was hard to distinguish the dark shapes around them, but when they came to a drop in the terrain, he stopped, pulling her up short.

"Right down there." He could hear a faint murmur now, and there was no mistaking the glimmer of starlight on the ribbon of water that wound between the rocky banks.

"Is there a river?" she asked.

"Probably a spring somewhere. But this is enough for us."

He cast about for the easiest way down the six-foot bank and held tight to her hand while they descended, slipping and lurching. They reached the bottom still upright—a roaring success. He led her to the rivulet and hunkered down. Carmela crouched beside it.

Freeland scooped a handful to his mouth and tasted it. "It's good water. Drink all you want. We can fill the skin." It was nearly empty, and he had wondered if they would be able to make it to the next station if they didn't find more.

She drank several handfuls and then eased down, half sitting, half lying on the rocky ground.

"Tired?" he asked.

"I sure am. How's your head?"

"Not so bad, but I still feel it."

She nodded.

The water was only an inch or two deep. He searched his pockets and found he still had the handkerchief his mother had passed him as he walked out the door two days ago. He unfolded it and dipped it into the sluggish stream. He squeezed it out the best he could with one hand and held it out to her. "It's clean. It might feel good to bathe your face."

"Thank you." She sat up straighter, took it, and gingerly patted her sunburned cheeks. She let out a little sigh that he took to mean she had found some relief.

"We could rest awhile," he offered.

She looked around doubtfully. "It will get hot quickly after sunup. I would like to bathe my feet before we go on though."

"Of course."

She held out the damp handkerchief.

"Why don't you keep that for now and let me get your shoes off. Everything's just plain awkward with these cuffs on, but I think I could do that."

She opened her mouth as though she would speak then closed it for a moment. "All right, I won't argue."

He soaked the handkerchief again for her and squeezed it out. When she had it in her hand, she lay back, limp.

"I'm sure it will be an unpleasant job, but go ahead."

He smiled in the moonlight. "I don't think I'll notice any smells if that's what you mean."

He untied her ankle-high shoes and eased off the one nearest him. Carmela winced and caught her breath as he pulled it free.

"You're hurting," he said.

"I think I have a blister."

"You should've said something." Carefully, he eased the lace on the other shoe looser and gently pulled the shoe off. He started to grasp her stocking, but she sat up quickly when he touched her ankle.

"I'll do it."

"All right." He sat back a little, keeping his left arm floppy so she didn't feel any resistance as she moved. He realized he was staring as she worked her stocking down and quickly looked away. "The stars are fading. Must be getting on to dawn."

She paused and looked up for a moment. "Likely you're right."

She kept working, and when she had both stockings off, she scooted closer to the water. As her feet slipped into the stream, she gave a little gasp.

"All right?" Freeland asked.

"It stings, but I'll be fine."

He wondered how far he could carry her if her feet gave out. Asking her to walk any farther rankled him. But they couldn't stay out here forever. He thought about taking his boots off and joining her in the footbath, but he wasn't sure he'd get them back on. Fatigue swept over him, and he leaned back on his elbow.

"I'm thinking we should try to rest a bit. Find a place to shelter and try to sleep."

She looked at him, her lips parted, and he realized he could see the warm brown of her eyes. "Are you sure? What if someone comes along and we miss them?"

"I don't think we would. But I could put my boots in the trail, so anyone would see them."

She smiled, a nice smile if not for the ugly markings on her face. "We could make an arrow in the dirt, pointing down here."

"Yeah, we could."

She pressed her lips together then met his gaze. "I think we should keep going."

He considered it and nodded. "All right, then, dress your feet."

She put her left foot across her knee to put the stocking on again, and he could plainly see pressure sores on her sole.

"Your foot's all raw. Why didn't you tell me?"

"It wouldn't have done any good."

Freeland exhaled and shook his head. "You must have learned that attitude when you were a captive. You shouldn't be walkin' on those feet."

She stared at him for a moment then turned her face away, but not before he saw tears well in her eyes. An ache grew in Freeland's chest. Here they were, out in the desert with no help in sight, and the girl had just lost her uncle to a band of cutthroats. She must have been horrified by Dix's deception and the idea that she might end up chained to a dead man if his head hadn't been so hard—not to mention what she went through years ago on that wagon train with her family. Then she'd been terrified by an Apache, and now he'd added another load to her distress.

"I'm sorry," he said.

"For what?" She turned toward him. "It's not your fault my feet hurt. Or that you're shackled to me. If you were alone, I'm sure you'd be at the next station by now."

He looked away, unable to confirm or deny that. "If I was alone, that Apache might have lifted my scalp."

Carmela sighed and finished pulling on her stocking. She worked the other on, and they sat in silence for a long moment. He hated to press her to put her shoes on and cause her more pain by walking, so he waited.

She pulled her feet up under her dark skirt so that her knees were bent and leaned forward, resting her arms over them. "I remember when I spoke in Tucson five years ago, right before the war broke out."

"I remember, too," Freeland said.

She eyed him sharply. "There was a boy. He came out in the alley behind the building, and he found me crying. He told me he had a brother who could help me."

Freeland sighed. "That was my younger brother, Will McKay."

She nodded. "He looked like you. Same hair, same eyes."

Freeland hesitated, not sure how to word what he ought to say now. "Will came to fetch me, but when we got back to the saloon, we were too late. You and Mr. Holden were gone. I hoped at the time that you would be all right, but I didn't see that I could do anything under the circumstances. I mean, I was new at the job and afraid to overstep my bounds. I was young. If I'd had the experience I have under my belt now. . . Well, anyway, the town was a little rowdy that night, and I had a prisoner in the jail." He shook his head. He'd been the practical one, set off against Will's idealism. "I'm sorry we didn't get there in time."

"Where is he now?" she asked.

He swallowed hard. "He was killed in the war."

Her eyes flared. "But he was so young!"

"Yes. Eighteen when he died. He was with Hood's Texas Brigade at Gettysburg."

Carmela didn't move for half a minute. Freeland remembered how badly his brother wanted to save this girl. Maybe now he had the chance to do that. Was that why God let him come on this odd journey and lose his prisoner?

"Were you in the war?" she asked.

"Yes. I went before Will. He was too young when it started. By the time I got home, he was gone. Mama was alone when she got the word. It was real hard, losing him."

He looked at her scuffed shoes. How could they go on with Carmela's feet in such bad shape? He was weak with hunger. He wouldn't be able to carry her far. But he wouldn't leave her out here alone. That was the last thing he would do.

"If I could wrap my foot, I think I could walk some more," she said.

"Are they both bad?"

"No, just the one. Maybe I can use your handkerchief."

"If you think it will help."

She smiled and glanced up at him from beneath her lashes. "Your brother gave me his handkerchief, too. I still have it. That is, it's in my trunk."

Freeland's eyes burned, but no tears came. Maybe he was just too parched to cry. "Guess we McKay men all have a soft spot for women in need."

Carmela gave a little laugh, a soft, musical chuckle that lightened his remorse.

The sun was rising now. She gazed toward the flagrant smears of red and orange in the eastern sky. "God is giving us another beautiful sight this morning."

Freeland looked toward it and watched the cloud shadows and hues change. "Yes, He is."

If he could just get the handcuffs off. Then he could be sure this wouldn't be Carmela Wade's last sunrise. He spotted a rock about the size of a potato and picked it up.

"Let me see if I can spring these things."

Carmela willingly adjusted her position so that he could set the latch on his bracelet against another rock.

"Do you think it will work?" she asked.

"No. It may just make it so a key won't unlock them, if I mash it too badly."

"What about the links? Wouldn't they be more likely to give?"

"We can try."

He hammered at the chain and the cuff for a good ten minutes. Sweat broke out on his brow and began to soak his shirt. Carmela watched in silence, her mouth tight.

At last he flopped back on the ground. "No good. If I just had a gun."

"We should drink and fill the water skin and then go on," she said quietly. "I'll put my shoes on."

❤

Carmela gritted her teeth and tried not to let her discomfort show on her face. The handkerchief in her shoe might help a little—or it might just make ridges of cloth to further irritate her tender foot. She could tear long strips from her petticoat; that might be more effective. She glanced at Freeland and decided she wasn't up to that right now. She had already exposed her limbs to him and endured the humility of taking care of her basic needs with him a foot away. She would limp onward the way she was, for as long as she could.

Freeland. It was a good name. Strong and suggestive of independence and optimism. Still, she wasn't sure she could call him that. She would work on it mentally, until she got used to it. His brother Will's name had been much easier to handle—but then, she hadn't known Will's last name.

A wave of sorrow for the gallant boy surged through her, and her hands trembled as she tied her shoelaces.

"Are you sure you're all right?" Freeland asked.

"Just hungry, I guess." She finished the job and leaned toward the stream with him while he let water run into the leather bag.

"If we could find some herbs, it might help my blisters," she said.

"What kind of herbs?" His eyebrows drew together.

"I learned what the natives use for medicines. I believe if we could find the creosote bush, a poultice might help."

He frowned. "Is that what we call chaparral?"

Carmela ran through the mental catalogue of plants she had studied. "I don't know. The Yavapai use it for skin problems and as an analgesic. It might help relieve the sunburn, too, though I think aloe is best for that."

"Yavapai?" Freeland cocked his head toward his right shoulder. "Is that who you were with?"

Carmela hesitated. "I'm not really sure. The Indian agent where the troopers first took me said my tattoos might be Yavapai. Or another tribe that they traded with."

"Mojave?"

"I really don't know."

He nodded slowly. "So, this creosote bush, or aloe?"

"There's another plant they would dry and powder for poultices— curly dock."

"Sure, I know it. I don't think there's enough water for it here."

"That's what I thought," she said. "But the creosote bush. We might find it. I looked it up after Uncle Silas took me home, and it's a good one."

"I'll keep an eye out for it." He held out his hand, and she took it, using his leverage to help her rise. She eased weight onto her left foot.

"Well?" He bent his head and peered anxiously into her eyes.

"I can do it."

They set out slowly, and she couldn't help favoring her injured foot. They regained the trail and headed northwest. By the time they had gone a hundred steps, her limp was so pronounced, Freeland stopped.

"No offense, ma'am—Carmela—but if we're going to make it, you need to lean on me. If I could carry you, I would, but I don't know if that's possible with these bracelets. Just hold on to my arm, and I'll give you all the support I can."

"A–all right." She raised her right hand and tried to take his elbow, but the short chain between them wouldn't allow it. So she looped her wrist instead around his forearm and grasped it firmly, feeling his muscles tighten.

"That's it. Now, put as much weight on me as you can."

Their gait was awkward, but she soon found a rhythm, and using Freeland's arm as a walking stick did help. If he'd been on the other side, she might have been fairly proficient. As it was, they made better progress than she had hoped.

"So you've been with your uncle since your ordeal with the natives?"

Carmela's pulse picked up, and the back of her neck tingled. "Since after my parents died. He came to get me at Fort Yuma."

"But you were with the Indians quite a while."

She hesitated, not wanting to lie to him. "I am told it was five years." By Uncle Silas. Her own heart knew the truth.

"That's a long time."

She nodded and concentrated on the rough trail. How different would her life have been if not for Uncle Silas? He was not the benefactor he made himself out to be. If he had really wanted to help her, he would not have exploited her and forced her into a life of deceit. She was twenty years old now. Other girls her age were courting, marrying, starting families of their own. But she was obligated to do her uncle's bidding.

Without Uncle Silas, she might have found love by now, or at least a pleasing arrangement with a husband. So long as he was a decent man, provided for her, and let her be honest, she wouldn't insist upon love.

She glanced up at Freeland, and his eyes met hers for an instant. He seemed like a decent man. He had been nothing but courteous to her during this awful odyssey. He hadn't blamed her for what Dix did, binding them cruelly together. If her life were different, if she weren't Uncle Silas's ward, she might have met a man whom she could love and share the future with—maybe a man like this one.

Her chest felt tight and she tried to pull in a deeper breath. Would she ever see Uncle Silas again? He may have bled to death by now, or the outlaws may have finished him off to get rid of him. What would she do if he never returned? She knew nothing about making a life of her own.

"We must be near the station," Freeland said.

She halted and looked up at him. "You've made this journey before?"

"Yes. I think we're close."

"And if that station was burned, too?" she asked.

He sighed and looked up the trail, as far as he could see. The ground rose before them, the path a beaten track of red clay. Across the hillsides grew clumps of brush and prickly pear, and saguaro cacti standing tall like sentries.

"We'll have to take it as it comes," he said.

She nodded. "Let's get there, then."

"Your feet?"

"Not too bad."

He grasped her hand. "You've got heart, Carmela. Most women would have folded up by now."

She smiled. The burned skin of her face hurt, and her lips cracked, sending out more shoots of pain, but she was ready to go on.

"It we make it to the top of this rise and we can't see the station, we'll rest, all right?" he asked.

"Fair enough." She set out, determined to make it to the top of the long slope. Her breath soon came in quick gulps, and she clung to Freeland's hand to steady her wobbly steps.

"Want to stop?" he asked.

She shook her head. Another hundred steps and they would top the hill.

At last they stood looking out over more of the same—dry, barren acres, with no sign of life or habitation.

"I guess we should sit for a while."

He guided her off the trail, into the shade of a large rock formation. They sat down side by side, and he passed her the water skin.

Carmela took a drink, not nearly as much as she wanted. She

passed it to him, knowing they both wanted to make it last until they got to the stage stop. There might be a stream or a well by the station. Most of them were built near a water source, so the teams could be kept comfortable.

"Rest now," he said, corking the bag.

She leaned back, with the unyielding stone behind her, and closed her eyes. What a sight she must make. She had lost her frivolous hat somehow, probably where they had tried last to sleep. Her foot throbbed, but she was thankful. Only one foot hurt. It could have been so much worse.

Freeland lifted his hat and settled it farther forward on his brow. He leaned back and started to fold his arms, dragging Carmela's wrist along with the motion.

"Sorry." He lowered his left hand to the ground between them.

"It's all right." She didn't open her eyes. If she could just sit still a few more minutes, she would drift into sleep.

A metallic click brought them both upright and alert. Her eyes flew open. Dix stood six feet away with Uncle Silas's derringer aimed at Freeland's chest.

Chapter Seven

*D*ix laughed. "Well, look at you two. Cozy as two peas in a pod. You must be getting pretty well acquainted by now."

Freeland clenched his fists. What was Dix doing here? If he hadn't been chained to Carmela, he would have lunged at the escapee. He made himself sit still, knowing the wrong move could endanger Carmela even more.

"Have you got the key?" he asked.

"Who, me? I didn't steal your key. The little lady took it."

Carmela's jaw dropped. She glanced at Freeland and snapped her lips together, turning her face away.

Good, Freeland thought. *Just keep quiet. Don't let him get to you.* He took stock of the man. Dix looked played out. His skin, kept from the harsh sun for several weeks while he was in jail, had burned and begun to peel.

"I thought you went after a loose horse," Freeland said.

Dix's mouth twitched. "Yeah, well, I never did get the horse. I've been walking, same as you. When I went back to where we were held up, you were gone, and I figured you were headed for the next stop, so I followed along. No sense trying to go all the way back to Tucson."

"You'd never have made it," Freeland said.

"That's the way I saw it. Figured I might get a horse at the next station."

Steal one, you mean, Freeland thought.

"You got anything to eat?" Dix asked.

"Nope. Haven't had anything but some cactus fruit." Carmela had spotted it. It hadn't filled their stomachs, but Freeland figured that at this point, anything was better than nothing.

That peashooter fired only a single shot. He could overpower Dix if his hand were free. Maybe he still could, if Carmela caught on and didn't hold him back. It would be worth the chance if he could get the gun from Dix.

"Reckon we ought to move on." He stood cautiously, giving Carmela a hand to help her rise. He looked meaningfully into her eyes and then away. Would she understand?

Apparently she did. As she got to her feet, she scooped up a stone with her right hand and concealed it in the folds of her skirt. Freeland quickly looked away so as not to draw Dix's attention to her movements.

"Go on." Dix waved the derringer toward the trail. "I'll be right behind you."

Freeland knew his chances to act would drop if he began walking in front of Dix. He paused, seeming to defer to Carmela, sending her a glance. She gave an almost imperceptible nod.

He stepped forward, closer to Dix than necessary to pass him. As the man started to draw back, Freeland pounced, grabbing Dix's forearm with his free hand and shoving it away, so the small gun no longer pointed at him. His rush carried them both to the ground. He felt Carmela thud down next to him. In his struggle with the escaped prisoner, he was too busy to worry about her, or if he was straining her wrist by yanking on the chain. He and Dix wrestled in the dirt, with Freeland concentrating on forcing his opponent to drop the derringer.

Carmela scrambled beside him. She pushed on his back and shoulder, working her way up to his head. Freeland could scarcely believe it when she reached over him and whacked Dix smartly on top of the head with her rock. Dix stared up at her and then gave a low, feral snarl.

Though she hadn't struck Dix hard enough to knock him out, Carmela had given Freeland the opportunity he needed. He drew his fist back and punched Dix as hard as he could in the jaw. The prisoner sagged back on the ground.

Freeland pulled in a deep breath and looked into Carmela's face, just inches from his.

"Thanks."

"I should have hit him harder." She gave a rueful laugh and rolled away from him, pushing back her disheveled hair.

"You did fine."

"I didn't want to break his skull." She rubbed her wrist, where the handcuff had chafed.

"Let's see if we can get these things off." Freeland stretched beyond Dix's lax hand and picked up the derringer. He cocked it and squinted at the barrel. "Great. Just great." If he were a swearing man, now would be the time.

"What is it?" Carmela pushed up on her knees and laid her hand on his arm.

"It's empty."

She gazed into his face for a long moment and swallowed hard. "Perhaps he really does have the key."

As quickly as he could with the awkward handcuff arrangement, Freeland checked the unconscious man's pants pockets.

"It doesn't seem to be here. He probably dropped it somewhere in the desert so we'd never find it."

Carmela sat down heavily. "What do we do now?"

"I think we'd better pick up the water bottle and my hat and start walking again."

"He might wake up and follow us."

"Probably," Freeland said, "but we don't have any way to restrain him." Technically, that wasn't true. He supposed they could tear strips from their clothing and tie him up. But he didn't want to leave him here to die, the way he and Carmela had been left. He looked around. "We can put him in the shade of the rocks. Maybe he'll wake up by the time the sun gets around them."

"I don't want you to have to fight him again."

Freeland flexed his jaw. "We should reach the station before he comes to and can catch up to us."

"All right. Let's move him. Tell me what to do and I can help you."

The sun hung in the dome of the sky almost directly above them for what seemed like hours. Carmela trudged beside Freeland, her mind racing as her body cried out for rest. He kept looking at her, and she wondered what was going on in his mind.

"What is it?" she asked at last.

"Sorry. I didn't mean to stare. It's just that. . .well, your tattoo on this side looks a little faded."

Her heart lurched, and she stopped walking. Freeland stopped, too. He took her chin gently in his hand and turned her head.

"I hadn't noticed that before. The left side is darker than the right." He let his hand drop. "Sorry. I didn't intend to embarrass you."

She put her free hand up to her cheek and touched it lightly. The skin was taut and painful. How much of the tattoos would peel off with her sunburn? Maybe it was time to tell Freeland the whole truth.

"Could we sit for a while?"

"Sure." They found scant shade beneath a Joshua tree, but its branched stem and spiky foliage did little to relieve the palpable heat. Carmela gazed at Freeland for a long time, and he looked back, waiting patiently for her to begin when she was ready. She felt fairly comfortable with him now. She had trusted him from the start, especially since he confirmed he was Will's brother, but now she was ready to confide in him. What he did with her secret was up to him.

"When my parents died, Uncle Silas was made my guardian. He's my mother's older brother. I didn't know him very well before. . .before he went to Yuma to get me. On the way back, he hatched this plan. Or maybe he'd been thinking of it all the way out from New England. It took him weeks to get there."

Freeland nodded, and she supposed he knew how difficult travel was in the West. Uncle Silas had been able to get a train to the Mississippi, but after that it was stagecoach most of the way, and he'd had plenty of time to think.

"What sort of plan?" Freeland asked.

"He wanted me to give speeches for money."

Freeland blinked. "That's what you do now."

She nodded. "I've been doing it a long time."

"All through the war?"

"Yes. We made a long trip through the Midwest, down to Texas and through New Mexico. When we left Tucson five years ago, the war was just starting. We went back to the North as fast as we could, but once we were out of the South, Uncle Silas started setting up more engagements for me. We stayed away from the conflict, and he always seemed to be able to find an audience. I had to tell about my parents dying and Indians capturing me. Lots of things. Sometimes I spoke twice in one day."

"Sounds tiring."

"Yes."

"Do you enjoy it?"

She couldn't help the twist her lips took. "I hate it, but I was young. Only twelve when it started. I didn't know how to get away from Uncle Silas and put an end to it. He was my legal guardian after my folks died on the trail."

"You mean, after the Indians killed them?"

Carmela hesitated. Should she tell him the entire, shameful truth? She decided to slide over that point if Freeland would let her.

"Before we heard about Fort Sumter, Uncle Silas wanted to continue on with our western tour, hitting all the major towns. He thought we could go as far as San Francisco then head back toward Missouri. But with the war going on, he thought it was better to get to Albuquerque and then Santa Fe and up to Denver, so we turned back shortly after I spoke in Tucson and met your brother. But all the way east, he booked presentations wherever he could. I think we made quite a lot of money—though we often had to stay extra nights in a city to do it, and that cost more for the hotels and meals."

"Sure."

"By the time we got to St. Louis, travel was becoming difficult. The farther east we went, the more crowded the trains were. He rented a house in Massachusetts, outside of Boston, as a home base, and we lived there off and on throughout the war, traveling for my engagements."

"You're from Massachusetts?" he asked.

"Maine originally, but. . .he didn't want me to speak in Maine."

"Why not?"

Why not, indeed? She was too naive to realize it then, but Uncle Silas was afraid of being caught. If people who knew her family personally heard her speak, they might know her claims were false. They would know the family had left their area much later than she claimed in her speeches. Better to stay a few hundred miles away from those who knew them best. But she hadn't put that together then.

"I thought it was because we could make more money in a more populated area," she said, not meeting Freeland's eyes.

"I don't understand why some people are so eager to hear about others' troubles," he said softly.

"Me either. But he wanted me to make it sound exciting." She shifted and rearranged her skirt. "Have you heard of Olive Oatman?"

"Sure. She was held captive in roughly the same area you were, I'd say."

Carmela nodded. "Yes, but before. . .before what happened to me. Uncle Silas had heard her speak once, several years previously. People paid good money to hear her tales. He insisted I do the speaking to earn 'donations' to repay some money my father owed him."

"I see."

"I don't. My father never mentioned owing money to his brother-in-law."

Freeland's lips pursed. "You were young, as you say. Do you think he would discuss it with you?"

"I don't know. My father and mother seemed carefree when we headed west. They were starting a new life together. I heard nothing about debts and obligations back home."

"So, all through the war, you did this speaking in Massachusetts?"

"Yes, and Connecticut and New York. We even made trips to Ohio and Indiana. But we stayed well away from the battle lines. If the audience was small and the receipts were too little to pay for lodging, someone among the organizers would give us a meal or invite me to stay in their home."

"What about Mr. Holden?"

She shrugged. "Where I was welcome, Uncle Silas went, too."

"So. . .do you still owe him money?"

Carmela eyed him sharply. Freeland McKay was a good man, and a lawman. She couldn't bring herself to tell him outright that she had never been a captive. That would be fraud. But she would dearly like to know if Uncle Silas's demands on her were legal.

"I started keeping track of the receipts as soon as he told me what my father owed him. We passed the mark last fall." Ten thousand dollars was a lot of money, she reflected. She swallowed hard. Her uncle, and before him her parents, had told her many times not to discuss family finances with outsiders. But Freeland could tell her what she wanted to know without being privy to the amount. "When I said something to the effect that I had earned back my father's debt, Uncle Silas said I still owed him money for the expense my care had been to him."

Freeland's features darkened. "That doesn't seem right."

"That's what I thought, but he said that counted against what I brought in, and I was honor bound to pay it all back."

"I'm not sure a child is liable for debts their parents incur. But then, law varies from one place to another."

He was silent for a while, frowning, thinking. She watched his eyes. He wasn't happy with her story. Maybe he guessed the part that she hadn't told him, and if he had, maybe he was figuring what the law would do to them for defrauding all those good people. Or maybe he felt sorry for her, for all those years Uncle Silas had dragged her from pillar to post and forced her into a public role. He had no idea the hours she had put in memorizing the stories and studying all the material Uncle Silas brought her about the Southwest Indians. She had read all the captivity narratives he could get hold of, from colonial days to the present. She also read what little they could find on pottery, weaving, and herbal medicine, as those were some of the skills of the tribes in the area where he said she was captured.

"We'd better go," Freeland said at last. The sun had moved so that the Joshua tree no longer shaded them.

She rose stiffly and looked back. There was no sign of Dix.

Freeland took her hand and led her up the trail. Each step was harder than the last, with the punishing sun beating on her head and her foot lancing with pain. Without the deputy's firm lead, she might have given up. At last, she staggered the final few steps to the summit and looked out over the vista below.

Freeland lifted his hand and pointed. "There it is. The station is still standing."

Chapter Eight

*P*lodding along the trail, they took nearly half an hour to reach the stage stop. As they entered the yard, Carmela stumbled and Freeland whipped out a hand to catch her, surprising himself that he could still react that quickly. She righted herself and surveyed the station house and corral, where a half-dozen mules stood, swishing their tails and dozing in a tiny strip of shade afforded by a small outbuilding.

Carmela jerked her chin toward the animals, and Freeland nodded. Their presence was a good sign.

"Anyone home?" he yelled toward the station, but his throat was bone dry, and his voice cracked. He knew it wouldn't carry far. Fumbling for the water skin, he saw a flicker of movement at one of the small windows.

"Who are you?" came a male voice with a southern twang.

He put the flask to his lips and took a swallow of water then called back, "Deputy US Marshal Freeland McKay and Miss Carmela Wade."

"You off the stage?"

"Yes sir."

The shadow moved from the window, and the door opened. A short man, his face creased by years out in the weather, came out and walked toward them carrying a shotgun with the barrel pointed toward the earth. Two others came behind him, one a gangly young man whose pant legs and shirtsleeves were too short, and a burly, middle-aged man with a thick black beard. Both had sidearms, and the bearded man carried a rifle.

"I'm Price, the station agent. What happened?" the first man asked.

"We were attacked by outlaws. Five of them. Our driver and shotgun messenger were killed."

"Dwight Herder?"

"Yes, and Tom. I don't know his last name. Sorry."

Price's mouth twisted. "Any more passengers?"

"This young lady's uncle was wounded. The outlaws drove the stage off with him in it," Freeland said.

Price's eyes shifted to Carmela for a moment and appraised her quickly. He nodded.

"And. . ." Freeland hesitated, not liking to admit his own failure. "I had a prisoner."

"Her?" Price frowned at the handcuffs.

"No," Freeland said. "Fellow by the name of Dix."

"He tricked me," Carmela said. "Mr. McKay was unconscious, and Dix had got hold of a gun in the fray. He made me unlock the handcuffs, and then he hitched me to the deputy and left us there to die."

All three of the men from the station stared at Carmela as she spoke. The muscular man scratched his chin through his heavy beard.

"You was out cold the whole time?" His eyes flicked to Freeland.

"I'm sorry to say it's true," Freeland said. "I wasn't much help in protecting Miss Wade and her uncle."

"You got me here," Carmela said stoutly.

"Well, come on in and tell me ever'thing," Price said. He clapped the bearded man on the shoulder. "This here's Windle, our blacksmith. Reckon he can get you out of them cuffs." He jerked his head toward the young man. "That's Jerry. He's one of our tenders. When yesterday's stage didn't come through, I sent the other one off to take word up the line."

"I wish you'd sent him our way," Freeland said as they started toward the adobe.

"Couldn't do that. He might have run into them road agents between here and the previous stop."

"We weren't attacked there," Carmela said. "The last stop was burned by Indians."

Price swung around to look at her. "Now wait a minute. Was it outlaws or Injuns?"

"It was both, sir," Carmela said.

Freeland nodded. "Before we were attacked, we came into Westfield station, and it was abandoned. No team, no people. We rested and went on. When we got to the next one, it had been burned out and the men stationed there killed. We buried them and rested the horses. Shortly after we left there, we were attacked, but not by the Apache that burned them out. These were white men."

Price shook his head. "Hard to believe. You'd best come in and sit down. I reckon you two have had a hard day."

Young Jerry nodded sagely. "We knew they was trouble down the line."

With his tools from the shed, it took Windle only seconds to cut the chain on the handcuffs. Carmela pushed the bracelet back and rubbed her wrist.

"You all right?" Freeland asked.

"Yes. It feels good though."

He nodded. The constant pressure and frequent tugs on the chain had rubbed his wrist, too, until it was sore and swollen. He thought he saw abrasions on Carmela's skin.

He leaned toward her. "I expect you'd like to use the necessary."

She flushed. "Yes, thank you."

Freeland turned to the station agent. "Maybe you could escort Miss Wade out back while Mr. Windle tries to get my bracelet off."

"Sure thing." Price gestured with his shotgun. "This way, miss. And Jerry, you keep watch out the front winder. We don't know if them outlaws or the Apache will show up here next."

"Yes sir." Jerry took up his post with the rifle, and Price took Carmela outside.

Windle eyed the metal bracelet on Freeland's wrist and selected a tool. "So your prisoner got away. Where do you reckon he went?"

"He followed us when he couldn't catch a loose horse. Carmela and I managed to overpower him. We left him lying in the shade unconscious a few hours ago."

"So he might be our next visitor."

Freeland grimaced. "It wouldn't surprise me a bit."

"We'll block the door again after you folks are done out back," Windle said.

Freeland noticed a cupboard, two chairs, and a table that had been dragged near the front door to barricade it with. These men took the danger seriously, even when they didn't know its nature.

Windle followed his gaze. "We don't take to the idea of bein' scalped."

"I don't blame you." Freeland held his arm out for the blacksmith to work on it. "I don't know if you can pick the lock. I rather foolishly beat on it with a rock."

"Well, we'll see about that. Come sit down."

By the time Carmela and Price returned, Freeland's handcuff was off, and Price gave him some horse liniment to smear on his wrist.

Windle smiled at Carmela. "Come have a seat, young lady. We'll get that hardware off you in two shakes of a lamb's tail."

Carmela sat down where he indicated and placed her wrist on the rough wooden bench the blacksmith was using as a worktable.

"I expect you're hungry," Price said.

"We haven't eaten for almost two days," Freeland admitted.

"Soup. I've got some on the back of the stove. I don't usually keep a fire on hot days, but soup's the best thing if you haven't et for a while." He laid down the shotgun and moved about the end of the room near the cookstove, unhurried but purposeful.

"I'd probably eat it cold right about now," Freeland said with a grin.

"Well, here, boy. Here's some cornpone to gnaw on while you

wait." He shoved a square black pan into Freeland's hands. It was half-full of cornbread, and a knife lay in the empty part where the rest had been. "Don't have no butter, but we've got us some applesauce in the crock yonder." He nodded toward a shelf.

While Freeland puttered about finding plates for himself and Carmela and heaping them with cornpone and applesauce, Price laid the fire in the stove.

"Man, do you have to light the fire?" Jerry whined from the window. "It's already an oven in here."

"I can eat cold soup," Carmela said quickly.

"Me, too," Freeland said.

"Well, I got to say, it's not really cold." Price took the lid off his stewpot and frowned. "It's as warm as you and me. I made a big batch yesterday, expecting the stage passengers."

Freeland peeked over his shoulder. "That looks fine. Dish it up."

"Aw, we need coffee, anyway," Windle said, not looking up from where he was working. "Heat it, Ed. Don't make the lady eat cold stew."

Price muttered to himself and added kindling to the firebox.

Freeland took the two plates to the table and found utensils.

"Did I get you?" Windle asked Carmela anxiously after his tool slipped.

"No sir; I'm fine."

"Good. I'm almost done." He filed away at the metal on Carmela's wrist.

Freeland took the opportunity to scrounge up two cups. Just as he set them on the table, Windle cried gleefully, "There you go!"

Carmela jumped up, smiling and working her wrist back and forth. "Thank you, Mr. Windle. I can't tell you how much I appreciate it."

"Oh, I got a good idea how much." The blacksmith gathered his tools.

"Breakfast," Freeland said, smiling at Carmela. "Or maybe it's lunch."

Price chuckled. "Afternoon tea. Enjoy."

Carmela came to the table, which was crowded against the other furniture near the door. Freeland had decided not to move it in case they needed the barricade, but he had set two chairs down for them. She eyed the tin plate before her with satisfaction then glanced over at Freeland.

"Would you ask a blessing, please?"

Freeland didn't mind, though he felt his face heat a little, knowing the other three men were listening. He nodded and bowed his head.

"Dear Father, we give thanks for our safe arrival here. We thank Thee for this food, and we ask Your blessing and safety for those in this house. Amen."

"Amen." Carmela smiled at him across the table.

A few minutes later, Price brought two cups of tepid coffee to the table.

"Here, miss. It ain't real hot, but you might need something to wash the pone down with."

"Thank you," Carmela said. "Your cornpone is delicious. Did you make it yourself?"

"Yes'm. Have to provide a meal for the passengers."

"I'd like to get your recipe, if you don't mind. I don't think I've ever tasted any as good."

Price smiled, and his eyes gleamed. "That's right nice of you, miss. Of course, you's powerful hungry. Everything tastes good when you're hollow."

She laughed.

"It is good," Freeland said. "So's the applesauce."

"Thankee." Price pulled the bench over and sat down between them at the end of the table. "That stew'll be ready right soon. So, what's your plan now, Deputy?"

Freeland sipped his coffee, thinking about it. Carmela would be safe here with Price, Windle, and the boy, Jerry. At least, she'd be much safer than she had been out on the desert with him.

He eyed Price, trying to read the older man's expression. "I'd like to go back and see if I can recapture my prisoner. Would you lend me a horse and a gun for a few hours?"

The station agent ran a hand through his shaggy, graying hair. "Well now, I'm not sure as I could do that, Deputy. We're short on assets right now, and we need to keep our one good team ready for when the next stage makes it through, whenever that may be. You saw how dangerous it is to get to a station and not have a fresh team waiting for you."

Freeland's heart sank. This was the answer he had expected. "You must have a saddle horse, and I'd come back before dark if I didn't find him."

Price shrugged. "Or he might find you and ride off on my horse. No, I can't let you do that. What with that desperado out there, and the Apaches that burned the last station, and an outlaw gang that held you up yesterday, well, that don't sound like very good odds to me."

Freeland pulled out Silas Holden's derringer. "You got any cartridges that would fit this thing? It's the only weapon I've got."

"You going to commandeer my horse if I do?"

"No sir," Freeland said.

Price nodded. "I'd sell you a few, but I don't reckon you've got any money left."

"I have a bit," Carmela said. "How much are they?"

Price looked at her in surprise. "Held out on the road agents, eh? Good for you. I'll let him have half a dozen for a dollar."

"Do you have scissors and a needle and thread?"

"Surely." Price fetched a small basket and handed it to her. He nodded toward a curtained doorway. "My cot's yonder. You can rest in there after you're done eating, miss."

"Thank you." Carmela rose and went through the curtain carrying the basket.

"Spunky gal." Price went to the stove to stir the stew. "Guess this is ready." He brought Freeland a bowlful.

"That smells real good." Freeland picked up his spoon.

Jerry turned from his post at the window. "Can we have some, too?"

"Hold your horses," Price said. "Let the guests eat. If there's some left, and I reckon there will be, you'll get it for your supper. Now, you're supposed to be keeping watch."

Jerry frowned and turned back to the window.

Carmela returned soon and gave Price a dollar.

"Why, thankee," Price said with a grin. "I'll get your stew. It's nice and hot now."

She was quiet while they ate. Freeland didn't press her. He was weary beyond conversation himself. And yet, they should settle what would become of her. With her uncle out of the picture, he felt responsible for her well-being.

When they had finished and Price took their dishes away, refusing help with the washing up, she headed toward the curtained doorway. Freeland rose and followed her.

"Carmela," he said softly before she could enter the other room.

She stopped and turned to face him. "Yes?"

"I need to talk to you."

Something flickered across her face—disappointment? Apprehension. No, he decided, she was afraid.

"Are you going to leave me alone here with them?" she asked. "Please tell me if you are."

Freeland shook his head, angry at himself that he had even considered going off and leaving her with three strange men. No matter how kind they appeared to be, he couldn't do that.

"I'll wait," he said. "I'll make sure you're safe at the next town."

She hesitated. Her lower lip trembled. "Uncle Silas—"

"We can't do anything right now. I'd need more men. Price is right about that. It's too dangerous."

"So, you'll get me to Prescott?"

"The next town is Wickenburg," Freeland said. "It isn't much, but there'll be more people than there are here."

"Will they have a decent place for me to stay?" she asked.

Freeland thought back to the last time he'd ridden through the cluster of tents and a few huts at Wickenburg. He couldn't remember seeing any women there, unless there were a few barmaids in the makeshift saloons.

"I'm not sure." Wickenburg might be far more perilous for Carmela than here at the isolated way station. "I won't leave you there if there's not." As soon as he'd said it, he knew he'd made a promise he might regret, but how could he do otherwise?

Her smile was his reward. "Thank you. That means a great deal." She pushed the curtain aside and went through. He had a brief impression of a small dim room with crates of supplies piled high on one side and a bunk on the other.

He went back to the table. Jerry and Windle were drinking coffee now, and Jerry had a bowl of stew in front of him. Price had taken his place at the window.

"Not much in Wickenburg," Windle said.

So he had heard.

"How far is it?" Freeland asked.

"Forty miles or more."

"Fifty," Price called.

Windle nodded. "It's a rough stretch. There's one more station between here and there, to change teams. They haul in the water."

"Long stages," Freeland said. "I remember. I made the trip once before by stage, and I've ridden it a couple of times."

Jerry slurped in a spoonful of broth.

Windle sipped his coffee and wiped his mouth and mustache with the back of his hand. "What you plan to do about the girl's uncle?"

Freeland shook his head. There was no good solution. "He may be dead. I can't face a pack of outlaws alone on the chance he's alive. I'll take her with me to the territorial marshal, I guess. He can decide what to do."

"He's your boss," Windle said flatly.

"Yeah. I'm hoping he'll get up a posse to go after Dix right away, and maybe we can find out what happened to her uncle."

"Maybe that Dix fella will come to you here," Jerry said.

Freeland hoped so, in a way. He didn't want anyone to get hurt, but if Dix came looking for a horse, surely the four of them could capture him. One way or another, he had to get Carmela to safety. He didn't like to admit it, but he might have to go with her all the way to Prescott before going after Dix. She was his responsibility now, and he had to find her a safe place to wait until the marshal could find out if her uncle was still alive.

♥

Carmela lay on Price's bunk, staring at the rafters above. What outcome did she wish for in this unforeseen predicament?

She didn't wish Uncle Silas dead, and yet she might be better off without him. If he died at the outlaws' hands, what would she do? What *could* she do? She didn't have enough money now to go back to New England, but she couldn't stay out here in the desert.

Perhaps when she got to the capital, she could find a place to live, and maybe even a job. But what skills did she have? She could sew passably, and she could cook a little if necessary. She had practiced weaving baskets to lend authenticity to her speeches, and she had read many accounts of pioneers and explorers, anything to be had about the southwestern Indian tribes. She had even tried her hand at pottery in New Hampshire, where a skilled potter had given her lessons that Uncle Silas paid for. Part of the debt she had run up, she thought bitterly. But she couldn't very well set up a pottery shop in Arizona.

How would she support herself? The idea of going on alone and fulfilling the speaking engagements her uncle had scheduled repelled her. Without Uncle Silas, she would stop doing that immediately. That was one thing she positively knew.

Her mother had always taught her that things turned out best for those who loved God. That was hard to accept now, with her parents gone and the deception she'd been forced to live for the past eight years. Now she was utterly alone, but she couldn't shake off her faith. Bad things happened to God's people, she knew that. She wasn't sure why He allowed suffering, but somehow, all of this was supposed to lead her to a good outcome—if not in this life, then in the next.

This life might be one long test. If she held fast to her belief, she would find peace in heaven. She hoped it was more than that. She hoped she would see some resolution for herself, Uncle Silas, Freeland, and the other people trapped at this way station.

She formed a silent prayer in her mind and drifted off to sleep thinking, *Lord, I believe You care about us. Please show me what to do.*

Chapter Nine

When Carmela entered the main room in the morning, Jerry stood over the stove, stirring something in a frying pan. Price lay rolled up in a blanket in a corner, Freeland stood on guard at the window, and Windle sat at the table nursing a cup of coffee while he waited for his breakfast.

"Good morning," she said.

"Morning, miss." Windle's teeth showed amidst his luxuriant beard.

Jerry waved his spatula. "Grits and bacon coming up, ma'am."

"Thank you, Jerry."

She walked to the window, and Freeland turned toward her. He appraised her face and gave her a tired smile.

"Sleep well?" he asked.

"Not bad. How about you?"

"Not so well. I finally got up and relieved Price a couple hours ago, so he could rest."

Jerry fixed their plates and sat down with Windle and Carmela. He wolfed his food and then fixed a portion for Freeland so he could spell him at watching.

Freeland sank down in the chair beside Carmela with a sigh

and reached for his coffee. She was nearly done with her meal, and Windle had cleaned his plate. The blacksmith rose and took his dish to the stove.

Freeland closed his eyes for a moment. When he opened them, he caught Carmela watching, and his lips quirked. She hoped her cheeks didn't bloom crimson, not that it would matter much with her sunburned complexion. Windle returned, his plate holding a second serving nearly as large as his first.

"So what's the plan?" he asked as he plunked down onto the bench. "You folks sticking it out here?"

Freeland nodded as he loaded his fork. "I've thought it over. I think we should stay with you until either another stage comes through or a party from Wickenburg comes to find out what happened."

"Probably wise." Windle plunged his spoon into the mound of grits on his plate.

The two men talked a bit more, and when he had finished his food, Windle announced that he would go out to feed the mules. He took his dishes to the washing area and went outside, wearing his holstered revolver and carrying the shotgun.

Freeland leaned back and looked at Carmela. "Get enough to eat?"

"Yes, thank you."

He smiled. "I imagine grits isn't your first love, being from the North and all."

"I've encountered it in my travels. It's not much different from the cornmeal mush my mother used to make." She rose and brought the coffeepot from the stove to refill his mug.

"Thanks." Freeland took a drink. He winced slightly, and she didn't blame him. The liquid was bitter, and by now it was probably not as hot as he'd like it, since Jerry had let the stove begin to cool down as soon as he'd finished cooking. She topped off her own mug, though she didn't really want more, but it would give her an excuse to linger at the table. She preferred Freeland's company to the comparative privacy of Price's room.

He set his mug down. Carmela had resumed her seat, and he

gazed at her across the rough pine table. "So, you've been back what—six years?"

"Closer to eight." As soon as she spoke, she realized that might not tally with what she had told him before, or what she had let him believe about her ordeal.

"Did you find it hard to come back to civilization?"

She lowered her eyelashes. She hadn't expected him to dive into the topic of her captivity. Her re-assimilation to the white culture was a favorite subject during question time at her lectures. To make the topic less painful, she compared her life before her parents' death to her life with Uncle Silas.

"In some ways," she said, hoping the vague answer would prompt him to drop the subject.

He leaned toward her and dropped his voice. "I know it's difficult for you when people stare. I saw Jerry gawking at you last night."

"Did he say anything after I retired?" she asked.

"Oh yeah. Asked me all about it. I told him I didn't know much, but that you'd spent time with one of the tribes. I hope he won't bother you, but don't be surprised if he tries to strike up a conversation about it."

She nodded. "Thank you. I'm forewarned."

He sat back. "I expect you're used to it. People can't help but wonder."

Tears sprang into Carmela's eyes. She would never get used to it, the staring, the questions, the smirking and leering. People thought they knew so much when they knew nothing, nothing at all.

"I'm sorry," Freeland said. "I didn't mean to upset you."

"No one ever does." She managed a weak smile.

His gaze fell, and she knew she had made him feel guilty. He'd been kind to her, and she didn't wish to make him feel bad. In fact, he had saved her life when it came down to it. If he hadn't rallied and brought her here, she'd be dead by now. And if she had let the Indian free her from the deputy, where would she be? Living out her nightmare—the lie she had told for the last eight years. Freeland deserved to know the truth.

She glanced around to check on Jerry, at the window, and Price, who let out occasional snores from his blanket cocoon near the hearth. Windle was still outside. She ought to have told Freeland everything when they were alone in the desert, but as things stood now, she probably wouldn't have a better time than this.

She leaned forward. "My tattoos—they're not real."

He blinked and leaned in, his face only inches from hers, his blue eyes keen. "Did I hear you correctly?" He flung a look over his shoulder. "They're fake?"

She nodded.

He sat for a moment, studying her chin. "What about the rest of it?"

She hesitated. Once she said it, she couldn't take it back. Gazing into Freeland's eyes, she wanted desperately to end the lie.

"I was never with the Indians," she whispered.

Freeland stared at Carmela. She scrunched handfuls of her skirt in her lap, not returning his gaze. Her brown eyes had a feral look, as though she might bolt at any second.

He wished he could take her outside for a walk, away from the others, but the chance of outlaws or Apache swooping down on them was too great. He rested his arms on the table and said softly, "Tell me about it."

Carmela sighed. "My father took us on a wagon train. He wanted to set up in California. He'd heard the best land was there. All of that's true. We traveled all year, from spring to October. We were getting close, Pa said. And then he got sick. He and Ma both came down with it, and my brother. The wagon train stopped. They talked about what to do. We weren't the only family that caught the sickness."

"What kind of sickness?" Freeland asked.

"I don't know. They just said fever. Now I think maybe cholera."

He nodded. "Go on."

"They left us and two other families. My pa died, and they buried him before the rest of the train left. By the time we were done, there was me and a man named Mr. Basford and one of his boys. The whole Jessup family died, and my ma and brother. Mr. Basford took me into his wagon with his son. He was awfully weak, and so were Tommy and I, but we made it to Fort Yuma. When they were stronger, they went on. They left me there with the army chaplain and his wife. They sent for Uncle Silas, and he came to get me." Tears trickled down her cheeks.

Freeland frowned. "So you were with the chaplain and his wife after your parents died, not after. . ."

"There was no ambush." She looked down at her hands.

"So why did you say there was?"

"Uncle Silas."

"This was all his idea?"

She nodded. "He made up the story. What I told you before was true, about Olive Oatman. He got the idea from her. He figured we could get rich—that is, *he* could get rich—if he could train me to tell a good story."

Freeland's breath puffed out of him and he sat in stunned silence. After a long moment, Carmela stirred.

"Will you arrest me, Mr. McKay?"

He stared at her. "Whatever for?"

"Fraud. I lied to thousands of people, and we took their money."

"You didn't have a choice, did you? That's what Will meant when he said your uncle made you do things. He made you lie so he could rake in the money."

Her lips trembled and her chin sank. "That's right." Her tears flowed freely now.

"You were a kid." Freeland scowled and tried to figure the years. "You told me you were twelve, right?"

"Yes. It took us a while to get ready. I had to study, and Uncle Silas spent months planning everything out. He made me say I was younger when it happened, to account for my time with the savages, you see."

"Sure."

She swallowed hard. "He made me say I was with them five years, but it isn't true. When people heard I was younger at the time of the. . .tragedy, it seemed more plausible that I stayed with them and didn't escape. I was too young to know better, according to Uncle Silas."

"But if you were twelve, and you knew what you were doing was wrong. . ." He let it trail off.

"Yes, I knew. I didn't want to do it, but he forced me."

"How?"

"I told you. He said my father owed him ten thousand dollars."

Freeland's brain was reeling. She had told him earlier that her uncle claimed her father owed him a lot of money, but ten thousand dollars? That was astronomical.

"Where would he get that much money?" he asked. "And why would your father borrow that much?"

"I don't think he did," she said with a glance toward Jerry. The young man slouched by the window, giving no sign he could hear them. "At first I was too shocked and frightened to reason it out, and I was only twelve. I couldn't really comprehend how much money that was. But now I think Uncle Silas made up the debt to use against me."

"Did he threaten you otherwise? What if you'd just said no?"

Her mouth twitched twice before she spoke. "I did at first. He. . . he hit me. Not on my face, but he hurt me awfully. He said if I didn't do as he said, it would be worse."

"But you seemed so—so cordial to each other."

"It's been a long time," she reminded him. "I stopped fighting him years ago. It was useless. We came to an understanding. I would work off the debt, and then I could do as I pleased, if I was of age. That won't be for another year. I just turned twenty, and I've worked off the ten thousand."

Freeland nodded. "And he told you your expenses went beyond that. You did say something about that."

"Yes. But I made up my mind that the day I turn twenty-one, I will leave him. If he tries to make me stay, I'll go to the authorities. But now..." She faltered. "Mr. McKay, what am I going to do?"

"Easy, now. And you don't have to stop calling me Freeland because you told me the truth." He reached over and patted her arm awkwardly. "It's not your doing. As far as arresting you, Mr. Holden's the one who committed the fraud."

"I told the lies."

"Under duress," Freeland said.

She inhaled deeply. "Yes."

He had no doubt she was telling the truth.

"I was clumsy at first, and I knew so little about the Indians. Uncle Silas made me memorize speeches. When we got back to New England, I spent the first winter studying. Everything he could find, I committed to memory. Some of the narrative pamphlets he bought were from the days of the colonies and the eastern Indian tribes, but that didn't matter. He told me most folks back East wouldn't know the difference, that savagery was savagery. But he found more and more accounts of the West—journals and articles and a few books. He scoured newspapers for new information and had me learn beading and pottery making."

Freeland put his hand up and rubbed the bump on the back of his head. It was getting smaller, but it still hurt some.

"Did you stay mostly in the East?"

"During the war, yes. We kept mostly to New England then. We made enough to get by, and Uncle Silas was eager to try a wider audience. Last summer, we went to New York and Philadelphia, then took the train west. And when we got as far as Texas, I realized how little I knew and how inaccurate some of my speeches were."

"What did you do?"

"Studied more. Uncle Silas has pushed me every single day. I wrote out descriptions of the activities in the Indian villages, so I could practice and get better at it."

"You've worked hard."

"Yes," she said with an uncertain air. "For the wrong reason."

"Maybe for the wrong goal, but it sounds like you had to do it. Don't blame yourself. And as to what you should do, wait and see if your uncle survives this, I guess." He pushed back his chair. "Why don't you get some rest? I think I'll go out and see if I can help Mr. Windle."

"That's probably a good idea." She stood and smiled ruefully. "Thank you."

He nodded and watched her walk to the curtained doorway, then he turned and strode to the window.

"Guess I'll go out and help Windle," he told Jerry.

"I'll cover you. It looks like he's putting the mules in the lean-to. Harder to steal them if they're inside."

Freeland glanced back at the curtain, but Carmela was out of sight. How on earth was he going to help that girl? He'd thought at first getting her to Wickenburg alive would be enough, but now he knew his commitment lay deeper. He'd reckoned on trying to rescue her uncle so that Holden could take care of her, but it looked as though he'd had it all wrong. If Holden survived his time with the outlaws, Carmela might need protection from him.

Late that evening, Carmela lay on the bunk, reflecting on their day. Other than her conversation with Freeland, it had passed uneventfully—quite a boring day, actually. Her thirst brought vivid memories of their time in the desert. She had come to admire Freeland. He had looked out for her in many different ways. The man handled himself well and put the well-being of others ahead of his own.

She couldn't lie there all night thinking about the deputy marshal. She rose and patted the crate that served as the stationmaster's bedside stand for her candle. Surely no one would mind if she crept into the other room for a drink of water. Maybe after her thirst subsided she could sleep.

For modesty's sake, in case they were roused in the night, she hadn't undressed. She picked up the candlestick and felt her way to the doorway curtain. Now, if she could just make it to the stove and light the candle from an ember without waking the men, she could have her drink. She blinked, trying to orient herself in the faintest of light that came through the windows.

"Can't sleep, miss?"

The voice startled her, and she nearly dropped her candle.

"M–Mr. Windle?"

"That's right," the blacksmith said. "It's my watch."

She could make out his form then, silhouetted against the small window where the men took turns watching the yard.

"I thought I'd get some water," Carmela whispered. "I was going to light my candle."

"Let me help you." He walked toward her and touched her arm, and Carmela pushed the candlestick into his hands. He went over and opened the lid on the stove's firebox. She could see his face in the dim glow of the embers. On the floor across the room, one of the other men stirred and rolled over.

Windle came over and handed her the flaming candle. It seemed overly bright, since she had been in darkness so long. He went to the water bucket and dipped a ladleful for her.

"Thank you." Carmela took it and sipped the tepid water, wishing he would go back to his post.

"Them Apache that hit the station down the line weren't friends of yours, were they?"

She gasped. "What do you mean?"

"I heard the deputy say you was with 'em awhile."

"I wasn't with the Apache."

"Oh. All right, then."

She hoped he wouldn't press her about her captivity. He laid a hand on her sleeve and leaned in close.

"I reckon you got pretty friendly with 'em, hey?"

Carmela jerked away, dropping the ladle with a clatter. "I don't know what you mean." She whirled and made her way back to the small bedroom and sat down on the edge of the bunk. Her hand shook as she set the candlestick on the crate.

In the outer room, she heard low voices. So she had woken someone. Or maybe it was time for them to swap off the watchman.

She blew out the candle, rose, and crept to the curtain, where she stood trying to calm her pounding heart enough so that she could make out their words.

"Just leave her alone." That was Freeland, she was sure of it.

"I didn't do anything," Windle replied. "She came out here to get a drink of water."

"Shut up," someone whined from across the room, and she thought it was Price.

"Go back to sleep," Windle said, louder. "You, too."

Was he speaking to Freeland now? After a momentary pause, Freeland said, "I'm up next, and I'm wide awake. Might as well spell you now."

"Fine by me," Windle said. She heard footsteps.

When all was quiet, Carmela pushed aside the very edge of the curtain with one finger. After a moment, she could make out the placement of the two small windows. The man at the nearest one had his back to her, but she was sure Freeland held the shotgun now. She exhaled carefully. She would be safe as long as he was on watch. She tiptoed to the bunk and lay down as quietly as she could.

Chapter Ten

Carmela allowed Jerry to escort her out to the necessary the next morning. He was nothing but polite and embarrassed. Back in the station, she waited until Windle went out to feed the livestock before venturing to the cooking area for her breakfast. Freeland was still dozing, but Price grinned at her as he flipped a pancake in his cast iron skillet.

"Morning, Miss Wade. Care for a flapjack or two?"

She returned his smile. "That sounds good, thank you."

He nodded and eased two golden cakes from the pan onto a tin plate and held it out to her. "Bacon in the fry pan there."

"Thanks." She reminded herself that she must open the seam on her jacket hem before they left and give the stationmaster part of the concealed money. She didn't have much, but Price had been kind to her and deserved to be paid for the supplies he had shared with her and Freeland.

"You sleepin' all right on that bunk? The mattress is none too soft."

"It's fine," she said. "If I have trouble sleeping, it's because I'm worried about my uncle." *And my future*, she thought, but did not voice that concern. "Thank you for giving up your bed for me. I feel a little guilty."

"No sense in that." Price carefully poured more batter into the pan. "If the stage line takes off, we plan to expand and have a better place for the passengers to stop and for the drivers and tenders to stay, but right now we're just eking by."

She nodded. "I don't suppose you can invest too much until you know if it will bring a profit."

"That, and if the Injuns will leave us be." Price shook his head, and his gray hair swung about his cheeks. "I dunno if we can survive out here or not. Giving it a go."

"I admire your ambition," she said. "And I'm certainly glad you were here when Mr. McKay and I needed you."

Jerry had taken up the post at the window once more. He called without turning around, "Sounds like someone's coming!"

Price drew his revolver and yelled, "McKay! Company."

Freeland sat up at once and reached for his boots. "Do we know who?"

The door burst open, and Windle ran in, panting. "Looks like the celerity wagon's coming in from Wickenburg."

"Hallelujah," Price said.

They all trooped outside and stood in a row as the driver brought the team and wagon into the yard at a trot. The unpainted coach looked a bit road weary, but Carmela was delighted to see it arrive with four armed men riding inside and two more on the roof. Behind it came eight mounted men, also bearing weapons.

"It's the marshal," Freeland said. He stepped forward to greet the leader of the horsemen.

"Everything all right here?" the marshal called as he pulled his palomino in.

"We're fine, but there's trouble down the line," Freeland said. He quickly apprised Marshal Duffield of the situation while Price conferred with the driver of the celerity wagon. Carmela edged up beside Freeland and hung on the marshal's words.

"I suspect that bunch of outlaws is a splinter off the gang that pulled a robbery near Wickenburg last month," Duffield said. "Could even be connected to the ones who robbed the Texas State Treasury last June."

"Think so?" Freeland asked. "It's out of the way."

"Yup, but they never caught 'em, and there was up to fifty men in that gang. They're probably scattered all over."

"So. . .you want to go after the outlaws now?" Freeland asked. "I'd like to get that gold shipment back and see what became of Miss Wade's uncle."

His eyes were eager, and Carmela had a sudden fear that he would go back on his promise and ride off with the marshal and his posse, leaving her here with Price and his crew.

"I think it would be better to go after them than the Apache," the marshal said.

Freeland nodded. "Those Indians are probably long gone, into some canyon or other. I doubt we'd catch 'em, and if we did, they might be too much for us."

"All right." Duffield dismounted and handed his reins off to one of the other men. "Let me talk to Mr. Price and see what he needs to defend the station. Like I say, those Apache are probably gone, but I don't want to risk leaving him undefended until we're sure, since you tell me two other stations have been attacked."

The men gathered near the stagecoach to lay their plans. Carmela felt abandoned, but she decided it was time to grow up. These men didn't need her to decide what they would do, and Freeland was already steering them toward looking for her uncle. But she could do something that would encourage them and strengthen them before they set out—she could fix a fresh pot of coffee and start cooking a simple meal. By now she knew where Mr. Price kept his utensils and supplies. No use acting helpless. She straightened her shoulders and headed inside.

❤

Freeland had to admire Carmela. She didn't cry or insist that the men go after her uncle. She didn't sit around moping while they made their plans. Instead, she put on Price's stained apron and whipped up a batch of biscuits and fried some bacon so they could all have a bite before setting out. She was some woman!

"I've got a packhorse with some gear on it for the posse," the marshal said as they sat at the table. "We'll escort the stage on down the line to make sure they get through all right, and when they're safe, we'll go after those outlaws."

"Do you have a horse I can ride?" Freeland asked.

Duffield frowned. "Seems to me you'd best escort that young lady to Prescott. Can't leave her out here."

"But—" Freeland closed his mouth. More than anything, he wanted to recapture Dix. Maybe the posse could do that. But the marshal was right—he was responsible for Carmela's well-being now, and he couldn't abandon her. Maybe he wouldn't have to take her all the way to the capital. Maybe she could stay in Wickenburg while he rejoined the posse.

Carmela came around with the coffeepot to refill their cups.

"What do you say, young lady?" Duffield asked her a bit more jovially than the circumstances warranted. "Will you be all right with Deputy McKay, getting from here to Prescott while I go looking for Dix and the outlaws? I think we have a fair chance of getting your uncle back, depending on how bad his wound was."

Carmela gulped. "Yes sir. That would be fine. I don't think I can help him by staying out here, unless you have a mount for me."

"Nope, I don't." The marshal eyed Freeland thoughtfully. "I guess we can redistribute the gear and give you the packhorse. Can the two of you get to Wickenburg on it?"

Freeland shrugged. "I guess so, sir. It beats walking, and handcuffed together at that."

Duffield laughed. "I should say so." He glanced up at Carmela. "Tell me, miss, is he giving it to me straight? Was he really out cold when that transpired?"

"Yes sir," she said. "It's my fault. I never should have trusted that man, Dix. If I'd thought about it, I would have realized he wouldn't have killed me with his only bullet. If nothing else, he could have used it to shoot the chain off the handcuffs."

"True," Duffield said. "Well, don't fret over it. Dix is a clever man, from what I understand. He found a way to keep the bullet and get free at the same time, as well as slowing down the deputy from pursuing him."

"They both might have died out there," Price said.

"Yes, they might." Duffield reached for another biscuit. "If we catch him, he'll have assault and escape charges added to his list of crimes."

Freeland could think of no way to persuade the marshal to take him with him that wouldn't leave Carmela in a precarious position. Now that he knew Price, he was sure the stationmaster was a good man, but he wasn't sure he would trust Windle and Jerry. Carmela really needed to get to a town where there were other women and she could find decent lodgings. Of course, Wickenburg wasn't much of a town the last time he was up this way. Would he want to leave his mother or his sister there unprotected? He drew a careful breath, considering. He'd have to see how things looked when they got there.

"I'll give you some messages to deliver for me," the marshal went on. "We'll need to inform the governor of the situation and tell the stagecoach agents along the way. Price may have some messages for you to confer."

Freeland nodded. Until they got telegraph wires out here, it was part of his job to carry the news, good or bad, when he rode to other parts of the territory.

He drained his coffee cup and looked at Duffield. "After I see Miss Wade is safe and report the losses to the stage line and the governor, am I free to ride out and join the posse?"

"Sure. I'll leave word for you anyplace I can."

Freeland wished he could pass his assignment on to someone else, but he knew that wasn't possible. The marshal had made it clear. He wondered if he would have received the same orders if he hadn't lost his prisoner, but those thoughts weren't profitable. Might as well do his duty and get it over with.

He rose and went to the worktable, where Carmela was stacking the dirty dishes. "Sounds like you and I can share one horse and head for Wickenburg anytime."

She nodded. "I have no luggage. I'll help clean up here for Mr. Price while you get things ready."

"Ten minutes," Freeland said with decision.

"I'll be here."

The marshal had secured a pencil and an old envelope from Price. He tore open the envelope and wrote his messages inside.

"If the governor's in when you get to Prescott, tell him anything he wants to know," he said soberly as he handed the paper to Freeland.

"Yes sir." Freeland swallowed hard. "I don't suppose I could leave Miss Wade in Wickenburg and send the messages on by someone else?"

"No, you deliver them in person, McKay. I can trust you, but there are not many men in Wickenburg I can say that about."

"Yes sir. I'll do it."

Duffield nodded. "Come on outside, then. We'll give you the horse and a bridle. Not sure about a saddle."

Windle, who had been leaning against the wall near the table, took his toothpick from his mouth. "I can lend you a saddle," he said. "Just leave it at the stage stop in Wickenburg."

"Thanks." Freeland nodded at him and followed the marshal outside.

❤

They rode slowly to spare the horse. Once again, the heat soared, and riding double increased their discomfort. Carmela sat behind the saddle and kept only the lightest handhold on Freeland's belt, leaning back as much as she could without overbalancing, in hopes a breeze would waft between them.

After an hour, they came to a silvery stream that seemed to disappear into the ground beneath some jagged red rocks.

"Where does it go?" Carmela asked, staring at it.

"Underground. That's the Hassayampa. It means 'river that flows upside down.' When there's a rain, it'll flow more above ground, but most of the time, it's pretty much down below."

Freeland turned and grasped her wrist to support her as she slid down the horse's flank, then he swung his leg over the saddle and climbed down.

"You can nearly always find water here, and we'll follow it upstream to Wickenburg. Shouldn't have to get thirsty again on this stretch. Go ahead and drink, before I let the horse get into it."

She drank and bathed her hands and face, then went off among the weird rock formations for privacy while Freeland drank and watered the horse.

The stark beauty of the landscape still amazed her, though she wasn't sure she ever wanted to visit the territory again once she'd escaped this ordeal. She walked back to where she could just see the horse's rump as it greedily guzzled from the stream and found a wedge of shade beside a tall, creased rock.

Despite what Uncle Silas had done to her, she couldn't abandon him to the outlaws. If the marshal and his men didn't find him, she would have to arrange for a search party. After all, he had taken her in and educated her, though more in culture and history than anything else. He had tutored her in public speaking and trained her to behave like a lady. For the most part, he had made sure they lodged in decent establishments and had plenty to eat, and he had kept the crowds from mauling her. She supposed she owed him something beyond the money she had earned for him—some loyalty. Even so, she couldn't shake the thought that without his deception and the tattoos on her face, she wouldn't have needed much protection.

Freeland led the horse away from the spring toward the trail. He spotted her in the rock's shadow and walked over, with the horse clopping behind on the powdery red dirt.

"Ready?"

She nodded. "I was just thinking."

"About Mr. Holden?"

"Yes. If the posse can't find him—"

"They should be able to track the outlaws, and if your uncle isn't with them, the marshal can make them tell him where he is."

Carmela gazed into his blue eyes, letting that sink in.

"You think he's dead."

Freeland looked off toward the town they sought, northward. "I don't know. I didn't look closely at his wound. But it's easy to bleed to death from an untended body wound, and infection is common. Without a doctor. . . I'm just saying, maybe you should prepare yourself for bad news."

She smiled ruefully. "Is there ever good news out here?"

Freeland's cracked lips returned her smile. "Well, I did thank God when we found Mr. Price and the others alive, and when the marshal turned up with his men this morning."

"So did I. And when we overpowered Mr. Dix. We've shared a great deal of misfortune and fortune, Mr. McKay." His eyebrows arched, and she looked away. "Freeland."

He cocked his head toward his right shoulder. "I hope you won't think me too bold if I say there's no one I'd rather have survived with, Carmela."

She shivered in spite of the heat. Was he valuing her above the stagecoach driver and the others? If they'd all died but one, was he saying he'd choose her over Dix? Was it just because she was a woman and he was a gentleman? She'd never felt as though someone liked her as a person. Lots of people wanted to talk to her as a curiosity and get to know her because of her alleged past. Will McKay had cared about her. Had his brother come to respect her and even like her as well? She thought about that for a long time as they plodded along the shimmering trail, glimpsing the Hassayampa now and then, off to their left.

At last Freeland pulled the horse to a halt, and she expected him to call another rest. Instead, he leaned to one side.

"Look ahead, down the trail. Can you see it?"

Far below them, clustered along the riverbank, were dozens of tents. A few buildings were scattered among them, and she could see tiny dots of people and livestock moving about.

"Maybe you can stay there," Freeland said. "Fellow named Grant runs the stage stop."

"Does he have a wife?" Carmela hated the quiver in her voice.

"I dunno." Freeland nudged the horse forward.

On the last couple of miles into Wickenburg, he told her bits of information and legend.

"They say once you drink out of the Hassayampa, you can't tell the truth anymore," was one.

"Does that mean we're both liars now?" she asked.

"Maybe. It's because of all the false claims they've made—the miners. They've sold more worthless claims in this valley than anywhere else on earth, I reckon."

They passed some prospectors heading toward the mountains with their mules loaded with tools and provisions, and two Indians crossed their path as they came down into the tent city.

"Are they Apache?" Carmela whispered, trying not to stare at the grim faces.

"Yavapai," Freeland said.

"Are they friendly?"

"Some. Can't rightly trust 'em, the marshal says. The ranchers and miners in these parts have had trouble with 'em."

She exhaled carefully and clung tighter to his belt.

One of the rough cabins had a sign proclaiming that an assayer plied his skills there, but the rest of the buildings seemed to be saloons. Men went in and out of them, shouting to each other. Carmela cringed and tried not to meet any of the bearded miners' eyes, but she knew all of them stared at her. She wanted to bury her face in the back of Freeland's shirt, but that would be most improper.

At last they saw a cabin a little away from the tents and the noise of the settlement.

"Yonder's the stage stop," Freeland said. He pulled up before it and helped her dismount. They walked to the door together, and he pounded on it with his fist. "Grant?"

The door opened, and a bearded man of about forty eyed him closely. "McKay?"

"None other. This here's Miss Wade. Is there a decent place in town where she can board?"

"Yer joking, right?" Grant said.

"Well, I wasn't." Freeland sighed. "I reckon we'll head right out for Prescott, then. Can you give us a meal and rent me another horse?"

"Sure." Grant stepped back so they could enter the small, dark room. Carmela hoped he wouldn't ask about her tattoos or why she was traveling through this desolate area. He started out by asking what was going on down the line, and Freeland gave him a shortened version of the attacks on the stagecoach and stations.

"They'd best not try that here," Grant said.

"I doubt they would, with so many miners milling around," Freeland replied.

"So the young lady's not looking for work, then?" Grant said as he took a couple of tin plates from a shelf.

"No," Freeland said firmly.

"Too bad," Grant said. "Murphy's and the Silver Slipper are both looking for girls. Of course, them Injun markings don't help her none—although, some fellas might find 'em exotic, I s'pose."

Carmela clenched her teeth together and let Freeland give the man the answer he deserved.

Chapter Eleven

They were back on the trail an hour later, with two passable horses under them. Freeland had arranged with Grant to leave the marshal's borrowed horse and Windle's saddle there, and Carmela had surprised him by coming up with a dollar and four bits—enough to pay for their dinner and assure Grant that the horses they took from his corral would find their way back. Grant wasn't in the habit of loaning or renting out his horses, but Freeland's badge seemed to sway him.

As they headed through Peeples Valley, toward Prescott, Freeland kept an eye on Carmela. On the way out of Wickenburg, he'd found a Yavapai woman who was willing to sell a light, woven shawl. Carmela had gladly paid for it to keep the sun off her. They had no other comforts besides the refilled Apache water skin. She rode slouching in the saddle, her eyes nearly shut.

"We'll get there by nightfall," Freeland told her. "Grant says these horses are good for it."

She nodded but said nothing.

Freeland quickened the pace, and they trotted up the valley for an hour, passing a few people now and then. A rancher was driving some steers to Wickenburg to sell, and miners worked their way back and forth between the town and their claims. A pair of troopers from Fort Whipple stopped and talked for five minutes, very interested in Freeland's report of the outlaw gang and marauding Apache.

After they had moved on and gained another five or six miles, he led her down a well-worn path to the edge of Date Creek, so they could water the horses. He noticed that after she splashed water on her face she took one corner of the shawl and scrubbed fiercely at her chin and cheeks.

"You all right?" he asked as they prepared to mount again.

"Yes."

He smiled. She wouldn't complain. A couple of days ago, he'd have said it was because the Indians taught her not to. Now he realized she was just stubborn. She probably hurt in a million places, and he could tell she was exhausted, but she never once asked him to rest or how far it was to Prescott.

"I know it seems we're getting farther and farther away from your uncle, but I assure you, we'll do our best to get him back."

"Thank you." She tightened the girth on her saddle without looking at him.

Freeland cleared his throat. "The ink's less noticeable."

She met his gaze then. "Did I mess it up?"

"Not really, but it's lighter now. I bet it will all come off in a few more days."

She blinked twice, and he could see the sheen of tears in her eyes. "He renewed it every few days."

He reached out with one finger and barely grazed her cheek where the diamond pattern still showed but not nearly as pronounced as when he'd first seen her. She didn't flinch, but he felt suddenly he'd overstepped some invisible line. He let his hand drop. "Well, you don't have to do it again if you don't want to. Ever."

She let out a deep breath. "Thank you. We'll see what happens with Uncle Silas."

He nodded. She had to know she could do as she pleased now, and she didn't have to obey the bully any longer. But she was tenderhearted, and she was entrenched in the habit of obedience, even if her respect for her uncle had cracked and sloughed away.

"Did he make arrangements for you in Prescott?"

"I don't know." Her gaze slid off toward the jagged mountain peaks edging the valley. "He wrote a letter, but with no telegraph lines out here, I have no idea whether the townspeople expect us or not, or whether they have set up a lecture. They generally do, but it's all so. . ."

"Primitive?" he asked.

She smiled faintly. "It is a bit provincial. Uncle Silas is usually able to draw a crowd for us, however, even if we enter a town unannounced."

"The miners and ranchers out here crave entertainment," Freeland said. "I imagine you can have an audience without too much trouble. If you still want one."

Her lips twitched. "I would like nothing better than to drop the ruse of my captivity. However, I don't know how I should live if I did. The money I gave Mr. Grant was nearly the last of my hoarded coins."

"You're a nice young lady," Freeland said. "Decent, polite. We should be able to find a place for you to stay until we determine what's become of your uncle."

"Thank you. That's reassuring."

He gave her a quick boost into the saddle and mounted his dust-covered bay. As they jogged along up the valley, he tried not to think about Carmela's future. Instead, he thought about Dix. If the marshal didn't find him where they'd left him, or close to it, they would focus on tracking the outlaw gang. Maybe he would be able to hunt for Dix after they settled that issue.

His headstrong thoughts veered back to Carmela and the moment he had touched her cheek. He'd been tempted to kiss her, of all things. In the scorching heat, with many miles ahead of them, he'd been thinking of romance.

His involvement with Carmela had gone beyond satisfying Will's request, he realized. He didn't just want to see her safe. He personally cared what would happen to Carmela now. The depth of emotion he'd felt back there near the creek alarmed him. After all, he would probably never see her again after he found her a place to board in Prescott. He would let the marshal take her whatever news they learned of Mr. Holden.

The sun was setting as they rode into the capital, their horses' steps dragging.

The town had tripled in size since the last time he'd been there. Already the noise from the saloons dominated the atmosphere.

"Stay close," Freeland murmured. "There'll be a blacksmith closer to the governor's house."

Without mishap, he led Carmela past the street that was no more than a long string of saloons. They caught glimpses of restaurants and boardinghouses, a hotel, several stores, and even a newspaper office where the *Miner* was published sporadically.

"It's a city," she said in amazement. "I thought it would be like Wickenburg."

"Ranchers and farmers are moving into the valleys," Freeland said. "Still a lot of trouble with the Indians though. The mining companies trying to build stamp mills are attacked nearly every day."

"Why? Are the tribes angry that so many whites are moving here?" Carmela asked.

"Partly. Mostly they want to steal the livestock. Hundreds of horses and mules have been stolen in this area over the past couple of years."

At last they arrived in front of the governor's house. The solid log cabin was larger than most other buildings in town, two stories high, with room for a detachment of soldiers to bed down.

"It's built for a fortress if need be," Freeland told her. After he presented his badge to the army private at the door, they were shown inside.

They met the governor in a large and rustic inner room. The plain board floor and walls were decorated with rugs and pictures that lent an air of civilization.

"Welcome, Deputy," Governor McCormick said when the soldier announced him and Carmela. "Miss Wade. My wife and I are at dinner with Captain Johnson, who is here from Fort Whipple. Will you join us?"

Freeland glanced at Carmela, who was gazing at the dining table and the beautifully gowned woman who sat there.

"I'd be lying if I said we weren't hungry," Freeland said. "We've been traveling all day on a scant meal in Wickenburg. We're sorry to interrupt your dinner though."

"Nonsense," the governor said. "We were just about to begin."

Mrs. McCormick rose and came toward them. "Good evening. I do hope you'll join us. Miss Wade, would you like to freshen up first?"

"Thank you, ma'am," Carmela said. "I would like it more than I can say. This dust. . ." She glanced down at her discolored skirt.

"Isn't it awful?" Mrs. McCormick smiled and guided her to a door at one side of the room. "Come right this way, my dear."

"Have you had truck with the marshal?" McCormick asked Freeland.

"Yes sir. He's gone after the band of highwaymen that's terrorizing the stage line below Wickenburg. Unfortunately, some Apaches have also been at work there. Two way stations were attacked, one of them burnt. The agents and their men were killed. All the stock was run off of course."

"What a pity," the governor said.

The captain had joined them. "You'll have to tell us everything over dinner, Mr. McKay."

"Yes," McCormick said, "But first, I allow you'd like to wash up."

Captain Johnson summoned the private and detailed him to show the visitor where the men habitually cleaned up. When he re-entered the room a few minutes later, Freeland was glad to see that Carmela had returned. Her hands and face were clean, and she had combed her hair and shaken most of the dust out of her clothing.

After the governor offered the blessing, they were served a plentiful meal of roast beef, biscuits, corn, and applesauce, followed by a spice cake almost as tasty as the one Freeland's mother baked now and then. When his third cup of coffee was poured, he sat back in satisfaction. Carmela smiled timidly at him from across the table. She, too, looked sated.

"Now, tell us about your adventures," Mrs. McCormick said. "I'm very curious as to why you are traveling in these parts, Miss Wade."

"She was under the protection of her uncle," Freeland said. "Unfortunately, he was driven off in the stagecoach when the robbers took it, bleeding from a gunshot wound."

"Oh dear." The hostess's distress showed on her lovely features. She turned to Carmela. "Forgive me, Miss Wade. I did not mean to make light of your ordeal."

"Not at all, madam. You couldn't have known," Carmela said.

Freeland recounted their journey from Tucson, not elevating himself or leaving out his regrettable loss of his prisoner. He mentioned Carmela's reason for traveling as if it hardly mattered, and skipped over the more personal bits that he thought might embarrass her—notably, Windle's advances to her—but emphasized her pluck and perseverance during their difficult journey.

"Amazing," the governor declared when he had finished.

"My dear," Mrs. McCormick said to Carmela, "you must be exhausted. Do you have lodgings?"

"We hoped you and your husband might be able to recommend a quiet boardinghouse," Carmela said.

"There's one two streets over." Mrs. McCormick looked toward her husband. "Mrs. Finney."

"Sure," the governor said. "Mrs. Finney's a good sort. I've recommended her to ranchers bringing their families into the valley. You want to get as far away from Whiskey Row as you can. Otherwise, the noise from the saloons will keep you awake all night."

"I believe we heard the beginnings of it as we rode in," Freeland said.

"You'd best keep your head down. With the marshal out of town, you might be called on to help the local lawmen." Governor McCormick pushed back his chair. "I wish we could put you up here, but with Captain Johnson's detachment of soldiers, we've little room and less privacy."

"I can send a few men to escort you to Mrs. Finney's," Johnson offered.

"That would be most appreciated," Freeland said.

Mrs. McCormick stood, and Carmela and the men did likewise.

"Miss Wade, since you've lost your luggage and the daylight's gone, let me loan you a few things to make your overnight stay more comfortable."

"Thank you so much." Carmela's eyes filled with gratitude.

"Excuse us, gentlemen." Mrs. McCormick led Carmela out of the room.

"Bad business, with her uncle," Captain Johnson said, gazing after the women and shaking his head.

"Yes," Freeland said.

"You don't expect to get him back alive, do you?" the captain asked.

"Well, I. . ." Freeland knew it was unrealistic to expect Silas Holden to survive his wound, or for the outlaws to let him live if he did. "I didn't like to dash Miss Wade's hopes."

"Of course not," McCormick said. "You never know out here. Whiskey, gentlemen?"

"No, thank you," Freeland said. While the other two men filled their glasses, he sipped the last of his coffee and thought about Carmela. What would become of her now? She had no money and no one to look after her. But he couldn't stay here. He had to rejoin the marshal. A pang of guilt stabbed him, but he pushed it aside. He was responsible for losing the prisoner, and if there was any way he could recapture Dix, he needed to do it. If he could help bring in the outlaw gang as well, all the better. That meant Carmela Wade was far down his list, and he didn't like that.

"I guess I can take you in." Mrs. Finney stood in the doorway at her boardinghouse and looked Carmela up and down doubtfully, her gaze lingering on her chin. "Seeing as how a lawman brung you and you been robbed and all."

"Thank you," Carmela choked out.

The woman looked sturdy but dour, her gray-streaked hair pulled back into a severe bun. Her dress was of well-worn, dark gray linsey-woolsey, with a gathered skirt and fitted basque. Her face bore the wrinkles of a middle age made hard by labor. Apparently there was no Mr. Finney now, and Carmela suspected the landlady worked long hours to keep up her reputation for one of the few respectable boardinghouses in town.

"If you put in a bill for my lodging to the marshal, I'm sure he'll pay it as soon as he gets back," Freeland said.

Carmela didn't assume anyone would pay her bill. "I'll be frank. I don't have much left," she confessed. "Less than a dollar. I ask for your mercy until I am either reunited with my uncle or find another way to get on."

"Well, you can stay a couple of nights on that, dearie. We'll talk more tomorrow. Let's get you into bed, eh?" Mrs. Finney turned and shuffled to a small table that held several candlesticks. She took one and lit it from the oil lamp that brightened the otherwise stark front room. No plush cushions or upholstered chairs here. The décor was strictly frontier practical.

Carmela didn't care. All she wanted tonight was a bed. After the large meal at the governor's mansion, she was certain she would sleep well.

The boardinghouse was all one level except for a loft. Mrs. Finney handed the first candle to Freeland and lit another.

"Sir, I'm afraid all the rooms are full but one, and I'll give that to this young lady. But you may sleep in the loft with the three freighters who are up there now. I suppose you haven't any bedroll."

"No ma'am," Freeland said.

She sighed and walked to a large cupboard near the steep stairs leading above. Throwing open the door, she gestured toward stacked blankets and linens. "No pillows left, I'm afraid. There's a few straw ticks up there on the floor. You should be able to find one unoccupied."

"Thank you, ma'am." Freeland pulled out a blanket and headed up the stairs holding his candlestick carefully.

Carmela felt sorry for him, but she was too tired to spend much thought on his sleeping arrangements. Mrs. Finney led her down a corridor, off which doors issued on one side, six in a row. They walked all the way to the end, and the landlady opened the rough pine door.

"Here you are. Small but more comfortable than what the deputy's getting, and secure if you bar the door inside."

"Thank you." Carmela stepped in. The candlelight revealed a single spool bed, probably brought on some settler's wagon. The footboard was scarred and the varnish worn off in several places, but it was a proper bed.

"This mattress is all right," Mrs. Finney said. "Not the best, but it should do you."

The bed was made up with real sheets, and an extra blanket was folded across the bottom end. A small pillow in a linen case lay at the head end.

"I'm sure it will be more than adequate. Thank you."

Mrs. Finney nodded. "I'm up before sunrise, to cook for folks who want to get on the road. I don't know when the deputy wants to leave, but if you wish to sleep in, feel free." She picked up the metal pitcher from the washstand. "I'll bring you some water for washing. The necessary is out back. There's a door beside the kitchen that leads out there."

"Thank you."

When she had left the room, Carmela took the candle to the washstand. The steel basin was painted with chipped white enamel. No good china in Mrs. Finney's boardinghouse. She didn't mind, really. It must be hard to get hold of the basic furnishings and implements out here.

A small framed mirror hung over the washstand. She held up the candle and stared at her sunbaked face. Her skin tingled, but she focused on the hated tattoos. Freeland was right: they had faded somewhat, and they looked fainter on one side than the other. She could only imagine how horrible her face looked in bright daylight.

She put her fingers to her cheek and winced. Maybe when her sunburn peeled, the ink would come off with it. The thought of Uncle Silas insisting on re-inking her markings while her skin was this tender made her shudder.

Mrs. Finney tapped on the door.

"Got your water, dearie."

Carmela hurried to open the door and take the pitcher from her. "Thank you very much."

"Oh, you're welcome. Do you want to go to church in the morning?"

Carmela blinked. "It's Sunday?"

"Yes. I walk to the Baptist mission church. It's not far."

Carmela hesitated. The idea of attending church appealed to her—all too often she and Uncle Silas were on the road Sundays, or sleeping in after a late evening performance. But did she want people to see her like this, all sunburned? They would stare, as always, at her face, and it was not a pretty sight.

"I'm feeling a bit sun sick."

Mrs. Finney nodded. "I'm not surprised. You took a lot of sun, and it shows. No sense mincing words. Would you like some salve?"

"You have something that will help?" Carmela asked eagerly.

"A concoction I make from aloe plants. Works for burns, and I think it would ease your pain some."

"Thank you. I honestly didn't know if I'd be able to sleep, with my skin so tight and painful."

"I'll get it."

The landlady shuffled away down the hall. She was very kind. Maybe—if she was still here next week—Carmela would go to church with her next Sunday. She walked to the mirror again. How much would the tattoos fade by then? Should she re-ink them?

She heard Mrs. Finney returning with the aloe medicine. In a flash of decision, Carmela knew she would not renew the markings on her face—not ever.

Chapter Twelve

$\mathcal{O}$n his way south again, Freeland swapped his horse out in Wickenburg with Grant, taking the one the marshal had loaned him and Carmela. He pushed the animal to get back to Price's way station as soon as possible.

Price, Windle, and Jerry held their ground at the station, as watchful and skittish as when he had left them.

"The stage from Wickenburg came through this morning, with six outriders to protect them," Price told him in the yard when he rode up at sunset.

"I guess that's the way to go for now," Freeland said.

Price spat on the ground. "Yeah, but it's expensive for the stage company. They can't keep that up forever."

Since there was no new word from the marshal, Freeland decided to sleep there and head out at dawn. He had ridden all day, and Price still had no animals he could swap for. His horse needed a good rest.

He fidgeted after supper. He wanted to get on with it and catch up with the marshal. At least he'd succeeded in bringing Price word from Prescott that the line's owner would be down the following day to assess damages.

"He hopes to leave new workers at the two stations that were attacked and replenish the livestock," Freeland said. "Of course, they'll have to rebuild the one that was burnt. I got the idea he plans to do that right away."

"Is he sending any reinforcements here for us?" Price asked. "I'd like to have two or three more men here, just in case, and we really need another tender when the stage is running regular."

"He didn't say so." Freeland could understand the man's concerns, but with company employees coming through with extra guards and a crew working at the burned-out station, he doubted Price's place would be hit.

In the morning, he pressed onward. The place where the stage-coach was attacked and stolen was obvious. Two crosses made of cactus stems lashed together marked graves. Marshal Duffield and his men must have taken time to bury the driver and shotgun rider.

Freeland stood for a moment gazing at the markers. When this was over, he'd try to replace them with wooden ones, so the graves wouldn't be lost and forgotten. The two men deserved to be remembered. He closed his eyes and prayed silently.

Lord, thank You for those two brave men. I trust they're with You now.

He sighed and opened his eyes. The sun's rays were heating up now, and they reached through his thin cotton shirt to disturb his already burned skin. Time to move on.

He was about to swing into the saddle when he noticed a small cairn of stacked rocks. Curious, he walked over and carefully took it apart, one stone at a time. Between the bottom two was a small piece of folded paper. He opened it and squinted at the penciled words. The sun dazzled his eyes, glaring on the white paper, but he made out, *"McKay—go south. JD."*

Freeland smiled. The cairn was for him, and the message was written by the marshal.

He mounted the horse and followed the tracks of the posse southward. Now and then he could read the stage's tracks, too, where the ground was soft, but mostly it was rock or hard-packed dirt. They hadn't kept to the main road between Wickenburg and Tucson but had gone off on a course of their own through the desert. Must have a hideout of some sort out there, or maybe they knew a shortcut.

He wondered how Carmela was doing. Mrs. Finney was a good sort. She would take care of the girl. Freeland had told her privately that he would see she was paid for Carmela's stay if the girl's uncle wasn't able to do it. Mrs. Finney had fed him a wondrous breakfast before he rode out, and she loaned him her departed husband's canteen and pistol.

"Don't you worry about Miss Wade," was the last thing she said to him. "Just you watch your back trail."

Freeland swiveled his head as he rode and looked behind him. Nothing but barren, hot, cactus-studded desert. Even so, the thought of Carmela's encounter with the Apache brave who rode out of the Superstitions made him shudder. He gazed off toward the mountains in the far distance. He could barely see the highest peak from here, and soon they would be completely out of sight.

Carmela rose late, a bit ashamed of herself for sleeping in. She dressed quickly in the extra clothing Mrs. McCormick had given her and went to the dining room. It was empty and the table clear, but she could hear sounds of water pouring and dishes clinking from the kitchen. She tiptoed to the open door and peered in.

"Hello, dearie." Mrs. Finney, her arms up to her elbows in an enameled dishpan, smiled at her. She lifted her dripping hands from the water and wiped them on a linen towel. "Fancy some breakfast?"

"I'm so late, I doubt I deserve any," Carmela said.

"Nonsense. Sit down at the table, and I'll bring you something."

Carmela obeyed. She had met a wide variety of landladies and hostesses in her travels. Most boardinghouse proprietors had strict hours about breakfast and wouldn't serve it to latecomers. Some would leave out a few biscuits and slices of bacon. Few offered Mrs. Finney's brand of graciousness.

She looked down the long table with its empty chairs, and part of her wished Freeland had stayed. The other part was glad he had gone.

Mrs. Finney came in with a loaded plate. Carmela feasted her eyes on the mounds of eggs, fried potatoes, and ham.

"Thank you so much."

"Coffee? Or I've got tea or a bit of milk to spare."

"Milk? I'd love to have some."

Mrs. Finney smiled. "I have a milch cow that a neighbor keeps for me. She calved a month ago. Mr. Rowland milks her every morning and brings me part. I let him keep some. But unless I'm making custard that day, I usually have too much."

"I don't often get it when we're traveling," Carmela said.

She bowed her head and said grace while Mrs. Finney fetched her a glass, adding a special petition for Freeland. *Keep him safe, Lord.* The last thing she wanted was for him to go looking for Uncle Silas and get killed for his pains. Of course, he would look for his prisoner first. But the posse might have found Uncle Silas already.

She looked up as Mrs. Finney set the glass beside her plate. "How long do you suppose it will be before we hear from the marshal or Mr. McKay?"

"I couldn't say, child. News travels slowly across the desert, and men even slower. Mr. McKay told me some about your journey this morning before he left. Your survival is nothing short of a miracle."

"I know."

Mrs. Finney was eyeing her face critically, and Carmela put a hand up to her chin. A comment about the tattoos would come; one always did.

"Is the aloe salve helping?"

Carmela blinked, touched by the kindness in Mrs. Finney's voice. "Why yes, I think it is. I slept quite well last night."

"I'm glad."

Mrs. Finney went back to the kitchen, and Carmela made short work of her breakfast. When she had scraped every bite from the ironstone plate, she took it, with her fork, knife, and tumbler, to the kitchen.

"May I help you with the dishes?"

"Heavens, dearie, you're a guest."

"I know, but you must have a lot of them, and. . .well, I told you I don't have funds. I'd like to make up for that as much as I can."

Mrs. Finney pushed back a strand of her graying hair. "All right. There's an apron over there, on the hook by the back door. I've done up the breakfast things, but you can wash your own dishes and keep up with me as I do my baking."

"That sounds like fun." It had been years since Carmela had worked side-by-side with a woman in the kitchen, and she found herself enjoying the work and the conversation. The kitchen grew warmer than she would have liked as the landlady built up the blaze in the stove's firebox to cook her cottage pudding for tonight's dinner, but Carmela expected that and didn't complain.

As she worked, Mrs. Finney divulged tidbits about her other boarders, the luncheon menu, the governor, and his wife—"They met on a steamboat, of all places!"—and the young minister who would preach at ten o'clock.

"Oh, I forgot about church." Carmela truly had. "Isn't it ten yet? I slept frightfully late."

Mrs. Finney looked toward a small anniversary clock sitting on the top shelf of her pantry. "It's half past nine. I should get ready. Are you sure you don't want to go?"

Carmela hesitated, craving to hear God's Word, but then remembered how the people would stare.

"Thank you, but I think I'd best stay in today. Perhaps next week."

"Of course." Mrs. Finney took off her apron and hung it up. "Would you mind adding three sticks to the stove in an hour?"

"Not at all."

"Only three sticks, mind. I don't want those potatoes overdone."

"What about the pudding?" Carmela asked.

"It should be done just before I go. If it's not, I'll let you keep an eye on that, too."

Ten minutes later, Mrs. Finney was off, wearing a light, silvery

117

shawl over her black bombazine gown. Carmela had a feeling the lady wouldn't be seen in public—at least not at church—out of her mourning attire. She would have to ask how long since Mr. Finney had passed.

A man appeared in the kitchen doorway. "Breakfast all done?" He looked sleepy and a little bleary-eyed, but he jerked alert and eyed her critically. "Who be you?"

"I'm Miss Wade. Who are you?"

"Buck Chard. Been boardin' here six months, when I'm not on the road freightin'."

Carmela nodded. "I'm also staying here. I arrived last evening, and Mrs. Finney asked me to watch her cook fire while she's at church. I believe there's coffee in the pot on the stove, and I can fix you something quick."

"Thank you kindly." Buck seemed to know his way about the kitchen, and he snagged a thick mug from a cupboard and poured himself coffee. "Where you from, missy?"

Carmela had located the cast iron skillet and carried it to the stove. "New England."

He nodded. "You been west of here though." His gazed focused on her chin. "Are those Yavapai markins?"

"I—I've never been a hundred percent sure what tribe..." Carmela let the familiar lie trail off. She couldn't bring herself to say, *"I was with."* If she didn't stop lying now, when would she?

Buck grunted. "They kept you long enough to brand you theirs. How long were you with 'em?"

"I..." The words gagged her. She whirled to get the eggs. "I'd rather not talk about it."

Buck's eyes narrowed in speculation. "Sure. Well, I'll be at the table. Thanks for getting my grub."

She nodded, and relief washed over her as he left the room. As long as the ink remained, people would wonder. She'd had to be careful in her lies for so long, needing always to be consistent. Now she would have to be as careful in telling the truth.

Tears rolled down her cheeks, and she swiped her apron across her face. *Lord, I don't know what to say. Teach me what words to use.*

❤

Freeland saw their dust long before he could make out the horses of the posse or the men riding them. He urged his horse into a lope. They spotted him, and one rider detached from the group and rode back to meet him.

Benny Lassiter, another deputy marshal, grinned when he got close enough to recognize Freeland.

"Well, howdy. Took your time."

Freeland shook his head. "I'd like to see you ride all the way to Prescott with a civilian in your care, then apprise the governor of the situation and inform the stage company of its losses, then get back to the site of the holdup and track you down here any sooner. Oh, I admit I did stop long enough to sleep a few hours in Prescott and again at Price's station."

"Ah, that explains it. Lazing around to sleep." Benny laughed.

"What have you got?" Freeland asked.

"We think the outlaws have a hideout somewhere close by. So far we haven't located it, but we have found tracks more than once."

"See anything of my prisoner?"

"You mean your *former* prisoner?"

That tasted sour in Freeland's mouth. "Well, yeah. Dix."

Benny shook his head. "He wasn't where you left him. I reckon he woke up and walked away under his own power. We took a quick look around, but we couldn't pick up his sign, and we didn't want to take time to look for him. Figured we'd best go after the gang first. The desert will take care of Dix."

"Maybe. But we might never know." Freeland squinted ahead to where the marshal and his men were spreading out in ones and twos on each side of the trail. "So what now?"

Benny pointed back along the trail Freeland had ridden all day. "We caught sight of the stagecoach's tracks a couple of times. Haven't found where they took it off the trail, so we're assuming it's ahead of us. Of course, there were plenty of rocky places they could have gone, but it's hard to take a coach over terrain like that and not leave any evidence."

"You're sure?"

"No. Can't ever be sure."

Freeland nodded. They might have missed something, but with Duffield and seven other men on the chase, most of them experienced trackers, that seemed unlikely. They started their horses jogging along toward the posse.

Freeland pushed his hat back. "I thought you'd have gotten farther."

Benny shrugged. "We've had to go fifty miles south with the stage and ride back, and we've checked every side canyon and ravine since we crossed the Salt River. It takes time."

"Isn't there a settlement down here?"

"Yep," Benny said. "Some ranches. A few miners down here, but not so many as up around Wickenburg and Prescott. They's some over near Fish Creek. We might head there, unless we find some sign soon."

They reached the posse, and Marshal Duffield welcomed Freeland. "I'm not sure but we're wasting our time," he said dourly. "If there wasn't a payroll and a wounded passenger involved, I'd give it up and tell the stage company to cut its losses."

"You don't think we can find where they're holed up?" Freeland asked.

Duffield gritted his teeth. "I'd like to say we can, but we've got nothing yet. The question is, how much time do we spend on it?"

As night fell, they came to a small settlement that was more of an encampment on the bank of a sluggish stream. Half a dozen tents and a couple of huts made up the hamlet on Queen Creek.

While the others made camp and prepared coffee and supper, the marshal took Freeland with him to question all the men in the tent town. When they had gathered around, Freeland patiently described the stagecoach and team, the outlaws, and Mr. Holden.

"I didn't see no stagecoach," one man said, "but a couple of fellows came through here yesterday. Said they'd been to Florence, on the Gila."

The marshal and Freeland nodded.

"Well, they'd got a few supplies, but they were jumpy. Said a horse had been stolen in Florence. They hoped somebody was heading their way and would travel with 'em."

"Could be the outlaws made a visit there," Freeland said.

"Maybe." Duffield took his hat off and shoved his hand through his hair. "That's a ways. I hope we don't have to go that far."

"I mighta seen somethin'," another man offered.

"Yeah?" Duffield turned to him.

"Some kind of wagon tracks, about two miles up this creek. They crossed the water. Lot of animals. I wondered where in the world they were headed with a wagon out there. Could be your missing stagecoach."

"Thanks," Duffield said. "We'll check it out in the morning. I don't s'pose you'd ride along and show us where the tracks are?"

"I could, but if you ride upstream, you'll see it."

They thanked him and went to the posse's campfire.

"Better'n nothing to go on," Benny said when he heard their tale.

"That's what I figure." Duffield reached for his tin cup and held it out for coffee. "After you eat, men, get a good rest. We head out at dawn."

They set out before the sun sent its first rays over the desert, while the air was still cool enough for comfort. They skirted rocks and ridges, finally descending to the streambed and splashing through the water the last quarter mile. The miner was right. The vehicle's passage was obvious, with deep wheel ruts carved into the soft clay along the bank.

"It's them," Freeland said, eyeing the width of the wheel rims and the distance between them.

"Horses, not mules." Duffield was gazing down at the rounded hoofprints. "You said they had a team of horses, right?"

Freeland nodded grimly. "Four horses in harness when we were attacked."

"All right, let's go." Duffield raised a hand and gestured for the men of the posse to follow him southward, away from the creek.

They jogged along for two hours, stopping now and then to examine faint traces of the coach's progress. The outlaws' horses, along with those of the team, left a clear trail. Freeland was concentrating on the imprints when Benny, up ahead, gave a sharp whistle.

He and the marshal rode up to Benny, and the other men bunched their horses up behind them. In the distance, a lone rider moved slowly toward them.

"Think it's a trap?" Benny asked, drawing his sidearm.

"I dunno," Duffield said. "Sit tight for a minute."

While they watched the horseman, Freeland scanned the landscape around them, looking for signs of other men lying in wait. He couldn't see anything that didn't belong, or any movement other than the oncoming horse and a meadowlark it flushed from a clump of thorny brush.

Recognition hit him in an instant, and he straightened in his saddle, squinting at the rider in the bowler hat to be certain. He glanced at the marshal.

"That's Holden."

Chapter Thirteen

The closer the rider came, the lower he slumped over the horse's back. He had no saddle. The horse walked slowly, and when it passed a wisp of vegetation, it halted and stretched its neck toward it. Holden didn't respond.

"Come on." Freeland lifted his reins and urged his horse forward. When he was ten yards from the rider, he slowed his mount and shouted, "Mr. Holden!"

Silas Holden raised his head and blinked. His face was burned scarlet, and his clothing was tattered and bloody. He grimaced as he focused on Freeland. "Deputy?"

"Yes sir." Freeland rode up beside him. "Where are the outlaws?"

Holden started to twist in the saddle but moaned and inclined his head instead. "Back there. I got away from them, only because they'd been drinking hard last night. I was afraid they'd come after me and kill me before I got back to civilization."

"You were wounded when they hit the stagecoach." Freeland gazed at his gory shirtfront as Marshal Duffield and the others rode up to them.

"Yes," Holden said. "Thought I was about to meet my maker, but I felt stronger these last two days, and I was able to pull myself onto the horse by climbing on the tongue of the stagecoach." His eyes sharpened as he turned his gaze back to Freeland. "Are you going after them? Because I want my money back."

"We'll see about that," Freeland said. "Don't you want to know what's happened to Miss Wade?"

Holden stared at him for a moment and then dropped his gaze. "My niece. Is she. . . ?"

"She's safe, sir," Freeland said.

Marshal Duffield pushed his hat back, and Freeland hastened to do the honors. "Mr. Holden, this is the territorial marshal, and these other men are part of the posse looking for the outlaws that robbed the stage."

"Howdy." Duffield nodded. "We'll take a look at your wound, and then we'd appreciate it if you'd show us where the gang is hiding."

He set four men of the posse to watch Holden's back trail. One of the townsmen from Prescott, Ed Parker, settled Holden on a blanket on the ground and had him uncover the gunshot wound on his left side.

"Nasty, but it's healing," Ed noted. "It must not have hit any vital organs, or you wouldn't be walking today."

"I trust you're right," Holden said, "but the pain is fierce."

"We'll get you to a doctor to check you out as soon as we can," the marshal said. "Meanwhile, we're this close to the outlaws' nest, and we've got to strike."

"It's two or three miles back." Holden squinted up at him. "Honestly, Marshal, I don't know if I could stay on the horse's back to ride that far again."

"We'll give you a saddle." Duffield turned his head and called, "Benny! Throw your saddle on Mr. Holden's horse. You'll have to ride bareback until we sort out those road agents."

Benny frowned but obeyed. He was one of the younger deputies, and Duffield probably figured he had the stamina and coordination to pull off a raid riding bareback.

Holden moaned as Freeland and Benny hoisted him into the

saddle a few minutes later. Duffield had issued him a ration of whiskey, but he clutched his side and slumped low over the pommel of the saddle. Freeland was afraid he would tumble off to the side before they'd gone half the distance, but somehow the thin man stayed on horseback.

"Stop here," he said weakly after a couple of miles.

"Marshal," Freeland called to Duffield, who rode several yards in the lead.

Duffield turned his horse and rode back to them. Holden hugged his wound and breathed heavily.

"What is it?" the marshal asked.

"It's not far," Holden squeezed out between his teeth. "Go past those rocks yonder, and you'll be able to see a boulder where they keep a lookout. The hideout's just a bit beyond, backed up to a cliff. They've got a corral to the side."

"How many men are there?" Duffield asked.

"There were four after the holdup, but another man joined them." Holden glanced at Freeland. "That Dix you had on the stagecoach."

Freeland stared at him. "Dix is with the gang now?"

Holden nodded and moaned. "Came in yesterday on a stolen horse. He's none too happy with you, Deputy. I heard him say he'd go after you when he had a chance."

❤

Carmela went to the kitchen in the middle of the afternoon. Mrs. Finney had returned from church at noon, served them all dinner, cleaned up with the help of Carmela and a miner who was behind on his bill, and then retired to her chamber for a nap. Now she was back at work.

The older woman still looked tired. She stood by the drain board, peeling parsnips. Carmela paused in the doorway.

"May I help you with supper, Mrs. Finney?"

"I won't say no." She turned the vegetable peeling over to Carmela and started measuring out ingredients for an Indian pudding. They worked in silence for a while, and then she said, "I've heard something from one of my boarders."

"Oh?" Carmela looked up eagerly, but Mrs. Finney's grave face quelled her anticipation. The landlady was not about to tell her an amusing anecdote.

"One of the gents says he heard you speak your piece once. Not here. In Albuquerque."

Carmela's heart sank. Buck Chard came to mind, and his words with her that morning. But if he'd seen her before, surely he would have said so, and he'd asked about her captivity. He must not have heard her presentation, or he would have known more about her past.

"What did they say?" She concentrated on the parsnip she was peeling. She was glad to have something to occupy her during the conversation, but she wouldn't want to scrape the skin off a knuckle.

"Said he saw you with your uncle, only he thought you looked different. Like maybe your tribal tattoos were more noticeable."

"They might have been," Carmela said without looking at her. "They seem to have faded some over time."

"This was a month ago."

She swallowed hard. Uncle Silas had booked her for three nights in Albuquerque last month, and they had done well. Several hundred people had heard her talk.

"I expect he did hear me, then." Carmela stopped peeling and looked over at her hostess. "Mrs. Finney, I want to quit speaking, but I don't know how I'd make my living if I did."

The dour landlady tipped her head to one side. "Well, you're a right enough hand in the kitchen. Maybe you could hire out at a hotel. . .or a boardinghouse."

Carmela eyed her in surprise. Was Mrs. Finney offering her a job? She cleared her throat. "Are—are you saying I might work here for wages?"

Mrs. Finney stirred her batter. "I'm not as young as I used to be. I could use some help and a bit of female company. I'd give you the room and your board if you worked. . .say, three hours a day? One day off a week."

"That seems fair." Carmela smiled. "Thank you."

Mrs. Finney shot her a glance and nodded. "Right. You work with me until supper and help do the dishes tonight, and we'll call it square through tonight's room, eh?"

"That sounds wonderful. Then the marshal won't have to pay my bill."

"Yes, and we can go on that way until Mr. McKay or the marshal comes back to settle up if you want. We can wait and see if they find your uncle, and if they do, whether he has any funds or if those robbers took every penny."

Carmela sighed and picked up the vegetable peeler. "I expect they did. I'm not supposing they've treated Uncle Silas very well either." Tears filled her eyes, despite their history together. "He was bleeding profusely. I do hope they helped him and didn't just let him. . ."

"There, child. Take it to the heavenly Father, and leave it at His feet."

"Yes. I *have* been praying," Carmela admitted. No matter how Uncle Silas had abused her in the past, she wouldn't wish him to bleed to death, alone in a desolate country.

"And what does your uncle say about quitting, then?" Mrs. Finney asked.

"I haven't asked him, but I don't think he'd want me to."

"You bring in too much money for him to want that?"

Carmela let out a shaky sigh. "Maybe. But I'd like to be done with it. I want to live a normal life, not travel all the time and stand up before crowds and—and—give speeches." *Tell lies,* she wanted to say, but she didn't. Mrs. Finney most certainly would not want to hire her if she knew Carmela regularly and deliberately defrauded people.

"I'll add that to my list of prayers."

One tear spilled over and trickled down Carmela's cheek. She quickly wiped it away with her sleeve. "Thank you."

Mrs. Finney had a good heart. But would she be as kind if she knew all? Carmela doubted it very much. Mrs. Finney didn't seem the type who would put up with liars.

♥

"Please, Marshal, leave me here so I can rest." Silas Holden's face was tight and grayish, and beads of sweat had formed on his brow.

Duffield considered that for a moment. Counting himself and Freeland, they had ten able-bodied men. Freeland figured the injured man would only be in the way when they confronted the outlaws.

"I'd have to leave one of my men here with you, and I need every gun when we go up against that bunch."

"I don't think I can ride anymore."

"We'll find out, won't we?" Duffield turned away.

"You're going to get my money back, right?" Silas yelled after him. "I want every cent they took off me." When Duffield didn't respond, he looked to Freeland. "Tell him, McKay. I had the proceeds from our last several shows in the money belt they took off me. I'm entitled to that money."

"We need to get on," Freeland said. "You can discuss that later."

"I want assurance that I'll get back my property," Holden insisted.

"Holden, shut up and get ready to ride," the marshal called from where he was checking his saddle cinch. "We're wasting time."

"I want you to promise—"

Duffield strode over to him and glared at him. "You shut your trap or I'll have you bound and gagged." He looked around at the deputies. "I mean it. Gag him if he doesn't stop talking."

♥

On Monday morning, after the breakfast dishes were done, Mrs. Finney and Carmela sat down at the kitchen table with a pot of tea to talk about the dinner and supper menus. Only two boarders were expected to join them for the noon meal—John Ralley, who worked at the mercantile on Montezuma Street, and Clark Shifton, a freighter who would lay over another day while the cargo for his next run was being assembled and loaded.

"So dinner will be light," Mrs. Finney told Carmela. "We'll heat up the leftover ham from yesterday and fry up some potatoes." She frowned. "Though I'm low on potatoes. Maybe I should save them for the stew for supper. I guess we can make do with cornbread and turnip at noon, and dried apple pie."

"That sounds like plenty for the midday meal," Carmela said. She wasn't used to a large meal in the middle of the day.

They went on to discuss the dishes they would prepare for supper. A loud knocking on the front door drew Mrs. Finney up from her chair. "Just check on how much cocoa powder is left, would you, dear? I'm thinking we'll make a chocolate cake for this evening."

Carmela timidly opened several crocks on the shelf of baking supplies before she found the dark brown powder. She didn't think a cake would take more than a cupful, so there should be plenty. She heard a man's voice in the other room but paid little attention. Mrs. Finney's establishment seemed well known and attracted plenty of people who came in and out of town for business reasons. If they wanted a quiet place to sleep and could stay sober—Mrs. Finney insisted no boarders come in drunk—then this was the perfect place for lodging. From their earlier conversation, Carmela had gathered that she seldom had vacancies.

Footsteps came to the kitchen doorway, and she looked up.

"There's a gentleman here who'd like to speak to you," Mrs. Finney said.

Carmela's heart raced. Surely it couldn't be Uncle Silas. It was too soon for either him or Freeland McKay to be here.

"I'll bring coffee into the dining room." Mrs. Finney moved past her to the stove.

Carmela hastily removed her apron and smoothed back her hair. She walked quickly to the doorway and peeked into the next room. A bearded man she didn't know sat at the table, his chair pushed out away from it. His round head was nearly bald, and he turned a worn felt hat around and around in his hands as he waited.

When he saw her, he jumped up. "Miss Wade?"

"Yes sir. May I help you?"

"I hope so. Could I talk to you for a minute?"

"I suppose so." Carmela sat down across the table from him and glanced toward the kitchen. To her relief, Mrs. Finney approached with an enameled coffeepot in one hand and two mugs in the other.

"There we go," she said cheerfully, setting down the thick, white mugs. She poured out coffee for them both.

"Thanks." The man reached for the nearest sugar bowl of the three Mrs. Finney kept evenly spaced along the length of the table.

"This is Mr. Roote," Mrs. Finney told her. "He goes to my church."

Carmela supposed that was some sort of recommendation, or assurance that the man stirring two spoonfuls of sugar into his coffee wasn't out to harm her.

"How do you do?" she said.

"Not well." Mr. Roote frowned as he raised the cup to his lips. After a small sip, he took a bigger one then set his coffee down. Mrs. Finney had retreated to the kitchen. "It's about my daughter. Lucy."

Carmela blinked. "I don't understand."

Mr. Roote sighed. "She was taken last year by the Apache. My ranch is three miles out of town. I thought we were close enough to be safe, but I was wrong. She was out by herself one day, hoeing in the cornfield. Not far from the house, but far enough."

Carmela's heart ached fiercely at the pain in the rancher's eyes.

"They only had her six months," he went on. "Soldiers from Fort Whipple brought her back. But. . .she's not the same."

A dozen questions leaped to Carmela's mind. She opened her lips then closed them, unsure what he wanted of her.

"I thought maybe. . ." He picked up his mug and took a swallow.

Carmela also sipped her coffee, though she didn't really like the bitter taste. When she lowered her cup, Mr. Roote was staring at her.

"Could you talk to her, miss?"

"Me?" Carmela squeaked.

He nodded. "You know what she's been through. It's been real hard for us."

Carmela cleared her throat. "I'm not sure—"

"Please! We don't know what to do. She's all the time running off by herself, and she says she wishes they hadn't brought her back. My wife is at her wit's end, miss. Can't you just talk to her?"

"Wh–what would I say?" Carmela felt as though a great chasm opened before her. This man wanted her, because she was an "expert" at life as an Indian captive—to tell his daughter how to make peace with her re-assimilation into the whites' world. He assumed she had done it, had come to terms with her past and her present, had fit back in with what was left of her family. If Carmela Wade could do it and turn out such a poised, genteel young lady, so could his daughter, provided the right person talked to her and spoke the right words. But Carmela had no idea what those words would be, or if any words at all would help.

"Just tell her she's not the only one," Mr. Roote said. "Tell her you was with 'em a long time, but you're all right now. I don't know. How did you deal with it when you were returned?"

She sighed and stared down into her coffee. She wanted more than anything to tell the truth, but if she did, she would shatter his hopes that his daughter could recover—could be normal again.

"How old is she?"

"Fourteen. Lucy is fourteen. How old were you when you were taken?"

"Twelve," Carmela whispered. "My parents died when I was twelve," she hastily amended. He had asked when she was taken, and after all, she was "taken" then—taken by Uncle Silas. "You say Lucy wasn't with them long?"

"Only six months, but she thinks she's one of them now. Won't do the chores her mother sets her. Won't eat pork."

"Why not?"

"She says the Apache don't eat it."

This was news to Carmela, but it made sense in a way. They would prefer wild game—or beef. Stolen beef, much of it.

"It confounds me how she can be so loyal to them savages. They kidnapped her. They took her away from us, who loves her. They took away her clothes, every stitch, and made her wear what they wear and eat what they eat. I'm guessing she cried plenty those first few weeks."

"They wouldn't let her cry," Carmela said, and immediately closed her lips. That was something she had learned from the couple who had cared for her at Fort Yuma. The Indians taught their babies not to cry by leaving them outside the camp when they wailed. They were only brought into the loving family when they were quiet. She had wondered when she heard it how many were snatched by wolves when they lay outside the camp, crying their little hearts out.

Mr. Roote eyed her keenly. "See? You've been through it. Please, please talk to her, Miss Wade."

Carmela's stomach roiled. She didn't want to go on pretending. But if she refused this distraught man, she would look cold and unkind. No sounds came from the kitchen, and she was certain Mrs. Finney was listening.

"All right," she said at last. "I'll try, but I don't know if I can be any comfort to her."

His face cleared and he pushed back his chair. "Thank you, Miss Wade. I'll bring her this afternoon."

Chapter Fourteen

armela went back to the kitchen. Mrs. Finney was kneading her bread dough.

"I thought that might be what he wanted." She gave the lump of dough an extra punch.

"I don't know what good I can do." Carmela reached for her apron.

"That poor child. It might help her just to have someone to talk to who has an idea of what she experienced."

"That's what Mr. Roote said, but I'm not sure my experience was at all like Lucy's." Carmela felt her cheeks flush as she spoke. In fact, her experience was nothing at all like Lucy's, but she couldn't say that now.

"Just let her talk, if she will," Mrs. Finney said. "Her mother said sometimes she doesn't speak for days on end. She might open up to you."

"Maybe. Shall I start the cake?"

"If you would. I left the recipe on the table there."

Working with Mrs. Finney would have been pure joy if Carmela hadn't been so nervous about Lucy's impending visit. Whatever would she say to the girl? Her thoughts circled round and round in her mind, always coming back to the fear that she would be lying a great deal this afternoon. It would be like her speaking engagements but with an audience of one. Lucy, of all people, might realize that she was a fraud.

At last she turned to the heavenly Father, embarrassed to come before Him but desperate for a confidant of her own.

Lord, please show me what to say. If I can help Lucy, then I'll be glad to, but I don't want to lie to her or her parents. If there's a way I can be of some comfort without lying, then please, please show it to me.

She felt a little better then and worked steadily for the next two hours. When John Ralley and Clark Shifton drifted in for their dinner at noon, the ladies were well prepared.

Mrs. Finney sent Carmela to freshen up after the boarders had gone back to work. She brushed her hair and repinned it and made sure her hands and face were free of flour and smudges. She gazed into the mirror. Her face was still red-tinged, and her sunburn was beginning to peel. No way to hide that. Mostly she looked exhausted, with dark patches clouding the skin beneath her over-large brown eyes.

If she were going on stage, Uncle Silas would be glad. He never instructed her to wear makeup, but preferred to have her look natural, as though she had just ridden in from the Indian village. He liked it on days when she looked ill or emaciated, and he frequently admonished her to eat sparingly so that she didn't appear too well fed. The desert's damage to her complexion fit right in with her story.

When she emerged from her room, Mrs. Finney was just heading down the hallway toward her.

"Oh, good, you're ready. Mr. and Mrs. Roote have brought Lucy. They're waiting in the parlor."

Carmela followed her to the parlor door. She had only entered the room once before, on the previous evening, when a few of the boarders had gathered after supper. The room held Mrs. Finney's best furniture and decorations, but even so, it had a sparse feeling compared to the crammed parlors she had visited in New England. A small horsehair settee, a rocking chair, and four straight chairs comprised the seating. A wall shelf held Mrs. Finney's Bible and two other books—her entire library. Two oil lamps were perched on small side tables, and an amateur painting of the Chino Valley graced the board wall over the settee. A rock fireplace took up most of one wall, and two small windows let in some light.

Mr. Roote sat on one of the straight chairs, and he leaped up when Carmela arrived.

"Hello. Thank you for seeing us. This is my wife, Bertha, and this is Lucy." His sorrowful gaze rested on the girl.

Carmela smiled, trying for a friendly demeanor, but not too bright. "Good afternoon, Lucy. Mrs. Roote."

Lucy gave the smallest of nods. Her mother, thin and somber in black, looked into Carmela's face, her gaze pausing at her chin.

"Oh my. Thank heaven they didn't. . ."

She didn't finish, but turned away, flushing. Carmela knew what she was thinking. *Thank God my daughter wasn't given those ghastly tattoos.*

Lucy wore her long, light brown hair parted in the middle. It lay loose about her shoulders and flowed down her back. Her mother's hair, in contrast, was pulled back into a severe bun. Carmela couldn't help thinking how pretty Lucy looked, and how young.

"You were with the savages longer than our Lucy," Mr. Roote said.

Carmela said nothing, not wanting to agree with him.

His wife sat forward eagerly. "You have obviously been through a horrible ordeal. But you seem very calm now, and contented."

What was it about her that made these people think she was content, Carmela wondered. She supposed it was because she had schooled her features into placidity, and because she willingly wore her hair and clothing in the style of the white women. Of course, they did not know her stylish dress was a castoff of Mrs. McCormick's, kindly donated to replace her tattered traveling outfit.

"It takes a studied effort, every day," she said. That was the pure truth. Each day she pleaded with God to help her through whatever came her way. Meeting Uncle Silas's demands with grace, and his whims when it came to changing the program, adjusting her costumes, or adding new material to her speeches took great patience. She had learned that it was best to simply do what he asked, even when she doubted the wisdom of his ideas.

"Did it hurt when they put those marks on your face?" Lucy asked, staring unabashed at Carmela.

Carmela drew a sharp breath.

"Don't be rude, dear," Mrs. Roote said.

"It's all right." Carmela sat down in the rocker, and Mr. Roote resumed his seat. Had it hurt? She struggled with a truthful but credible answer. The worst pain had been the stiff neck she got when Uncle Silas made her hold still for ages while he renewed the ink. "Not a lot. It prickled some."

Lucy nodded, still gazing at the tattoos.

Mrs. Finney hovered in the doorway. "Mr. and Mrs. Roote, I wondered if you would like to take tea with me in the dining room while the girls chat." She smiled encouragingly at them.

"Oh, I don't know." Mrs. Roote looked sidelong at Lucy.

"That might be a good idea," her husband said, rising. "Let them get acquainted." He nodded at Carmela, as though they were conspirators.

"I'll bring you girls something," Mrs. Finney said, spreading her smile to Lucy.

Mrs. Roote looked at her daughter. "Will you be all right?"

"I'm fine, Mama."

Mrs. Roote reluctantly followed her husband and Mrs. Finney out of the room.

"It really did hurt, didn't it?" Lucy said, leaning eagerly toward Carmela. "You just said that so Mama wouldn't be upset."

"N–no, actually." Carmela moved over to sit beside her on the settee. "It wasn't very painful. The ink bothered me at first, but it doesn't now."

Lucy nodded, her eyes wide, still studying the markings.

"What about you?" Carmela asked. "Did the Apache hurt you?"

Lucy sobered. "Some. Not for long. I soon learned what they wanted of me."

"What was that?"

"Obedience, same as here. And hard work, to help with the food."

"Of course," Carmela said. "It takes a great deal of labor to provide food for the tribe."

"I didn't mind that part." Lucy raised her chin almost defiantly. "Once I got used to things and learned a bit of their language, they treated me like one of them. Like an Apache woman." Her gaze held a challenge.

"Ah. And in what ways did they treat you like a woman? For the people I was with, that meant more work."

"How old were you when they got you?" Lucy asked.

"I. . ." She couldn't bring herself to say it, so she fell back on the answer she had given before. "I was twelve when my parents died."

"When the Indians massacred them."

Carmela said nothing but gave a little shrug.

"Well, obviously, they didn't massacre my parents," Lucy said. "I suppose I might have hated them more if they had."

"What do you mean?"

Lucy met her gaze for a long moment. "I liked being an Apache. Once I learned the rules, I mean."

"The rules?"

"Sure. You know. How they wanted me to behave. It wasn't so bad. I liked it better than here. No weeding the garden all day long, and no school. And they didn't make you wear all these tiresome clothes." With a grimace, she ran her hand down her bodice and skirt. "Last summer, we girls wore short dresses and moccasins. Not stockings or petticoats and long skirts. And no threat of corsets, hey?" She smiled, and Carmela found herself smiling back into her winsome blue eyes.

"Well, there is that."

Lucy laughed. "Do you ever feel like you want to go back?"

Carmela pulled away from her. "No, never."

Sobering, Lucy cocked her head to one side. "They *did* hurt you, then."

Carmela's lips trembled. "Your father said. . . He told me you've run off since you came home."

She nodded. "Some days I think I can't stand it. Mama will set me to stitching, and it seems so useless. Or we stand for hours over the wash kettle, scrubbing clothes. The Apache don't do that. And Pa's planted corn again. I know what's coming. I'll be out there for hours and hours alone, hoeing."

"I doubt he'll leave you alone for long after what happened."

"I hope he does. I hope they snatch me again."

"No, Lucy."

"Why not? They told me—if I'd stayed, they said I'd be married. That's what they meant, anyway. I'd be a warrior's woman by this time."

Carmela gasped. "At your age?"

"Yes. But my folks say that's disgraceful and I mustn't tell anyone or even think about it. How can I not? They'll keep me close until I'm an old maid."

"You—you want to marry an Apache man?"

"It would be better than living here on the farm. I'd get to ride horses, and I don't mean old plodders like that team my pa has. And we'd go swimming every single day when it was hot—without any clothes! And I could ride with my husband if he went to raid."

"Surely not."

"Some of their women go."

"Not really?"

Lucy nodded. "I've seen it. I suppose they cook for the men. In fact, there was a woman in the party that snatched me last year."

Carmela didn't know what to say.

Lucy frowned. "It's so freeing. You understand. How can you like it here, when you were with them for years? You were part of their family."

She launched herself at Carmela, who caught her in her arms. Lucy sobbed once, then grasped handfuls of Carmela's dress and sat up.

"I won't cry. But I dearly want to go back. Tell me you understand."

Carmela shook her head. "I don't. I'm sorry, but I've never felt anything like that."

"You wanted to come back to this world?"

Carmela sighed. "My parents and brother were dead, but yes, I wanted to go home. We didn't live out here, like your family. We lived back East. That's where I wanted to go." *To civilization*, she thought. To hot baths and a soft bed and kind words. She wasn't sure what she had expected when Uncle Silas retrieved her. Did she think he would take her home to live with an aunt? That she would have cousins around her to play with each day? She had hoped to live with Grandma Wade, but her grandmother had died shortly after her family set out to join the wagon train. Still, she had believed without question that returning to the East would be better than the bleak wilderness around Fort Yuma.

How little she had known.

The army chaplain and his wife—Captain and Mrs. Owen—had treated her kindly. She now believed she would have been much better off with them than with her uncle. But savages? She couldn't tell Lucy that was not an option for her, but she shuddered even thinking about it. How could this child look favorably on a life as an Apache woman?

"Dear Lucy." She touched the girl's tanned cheek. "My dear, you mustn't think it would be all fun and play for you. I'm sure the women worked hard. Indian women must prepare food and animal skins. They do all the tedious jobs while the men hunt and raid."

"The women here work harder," Lucy insisted. "Look at my ma. Seven children, and I'm the oldest. When I'm not sewing or washing dishes or doing farm chores, I have to look after the little ones."

Carmela sighed. "And you think it would be better with the Indians."

Lucy blinked and then nodded. "Sometimes I just don't feel that I fit in here anymore—in the white world. People have welcomed me back, but I know they look down on me and think I'm dirty somehow because I've lived with the Indians. The tribe never made me feel that way."

"That part I understand." Carmela had endured the looks of pity and speculation from the civilized people who paid to hear her speak. It hadn't taken Uncle Silas long to catch on to the fact that the more sordid she made the tale, the more they wanted to hear. He made her say they had stripped her of all her clothing after they captured her from the wagon, and that she rode with them for two days wearing absolutely nothing. Her face always flushed crimson when she told that part. And Lucy had gone through it, or so her father said. Yet, she wasn't resentful. She wanted to return to the tribe. Had a few short months with the Apache robbed her of all sense of decency?

"I knew it." Lucy threw her arms about Carmela's neck and clung to her.

Carmela talked to the girl for another ten minutes, probing gently about her captivity. It seemed Lucy had been treated fairly well. She had been with the Apache through summer and fall the previous year, when food was comparatively plentiful. She admitted the Apache were sometimes hungry while she was with them, and they made Lucy work hard with the other girls and women sometimes to gather and preserve food.

"It's much worse in winter," Carmela assured her. "You're fortunate that the soldiers got you back before winter."

"Oh, I don't know," Lucy said. "We had put by an awful lot of food. Baskets and baskets full of dried meat and corn." She gave Carmela a conspiratorial smile. "Some of it was stolen. That's the easiest way to grow corn."

"But think of the people from whom it's stolen," Carmela said. "They will suffer, too."

Lucy frowned at that.

"What did you think last winter?" Carmela pressed. "You were in a warm house with people who love you. I don't expect you missed any meals."

"I felt like a prisoner."

Carmela sighed. Was she getting anywhere?

"Some days I still think about running away and going back to the tribe," Lucy said, watching her face. Looking for a reaction, Carmela surmised. "Please don't do that. Lucy, your parents love you dearly. They want to understand you and help you."

"I know, but it's so hard. Mama fusses over me all the time. I can't stand it."

"You can." Carmela held the girl's hands and looked deeply into her eyes. "You can be an adult in this world, too, Lucy. But respect has to be earned. Yes, our ways are different from the Apache's. Perhaps it's not as exciting. But you belong here. You are loved here."

She wasn't sure Lucy believed her.

When Carmela took Lucy out into the dining room, Mrs. Finney tactfully left her with the parents while she took Lucy out to see the kittens her calico cat had birthed in the woodshed a week before. Mrs. Finney's kittens were apparently much sought after by residents, as they grew up without fail to be excellent mousers.

"So what do you suggest we do?" Mr. Roote asked when Carmela had given them the gist of her conversation with Lucy, though not the details she felt they would find most painful.

"I'm not a mother, Mr. Roote, nor an expert in child-rearing, or even in returned captives. I know only what I have lived in my limited experience and what I have learned from others."

"Go on," said the anxious Mrs. Roote. "Anything you can tell us will be helpful."

Carmela hoped it was so and sent up a silent prayer to God for that outcome.

"I know it's hard, but perhaps you should allow Lucy more freedom. It's not her fault that she now finds your life constricting. I know you have expectations for her, and that you hope she will turn into a proper young lady. That may never happen."

Mr. Roote's mouth worked, but he didn't say anything.

"So long as she doesn't shame us," Mrs. Roote conceded, looking down at her empty teacup.

Carmela frowned. "And how would she shame you?"

"By running back to those heathens. By showing she prefers them over us. Or by running wild in the town."

"I don't see any Apache women running wild in Prescott," Carmela said, though she had been there only two days and had no idea what happened on Whiskey Row after sunset.

Mrs. Roote sighed.

"You're right," Mr. Roote said. "If we don't hold her so tight, maybe she'll get used to us again. And maybe I can drive her out into the hills sometimes, though it's dangerous."

"She likes to ride horses," Carmela said, "but your workhorses are too tame for her."

"No!" Mrs. Roote twisted in her chair to glare at her husband. "You will not get her a horse. She'd be gone in a minute if you did."

"There now, my dear." Mr. Roote stroked his wife's hand. "I don't say I'll get her a mustang. I think you are right about that. But we can be a little more slack about her clothes when she's at home."

"I won't have her going about with no stockings or undergarments." Mrs. Roote pulled away from him and folded her hands on the table before her. "It's not Christian."

"That's the trouble, you see." Mr. Roote's sad eyes met Carmela's gaze. "She acts as if she's not Christian anymore, and it grieves us."

Carmela's lips trembled. She was way out of her depth here. "Does she follow the Apache gods?"

"I don't know," he replied.

"She reviles ours," Mrs. Roote said bitterly.

"Have you spoken to the minister about it?"

"Many times." Mr. Roote pushed back his chair. "I expect we'd best collect our daughter and head home. Thank you, Miss Wade."

Carmela stood, as did the Rootes.

"I'm not sure I've helped her. . .or you."

He clasped her hand for a moment. "Just talking about her with someone who doesn't get all horrified is a help." He looked at his wife. "Come on, Bertha. The cows won't milk themselves."

Carmela stood with Mrs. Finney on the front porch and watched them climb into their wagon.

"You look troubled," Mrs. Finney murmured.

Carmela nodded. "I only hope they can find a way to live peacefully together and not regret Lucy's return."

Chapter Fifteen

arshal." Silas Holden turned his pleading gaze on Duffield once more. "I can't ride into a gunfight. I have no weapon, to start with, and I'm debilitated by this wound. I beg you to leave me here."

"And bring your money back," Benny said with a sour smile.

"That's enough, Lassiter," Duffield said with a disapproving look.

Holden clutched his side. "Please. I think it's bleeding again. I can't go any farther."

The marshal paused, frowning. After a moment he nodded. "All right. Ed, you stay with him, and keep your eyes open."

"Right," said Parker. He dismounted and walked over to Holden's horse.

"They got a lot of money off that stage," Holden said. "They took more than eight hundred dollars off me, Marshal. Robbed me while I was unconscious."

"That so?" Duffield asked.

Freeland thought of all the people who had paid this charlatan good money to hear the lies he'd forced his niece to tell. That was how he saw it, but this wasn't the time to share that information with the marshal. He wasn't sure yet if exposing Carmela and her uncle's fraud was best for Carmela. He didn't want to make her life worse.

"Is it so wrong to want back the money I earned?" Holden's brow furrowed as he leaned lower over the horse's neck.

"Be glad they didn't kill you," Duffield said. "Ed."

Parker stepped up and helped Holden ease down onto the ground. Freeland dismounted, unstrapped his bedroll, and carried it over to them. "Here, you might as well use this."

"Thank you." Holden managed to put a remnant of his former dignity into his voice.

Freeland stooped to arrange the rolled blanket under his head. "You said my niece is safe, McKay?"

"That's right."

"Where is she?"

Freeland met his gaze. Was the man truly concerned about Carmela, or was he just trying to keep track of his main asset?

"She's at a respectable boardinghouse in Prescott. She's waiting there for word from the marshal or me. To be honest, I didn't expect we'd find you alive."

"I was always resourceful," Holden said, and Freeland didn't doubt it. "Are you sure she's all right?"

"Absolutely."

"But the stagecoach. . . How did she get to Prescott?"

"I took her there. We walked to the next stage station, and we waited there until the posse came through. Then we rode to the capital."

"You. . .you were alone with her?" Holden said slowly. "How long?"

"As long as it took us to get to Price's station." Freeland decided not to mention the handcuffs, or the fact that he'd been overpowered by his prisoner, but he needn't have tried to save his pride.

"That man, Dix," Holden said, eyeing him narrowly. "He said he saw you together the day after the robbery."

"That's true," Freeland said. "I had to subdue him." He waited, but Holden didn't mention the fact that he and Carmela had been chained together. Maybe Dix had been too embarrassed to tell the others he'd been overcome by a man and a girl in handcuffs.

"A night and a day is a long time to be alone with a young lady." Holden's eyes narrowed. His calculating gaze disturbed Freeland.

"I don't like what you're implying, Holden."

"Oh, don't you? A strong man like yourself, out in the desert alone with an attractive young woman? Most men would take advantage of that situation."

"Close your mouth," Freeland said. "I know how you treated Carmela these last seven or eight years. If you want to talk about taking advantage, maybe you should think about that."

Pure hatred glittered in Holden's eyes. He sank back on the bed-roll and turned his face away.

♥

"You're Miss Wade, the one who was to speak at the Silver Cactus last Friday?"

Carmela swallowed hard. Yet another stranger had come to Mrs. Finney's to seek her out.

"What can I help you with?" she managed.

"I'm Alfred Cox. I own the Silver Cactus. I heard you was held up on the way here, and we had to cancel the performance."

"I'm so sorry." For the first time she thought about the other people affected by her misfortune. Mr. Cox, of course, would have taken a cut of their admission sales and also profited by selling lots of liquor in his establishment when she had finished speaking.

"But you're here now," he said. "Maybe you could speak this week instead?"

Carmela gulped. "You didn't sell advance tickets, did you?"

"No, but I had posters printed at the *Arizonan* office. I figured we could just change the date on 'em."

Carmela's chest felt tight, and breathing was difficult. She hadn't considered that she might have to honor obligations Uncle Silas had arranged.

"My uncle," she gasped. "He was shot in the holdup. I don't know yet whether or not he survived."

"Oh. Sorry, miss." Cox fidgeted with the wide-brimmed straw hat in his hand. "Well, you think about it. It'd give you some money, if you need it."

That was true. Carmela had settled a way to pay her bill at Mrs. Finney's, but she would need some income if she wanted to leave Prescott. Even if Uncle Silas came back alive, he probably wouldn't have a cent on him. She had no doubt the robbers had taken his money belt the minute they discovered him in the stagecoach.

"C—could I think about it?"

Cox grinned. "Sure. Why don't I come back in a couple of days? Maybe you'll know more then, and you can let me know."

"All right. Thank you for understanding."

She closed the door behind him and leaned against it, sucking in air. She should have refused. But then what would she do if she learned she was truly alone and destitute? She didn't think she wanted to stay in Prescott the rest of her life, and Freeland McKay couldn't be expected to fund her transportation back East. Even if she went, she had no home there now. Who would she stay with? How would she support herself, if not by speaking?

She heard Mrs. Finney clattering about in the kitchen. Carmela's three hours were done for the day, and she didn't need to do any more chores. That was good, because she felt lightheaded and short of breath. She hurried to her room and shut the door then walked slowly to the washstand. She poured water into the basin and splashed some on her face.

She gazed at her reflection in the little mirror for a long time. The tattoos were quite faded, although they were still noticeable, and people who had never seen her before wouldn't realize the difference. Why had she said she would consider Mr. Cox's request? She had already made her decision not to renew the ink. Her stomach clenched at the thought of doing that.

Squinting in the light from the window across the room, she studied her complexion. She was glad the markings were going away. For the first time in years, she could imagine herself without them.

Her adult face had never been clean but had always borne the inked pattern. But it could cause her trouble if people saw her with them now and then a few weeks later without it. If she let them continue to fade, the boarders would soon remark on it, and if she saw the Rootes again, they would notice the difference. How could she explain it?

And if she agreed to perform at Mr. Cox's saloon. . . Yes, she supposed she would have to redo the inking as best she could by herself. Would she be able to accomplish it? Uncle Silas always did it before each performance. Would Mr. Cox remark that they seemed more pronounced than they had today? And how would she explain to kindhearted Mrs. Finney? Would she want a boarder and kitchen helper who lied for a living?

An even deeper concern plagued her. Was she breaking any laws now? Even though she wasn't speaking for cash at the moment, she continued living the lie. She had let the Roote family believe the captive story was true. Without taking money from people anymore, she still might be crossing some legal line. Freeland had said it wasn't her fault, but she feared the marshal might still charge her with the past fraud she participated in with her uncle.

And what would happen if Freeland brought Uncle Silas back? That possibility scared her even more than facing the marshal. She admired Freeland, and she thought he would protect her if he possibly could. But he was a lawman, and he wouldn't cover up her history of crime, would he?

Tears filled her eyes. She sat down on her bed staring at the window without seeing it. If only she had someone to confide in. She supposed Mrs. Finney was the logical one, but she dreaded making the woman think poorly of her. What if Mrs. Finney turned her out of the house? Maybe she could borrow enough from Freeland or Mrs. McCormick to get her to Yuma by stage. If Captain and Mrs. Owen were still at Fort Yuma, they might take her in. That was far closer than any distant relatives she might still have in the East. The Owenses had been kind to her. But would they understand and forgive what she had been doing since they last saw her?

They would understand, she told herself. They would have to. Maybe she could hide at their house until her tattoos were completely gone. Then she could start fresh.

She sighed, knowing it was unlikely the couple was still at the fort. It had been nearly eight years, and she had a vague notion that army officers were moved around often. She and Uncle Silas had planned to avoid the town on this trip, just in case. And she still didn't know how she would provide for herself once she left Mrs. Finney's care.

Freeland McKay. He was the only one who knew the truth now, if Uncle Silas was dead. He'd had time to think about it, and he might have some insight for her. She wished more than anything that he was here. She could ask him what to do. He was a thinking man, she was sure. Every minute she was with him in the desert, he had acted nobly.

With a shock she understood how much she missed him and how deeply she cared for him. But he wasn't here. She might never see him again. The marshal might come back and tell her that Freeland had left his posse and headed on south to Tucson. She'd better not hope too hard that he would come back here.

A quiet knock on her door startled her.

"Yes?"

"It's me, dear," Mrs. Finney said. "You have another visitor."

Carmela's heart raced. Could Freeland be back so soon? She had expected his mission to take a few more days, at least. She jumped up and hurried to open the door.

"Not the deputy?"

"No, I'm afraid not." Mrs. Finney smiled in sympathy. "It's a young lady. Or a young woman, at any rate."

Carmela frowned. What could this mean? She followed Mrs. Finney along the hallway. To her surprise, her hostess had seated the guest in the dining room, not the parlor. The girl—for she appeared to be at least two or three years younger than Carmela—stood as they entered. Her calico dress was of one piece and somewhat ragged. It hung loosely on her thin frame. Her hair, in contrast to Lucy Roote's lovingly combed tresses, hung in wild disarray, with no part and some ratted clumps that gave her an unkempt look. Her eyes were large in the dim room, and she seemed to drink in the sight of Carmela.

"May I help you?" Carmela stepped forward slowly.

"Don't know," the girl said.

"Sit down, won't you?"

As the girl moved to resume her seat, Carmela noticed her feet. She was wearing worn deerskin moccasins. Her heart sank. This couldn't be another.

"I am Carmela Wade."

"Rilla Landis," the girl said.

Carmela closed her eyes for a second. *Dear Lord, help me! I can't keep doing this.*

When she opened them, Rilla had leaned forward and was staring at her face, so close Carmela could smell her breath and see smudges of dirt on her cheek. She pulled back.

"Not with the Apache, were you?" Rilla said.

"No."

"I thought not. Did they rape you?"

"I beg your pardon?" Carmela was so shocked, she couldn't move. She had never heard the word spoken aloud, except once when Uncle Silas was having a conversation with a man in the next room and didn't know she could overhear.

"The buck who caught me didn't waste any time," Rilla said.

"I–I'm so sorry." Carmela felt ill. She looked around for Mrs. Finney, but the older woman had disappeared, probably into the kitchen.

"They made me leave my baby there." Rilla's brown eyes held sadness and also a hint of defiance, as though she expected Carmela to condemn her.

"You—you had a child there?"

Rilla's gaze dropped. "Two, actually. The second one died."

Carmela sat in stunned silence for a moment. She'd known captives suffered, but this poor girl had been through too much. Would she have been able to bear such sorrow and pain? She doubted she would have kept her sanity.

"People here say they'll pray for me," Rilla said bitterly. "Praying won't help."

Carmela thought it might, but she was sure this young woman didn't want to hear that opinion. She took a deep breath. "Prayer can help us put things in perspective. It reminds us that God is there, even in our darkest moments, and that His own Son died a brutal death for us."

Rilla held her gaze for several seconds. "He wasn't there with me."

"I'm sorry. To be utterly alone. . ." Wasn't that what she'd thought she was experiencing, now that Uncle Silas and Freeland were gone? How foolish of her! Carmela had never been completely alone. Even in the awful days after her family's deaths, she had prayed, and she had known God was there. She hadn't understood why He had taken her loved ones, but she had never doubted that He was nearby, whether she lived or died. When had she lost sight of that?

"I believe God is real," she said at last. "And I believe He is with us at the worst of times. He sustains us. And if the time comes for us to die, as it did with my family, He takes us home."

"You truly believe that?"

"Yes."

Rilla pressed her lips tightly together and folded her hands in her lap. "Sometimes I think I've gone mad. There are times. . ." She looked up. Her dark eyes had a haunted look. "I blame my parents. I think it's their fault."

"For not protecting you?" Carmela asked.

Rilla nodded. "My pa. Sometimes. . .sometimes I think of killing him. But then what would I do?"

Carmela had no words to soothe her. She pulled in a shaky breath, trying not to let the horror overwhelm her. *Help me, Father! I can't advise her. I don't know what to say.*

"I don't know if I can do anything to help you, Rilla, but I want to."

The somber girl's eyes flickered. "Just talking to you and having you not say I'm crazy helps."

"Really? I'm glad. Will it upset you if I remember you in my prayers?"

Rilla shook her head. "I don't suppose it can hurt."

❤

When Rilla had left, Carmela went to the kitchen with tears streaming down her cheeks.

"My dear, what is the matter?" Mrs. Finney wiped her hands on her apron and came to her, opening her arms wide.

Carmela leaned against her and sobbed. The landlady's kindness brought her mother to mind so sharply that it took her several minutes to recover enough to speak.

"There, now." Mrs. Finney pulled a handkerchief from her pocket when Carmela was reduced to gulps. "Tell me, child."

"Oh Mrs. Finney, I can't bear it any longer. That poor girl! Her situation was so much worse than mine, and yet she came to me for help. I can't help her. I can't help anyone."

"Now, now, why do you say that?" As she spoke, Mrs. Finney guided Carmela to the dining room, where they sat down side by side. "It seems to soothe these girls to share their stories with you, because you have something in common with them."

"But I don't," Carmela blurted.

"What do you mean?"

Carmela took two deep breaths. "It's all a lie. I was never with the Indians. My uncle forced me to say it. I was earning money for him by telling lies. My parents died on the trail to California, but I was never a captive. Not for a single day."

Mrs. Finney stared at her. She was so still, Carmela wondered if she'd stopped breathing.

"Well," she said at last. "How miserable for you."

"Yes, but my misery was nothing compared to what Rilla and Lucy endured. Especially Rilla."

"I've heard tales," Mrs. Finney said darkly. "She bears a heavy burden, for certain."

"What am I going to do?" Carmela's tears welled up again, and she applied the soggy handkerchief. "I've prayed and prayed, but God hasn't shown me any way to get out of this mess without making people angry. And I don't want to get arrested." She sniffed and looked into the landlady's hazel eyes. Mrs. Finney looked sad, but full of wisdom and compassion. Maybe God had answered her prayer after all.

"My dear." Mrs. Finney leaned toward her and patted her hand. "You have had a most stressful upbringing. Might we pray together for God's guidance?"

"I would like that." No one who knew the whole truth had ever prayed with her before. She clung to the landlady's hand and bowed her head.

"Our heavenly Father," Mrs. Finney said softly, "You know this child's heartbreak. You know what she needs. We ask that Thy will be done. For the uncle, Lord, only You know what is best for that man. It seems to me he's a scoundrel, seeing the things he's put this girl through. But You know his heart. Only You can judge his motives. And so we pray that You would have mercy and spare him if that is part of Your plan for Carmela, but also that You would turn his heart to the right. And for Carmela, please give her a plain path. Guide each step along her way, dear Lord, even as You guided her across the desert and here to my house. For that, I thank You. Amen."

Carmela's tears flowed freely now. She could hardly believe Mrs. Finney's kindness and her acceptance. "Dear God," she choked, "thank You for Mrs. Finney. Please show me what to do." She didn't think she could say more, so after a moment, she squeezed the woman's hand.

"Amen and amen," Mrs. Finney said briskly. "Now, let's be sensible about this. Are those markings on your face permanent?"

Carmela swiped at her cheek with the handkerchief. "I don't think so, though I've lived with them for years. They grow fainter, and my uncle used to renew them often. I assume that, if left alone, over time they would wear off."

Mrs. Finney frowned, studying her face and turning her chin to the side. "Well, we wouldn't want to scour your skin off, but we could give it a good scrubbing and see what happens."

"I think some of it is peeling off with my sunburn." Carmela wasn't entirely sure of that, but she thought she saw a difference. "I didn't want to go to church until I saw what would happen."

"That's understandable."

"And they've faded enough already that, if Uncle Silas came back and redid them now, I think people would notice and realize they're false. You would, wouldn't you?"

"Probably so."

"But then I think. . ." Carmela frowned. "When the posse comes back, it might be better to face them with the ink on my face. Maybe it's best to face the marshal with it the way he saw me first, at the stagecoach stop. Otherwise, I fear he'll arrest me for fraud. But I can't do them myself." She grasped Mrs. Finney's wrist as fear welled up inside her. "Would you help me?"

"Me? Color your face? No, child."

Carmela's heart sank. Not only had she exposed herself to Mrs. Finney, she had asked the dear lady to take part in a crime of deception.

"I'm sorry. I shouldn't have asked that. Forgive me."

Mrs. Finney smiled gently. "You're confused and worried. But the heavenly Father is neither of those. Let us trust Him."

"So you think I should. . ." Carmela gazed at her with a tiny spark of hope in her heart, but it seemed infinitesimal beside the huge bulk of dark fear she carried.

"Stop lying." Mrs. Finney nodded. "That's always best. Always."

Carmela let out a pent-up breath. "How do I begin?"

"The minister, I think."

"You mean, go to church on Sunday?"

"No, I mean we'll go round and see him today. Tell him all. The Lord can use him to give us guidance."

Carmela's pulse raced. "Do you really think— Oh, I don't know! I'm not ready."

Mrs. Finney regarded her calmly. "When will you be ready, dear?"

"I—I'm not sure."

"As I thought. If you keep putting it off, you'll never be ready, and then trouble will hunt you down. Better to meet it head-on."

Chapter Sixteen

reeland checked the loads in his rifle and sidearm and mounted his horse. Benny had retrieved his saddle and put it on his dun. The men signaled they were ready for action by gathering around Marshal Duffield for instructions.

"You be sure you bring my money back, Marshal," Holden called from where he lay on the blanket in the meager shade. "If you don't, I'll see that the governor knows about it." When Duffield ignored him, Holden opened his mouth again. "I mean it. I'll see that you no longer have a job if you don't—"

"Gag him," Duffield roared.

Benny Lassiter dismounted to help Parker do the job. Meanwhile, Duffield turned his horse so that his back was to the struggle.

"All right, men. He said there's a lookout at a boulder up ahead. There's not likely to be much cover." He sent two men ahead to try to outflank the lookout and signal them to come on.

Cover was scarce in the area, but Freeland's group waited twenty minutes while the two men crept around to where they could outflank the guard. When the signal came—a bandanna waved from the top of the rock where the outlaw had been stationed—they rode forward.

As they approached a ramshackle cabin, Duffield separated them into three groups. Freeland's job, with Deputy Eph Knapp, was to get to the corral and run off the outlaws' horses.

He recognized the paint one of the outlaws had ridden in the robbery. The big, bony workhorses had pulled the stagecoach, which sat abandoned outside the flimsy fence.

They got to the gate without raising an alarm. Eph watched the back of the cabin, his six-gun drawn, and gave Freeland a nod. He pushed the gate open. He didn't want to make a lot of noise, so he led the pinto out. As he'd hoped, another saddlehorse followed. He went back into the corral. The team didn't want to leave, and they didn't have halters, but Freeland managed to drive them out. The last of the outlaws' mounts had just plodded reluctantly through the gate when gunfire erupted on the other side of the cabin. The horses squealed and ran for the nearest ravine.

♥

The preacher was away on Saturday, when Carmela and Mrs. Finney tried to visit him, and Carmela was tempted to take that as a sign that she should wait.

"Hogwash," Mrs. Finney declared. "He has a lot of people to help. We'll see him at church tomorrow."

And so Carmela went with her on Sunday, to the wood framing of what would be the church when it was finished. After each offering, the congregation bought what lumber they could with it. They added a few more boards each week. So far, they had two walls and the sky overhead showing between the bare rafters. Rain was so uncommon here that they met every Sunday, sitting on benches inside the skeletal church.

Carmela appreciated the Reverend Mr. Bardwell's message on God's leading. He mentioned how God had led each one of the listeners here, some for reasons they didn't even know yet. They might think they had come to find gold, or to build a ranch or a business, but God had plans for them besides earning a living.

After the preaching, Mrs. Finney pushed through the people to invite him and his wife to dinner at the boardinghouse. She was too late. The Frawleys had already extended an invitation, so Mrs. Finney secured the minister's promise to come on Monday. One of her boarders needed guidance, she confided to him. Then she introduced Carmela.

Reverend Bardwell gazed pensively at her face with its fading tattoos and agreed to come.

Monday afternoon they sat in the parlor, Carmela, the minister, and his wife, with cups of coffee close at hand. The other boarders had gone about their post-lunch business, and Mrs. Finney had retired discreetly to the kitchen.

Carmela wasn't completely certain she could trust the minister with her secret. True, he seemed to be a sympathetic man. Tall, with light brown hair that needed trimming, he seemed both unshockable and knowledgeable of scripture. In fact, with his soft brown eyes that were just beginning to show crow's feet at the corners and his slightly bent nose, he reminded her of her father. She wasn't sure that was good—it might induce her to trust him more than she ought. But Mrs. Finney had assured her that Reverend Bardwell was a good soul and could advise her as to what the good Lord would have her do, and so she haltingly made her confession to him. His wife, a plain woman who seemed kind but had the lines of chronic fatigue in her face, sat quietly and listened.

"The Lord knows all our thoughts and imaginations," the reverend told her when she had laid out the tale. "Have courage, young lady."

Carmela eyed him warily. "I *want* to tell the truth, but it's hard when I've let people believe otherwise for so long."

"It is," he said. "But God is there at your side. And Mrs. Finney and my wife and I will support you."

"This is the right thing to do," Mrs. Bardwell said with a faint smile.

"But—you think I should stand up at church and tell every-one how I lied?" The thought terrified her. People would condemn her. They would spread the story abroad. More people would come demanding that she return their money. Why, she wouldn't be sur-prised if a crowd stoned her.

"Just tell the truth to God's people," Reverend Bardwell said firmly but gently. "If they are truly God's people, they will understand. That doesn't mean they will condone what you did, but I shall remind them that they have all transgressed in the past, too. So. . .next Sunday?"

"I suppose so," Carmela said, but her insides felt like a jar of Mrs. Finney's cactus jelly. What if everyone hated her after Sunday? None of the churchgoers really knew her yet. Most of them had stared at her yesterday morning. The Rootes had greeted her, and Lucy had run over to her and given her a hug, but the other stares had seemed cool, if not hostile. Curious, of course, but cautious, as though they thought she would steal their wallets if she had a chance.

"Good," Reverend Bardwell said heartily, reaching for his cup. He drained the last of his coffee and stood. "We must be going now. If you have any questions, come round or send word."

They were gone before she could say anything more, and Carmela sank back on the horsehair settee. Could she really go through with it? Her biggest hope was that the marshal would return before then and she would have some idea of what her future would be. Maybe she and Uncle Silas could move on by next Sunday, and she wouldn't have to face the crowd with her shocking truths.

But that would mean she would continue the fraudulent life she had lived for more than eight years. And besides, as Freeland and everyone else seemed to agree, Uncle Silas was likely dead. One way or another, Carmela would have to face life on her own.

She had told the minister of her situation. He seemed to be on her side. So why didn't she feel good about this?

❤

Freeland hated going into a gunfight. He'd been in some wild free-for-alls before, and each time, he'd felt as though he was running in place in a bad dream. The explosions of gunfire, the thuds, the footsteps, the horses' squeals all seemed unreal, but at the same time urgent.

The cabin had no back door, but there was a small window, shuttered from the inside. He ran to the back wall of the structure and flattened himself against the rough boards. He could edge around the corner, slink along the cabin's side, and join the fray at the front. He wasn't sure where Eph had got to, but he'd best get into it. He hauled in a deep breath.

Before Freeland could move, the shutter on the little window thunked and swung inward. A filthy man with shaggy hair and beard and a torn shirt made colorless by dust ground into it, stuck his arms, head, and shoulders out and tipped up to slide down to the ground.

Dix.

Freeland stepped closer and placed the barrel of his handgun behind his ear as he hung there, half-in and half-out of the window.

"Don't move, Dix."

The man twisted his head and looked up at Freeland, his mouth twisted in a grimace, his gray eyes huge.

"Don't shoot."

"I won't if you slide down peaceful and stay down."

He wriggled out and hit the ground hard. Freeland took a fleeting glance up at the window. Nobody else appeared in the square hole.

"You got a gun?" Freeland asked.

"Empty," Dix croaked.

Freeland saw it, stuck in a holster on his far hip.

"Take it out, nice and easy."

Dix's right hand moved slowly toward his hip.

"Don't make a move, or I'll blast you," Freeland said.

As the last words left his mouth, Dix twisted away from him and pulled the revolver at the same time. On instinct, Freeland let loose a round from his Colt then made himself wait as his brain registered the result. Dix's revolver flew from his hand and landed a few feet away in the dirt while the prisoner pulled his arm in to his stomach and clasped his wrist with his left hand. A string of oaths came out of Dix's mouth.

"Shut up," Freeland said. "Now stand up."

"I'm shot."

"In the hand. Stand up, you fool, and thank the Lord I didn't blow your head off."

The gunfire on the other side of the cabin had stilled, but Freeland heard a few shouts from that direction.

Benny Lassiter came charging around the corner, his revolver in his hand. He jerked to a stop when he saw Freeland and the prisoner.

"You all right, Free?"

"Yup. Did you get the others?"

"All accounted for but this one, and you got him."

"Where's Eph Knapp?" Freeland asked.

"With the marshal. One of the outlaws creased his shoulder."

Because of his wound, Freeland didn't put handcuffs on Dix. He bent to retrieve the revolver and had Benny cover him while he searched the prisoner for more weapons. He didn't find any and concluded the outlaws had not been generous on that score but had given Dix a handgun to help them defend the hideout.

"Let's go. We'll bandage you up before we take you in." He and Benny herded the bleeding prisoner around the cabin to where Duffield was taking stock and giving orders.

A knock echoed through the rooms of the boardinghouse as Carmela put away the breakfast dishes the next morning. Mrs. Finney had gone out to make some purchases. She had invited Carmela, but she had opted to stay home. A little more time, and maybe the pancake powder the saloon girls wore would cover her tattoos.

But now she was alone in the house and had to deal with whoever was at the door. None of the boarders would have knocked. It might be someone hoping to engage a room. Or it could be the preacher. Carmela went to the door and opened it cautiously.

"Miss Wade, I was hoping you were still here."

"Mr. Roote." Lucy's father stood on the stoop, eyeing her gravely. "May I help you?"

"It's Lucy. She's gone."

"Gone?"

"Run away."

Carmela drew in a sharp breath. "Oh no." The girl's words about wanting to go back to the Apache were carved into her memory. "I'm so sorry." She stepped back. "Won't you come in? There's coffee in the kitchen."

He followed her through the long dining room into Mrs. Finney's cozy domain at the back. Today the kitchen was a bit too cozy, since the heat outside had risen steadily since sunup. Carmela poured mugs of coffee for both of them and sat down with him at the plain pine table where they did their food preparation.

"Tell me everything."

Mr. Roote gave a big sigh and sat there with his large hand holding onto the ironstone mug but not taking a drink. "She must have gone in the night. She was there at supper, and maybe an hour later she went to bed. This morning she was gone."

"Is there any chance the Apache came and took her?"

He shook his head. "She left a note: 'I'm sorry, but I can't live this way. I'm going back to my people.' And all her Indian clothes and things were gone." He shook his head. "I knew we should have burned them! *'My people.'*"

Carmela's heart sank. "Will she know how to find them? Is there an Apache village nearby?"

"There was some camping by the river a week ago, beyond where the Yavapai stay. Not many, just a few who came to trade in town. I think they're gone now, but she might try to catch up to them."

"Have you—" Carmela stopped. She was going to ask if he had told the marshal, but Duffield was out of town. "Is there a deputy marshal about?"

"Yes. He's getting up a posse, mostly our neighbors and men from our church, to go after them. Will you go with us?"

The back door opened, and Mrs. Finney came in carrying two bulging sacks of groceries. She quickly took in the scene.

"Oh, hello, Mr. Roote. Is anything wrong?"

"Our Lucy's run away. Back to the Indians."

"No." Mrs. Finney set down her burdens and came to the table. "What can we do? Besides pray, I mean."

"They're gettin' up a posse. I hoped Miss Wade would ride with us." Mr. Roote took out a pocket watch and frowned at it. "I need to go. We're leaving right away."

"I don't have a horse," Carmela said.

"I brought an extra, in case you'd say yes."

She looked to Mrs. Finney.

"Miss Wade can't go tearing about the desert with a bunch of men," the landlady said. "I'm surprised you'd ask that of her."

"Where is the posse gathering?" Carmela asked.

"In front of the Juniper House, on Montezuma Street."

Carmela stood, her mind made up. "You go on, Mr. Roote. I shall be there in ten minutes."

"My dear! You should wait for the marshal to return," Mrs. Finney said.

Mr. Roote shook his head. "There's not time. We could lose all sign of her."

Mrs. Finney's tortured features played on Carmela's fears, but she placed a hand on her friend's arm.

"Pray for us, as you said." Carmela dashed to her room and threw on the tattered dress she had worn on the ill-fated stagecoach journey. She pulled back her hair and tied a bandanna around her neck. What else had she wished for when she was out there with Freeland? She pocketed the derringer Freeland had returned to her after their arrival in Prescott. It was loaded, but she had no extra rounds for it. She grabbed the shawl she had bought from the Yavapai woman and hurried out to the dining room.

Mrs. Finney met her as she entered, her arms full of bundles. "I'll walk over with you. You'll need this blanket, and I've filled a water bottle for you and packed some vittles."

Carmela was amazed that she had done so much so quickly. "Thank you." She kissed Mrs. Finney's cheek. "I can carry it. You stay here. You'll have to get dinner for the boarders by yourself."

Tears shone in Mrs. Finney's eyes. "Take my hat that's hanging by the door. And you take care. I shall pray my hardest."

Chapter Seventeen

$\mathcal{T}$he deputy marshal in charge of the posse looked old and frail. *Probably why Mr. Duffield left him behind when he went after the outlaw gang,* Carmela thought.

Mr. Roote beckoned to her, and she joined him in front of a saloon, where he had two rawboned horses saddled and tied up, waiting.

"Mrs. Finney gave me these."

He grunted, took the blanket from her, and tied it behind the saddle. "What's in the poke?"

"Food."

He took it and tied it with his saddle strings. "Hang the water bottle on your saddle."

She did as he said, and he untied her horse's reins and handed them to her. She got her foot up to the stirrup before she realized she would again be riding astride.

"Need a boost?"

Carmela was about to say no when he placed his hand on her thigh and shoved her up and over, into the saddle. She felt her face go scarlet, but he had already turned away, to mount his own horse. *Well,* she told herself, *he has daughters, after all.*

They rode over to where the deputy marshal was trying to organize the party.

"Mr. Orland," Mr. Roote called as they drew near, "I've brought Miss Wade."

The older man looked her over, frowning at the markings on her face. "Thank you for coming, miss. I understand Lucy has an attachment to you."

Carmela opened her mouth to explain. She had only met the girl twice, and she wasn't sure they had connected all that well, or else Lucy wouldn't have run off. She decided silence was the better course for the time being and nodded.

The deputy looked around at the other mounted men—only half a dozen besides Mr. Roote. He lifted his hat and scratched his head through his silvery hair. "This it?"

"Looks like," Mr. Roote said.

Orland nodded and looked over at a man in a white apron, standing on the doorstep of the saloon. "Harland, you get word to the marshal the minute he rides in. We're heading west from Roote's place. That's the way he thinks the girl went this morning."

"I'll tell him," Harland replied.

Orland urged his horse into a jog, and the others fell in behind him. Carmela and Mr. Roote ended up in the middle of the pack, which suited her. She didn't want to lag behind, but she didn't want to bear the deputy's close scrutiny. Perhaps he had seen Indians or other captives with tribal tattoos and would suspect hers were spurious. Or he might question her about her captivity, which could be even worse.

After they had left the center of town behind and were headed out Gurley Street, Mr. Roote pointed his chin toward the hill ahead. "That's Thumb Butte."

Carmela could see why they called it that. Many of the rock formations and mountains of the area were named for their shapes.

"Orland said he expects Marshal Duffield back soon," Mr. Roote said.

"How can he know?" Carmela asked.

"He can't. He's guessin'."

"Oh." Remembering the difficult terrain and the vast landscape in which the outlaws could hide, she decided not to count on the marshal returning quickly.

"Course, they mighta gone all the way to Tucson."

Carmela nodded. "They say someday we'll have telegraph lines all over the country. Then we can get messages to each other more efficiently."

"Not out here," Mr. Roote said with certainty. "Too hard to string 'em. Just think of bringing all those poles in, and the work to sink 'em, not to mention the Injuns interferin'."

"You think they'd cut the lines?"

"They hardly let the mines operate. They're having a terrible time settin' up a stamp mill. The Apache keep runnin' off their horses. Can't live out here without horses. Or mules."

It was true. She knew that firsthand. She and Freeland would not have lasted long if Price's station had been burned and the posse hadn't come riding along the next day.

"My uncle said they'll build a railroad," she said a bit doubtfully. "I mean, Prescott *is* the capital."

He laughed shortly. "Be a long time afore we see a railroad, I'm a-thinkin'."

They rode for half an hour, until they came in sight of a flat plain near the river. The ground was disturbed, and the remains of fire pits could be plainly seen.

"The Apache packed up and hightailed it," one of the men said to Mr. Orland.

Carmela's heart beat so strongly in her throat, she wasn't sure she'd be able to breathe much longer.

"Butler, you scout ahead," Orland said. "Come back and tell us what you find."

The man called Butler, who wore the work clothes of a laboring man, shot Carmela a sidelong glance before he rode off, following the rather obvious trail of the villagers. She wondered why he looked at her. Maybe it was only because she was an oddity.

She was still afraid, even though she had earnestly asked the Lord to calm her and protect her. Although she feared that everyone would hate her when they knew the truth, an even deeper fear haunted her. She had imagined Lucy and Rilla, especially Rilla, being disillusioned enough to do something rash. But she hadn't told the crowd yet, and it had happened anyway. Lucy had fled her loving parents to return to the savages. Their heart-to-heart hadn't helped, and apparently Carmela's prayers hadn't either.

Orland rode down onto the scarred earth the Apache had left. Wouldn't they cover the evidence of their sojourn? A lot of the early accounts she had read about native tribes were exaggerated, she knew. Fresher, more detailed writings had dispelled some of the myths of the noble savage. And yet, she had a distinct impression they had left in a hurry. Had Lucy ridden out here to join them? If so, perhaps they knew Lucy's family would not let her go easily.

Orland dismounted and kicked at the remains of a campfire. The other six men and Carmela remained in the saddle. The deputy crouched and poked the ashes with a stick.

"What do you think?" The man who spoke had the build of a blacksmith—muscular, broad chested.

"There's still coals here. They left this morning early."

"Seems odd," another man said.

"They've probably got the girl," the first man countered, shooting Mr. Roote a glance.

Orland mounted and led them along in Butler's wake. A few minutes later, the scout came back, loping his horse. He pulled up near Orland and turned his horse to jog along beside him. "There's tracks up here a little ways, where a small bunch rode in. I'm thinking a hunting party joined them, something like that. Maybe they gave them some news that caused them to pull up stakes."

"Any idea how far ahead they are?"

Butler shook his head. "A few hours? No way to tell, really. But some of them were in town yesterday, trading."

"Any sign of my Lucy?" Mr. Roote called.

Butler swiveled in his saddle. His eyes picked out the grieving father. "Nothing I could tell for sure." His gaze settled on Carmela. "Aren't you that captive girl people are talkin' about?"

Carmela's mouth went dry.

"Yeah, she is," Mr. Roote said. "My Lucy likes her. That's why I brought her along."

Butler grunted. "Maybe she can translate for us."

"I—I don't speak Apache," Carmela managed.

Another man rode up beside her, staring at her face. "I wondered about them marks on yer face. Howdy. I'm Del Filmer."

Carmela nodded and tried to concentrate on her horse's movements.

"I heard her give a talk once," Butler said, louder than before, as though to make sure everyone heard. "She knows all about Indian ways."

"Then maybe she should scout for us instead of you, Joe," said the ruggedly built man, and the rest laughed.

Butler looked disgruntled, but he said no more for the moment, and Carmela was glad. This might be a bad time to reveal the whole truth. She wanted to help Lucy, but she felt cornered. She couldn't lie to them now and stand up at church to give her confession on Sunday. They would despise her for sure, and they would wonder why she thought she could help on this expedition if she really knew nothing about Indians. She wished she had stayed home.

Lucy needs you. She squared her shoulders. She was here for the girl.

Mr. Roote squinted at her in the bright sunlight. "Your markings don't look as bright as they were the day we brought Lucy to see you."

Carmela's throat constricted, and she thought she would strangle and fall from the horse.

Freeland and Benny managed to catch two of the horses from the stagecoach team and three of the outlaws' mounts. The rest were probably still running.

"We shouldn't have run them off," Ben said mournfully as he

grappled with the harness.

"Yeah, but we didn't know it would be over so quick," Freeland said. "If Dix had made it to the corral and those horses were still in there, he'd have got away." He laid the straps over one of the big horses' withers and adjusted the back band and tugs.

"Think these two can pull the stage all the way back to Wickenburg?" Benny asked. Normally four to six animals pulled the coach over the rough trails.

"I don't know. I doubt they got much to eat out here the last few days. If we get as far as Price's station, maybe he'll have a team we can swap out for, and these can stop there and rest and eat."

"I s'pose we got to take that whiny old man along." Benny spat in the dirt and picked up the near horse's bridle.

"Mr. Holden?" Freeland said. "Yeah, he's Miss Wade's uncle. We have to take him."

"You seem to set some store by this Miss Wade." Benny cocked an eyebrow at him over the horse's back.

"She's nothing like him." Freeland walked over to the stagecoach, partly to get away from Benny's comments. The marshal was over-seeing the loading of all the loot they had recovered from the cabin into the strongbox in the driver's boot, and two of the deputies were digging graves a short distance away.

"Reckon the stage is in good enough shape to make it back?" Freeland asked.

"Seems to be. And we've recovered nearly all of the payroll that was lost. I'm just sorry we couldn't save the driver and shotgun rider."

"Yeah." Freeland frowned, remembering Dwight and Tom, both good men.

They set out with the outlaws confined inside the stagecoach. When they got back to where they'd left Silas and Porter, Silas was dozing in the scant shade of a mesquite bush. Porter sat nearby with his back to a rock and his rifle resting on his knees.

"'Bout time," he said, rising. "I heard the gunfire. I reckon it went all right." He looked down the line at the horsemen and the stagecoach that trailed them with Benny driving and Eph sitting with him on the box. Several of the posse members led extra horses.

"You got 'em all?"

"We sure did," the marshal told him. "Get ready to ride. Mr. Holden, you still with us?"

Silas opened one eye then sat up slowly, his hand clasping his wounded side. "Do you have my money?"

"Take it easy," Duffield said. "We'll discuss that when we get back to Prescott, where we can parley with the stage company's managers."

"I don't see why I can't have my own property back now," Silas snapped.

"I don't care whether you see or not. Do you want to ride with us or share the stage with the gang?"

A flash of terror flickered over Silas's face. "I surely don't want to be shut up in the coach with them!"

"Pick a horse, then," Duffield said.

"You got prisoners?" Porter asked.

"Yep." Duffield looked smugly over his shoulder. "Three of 'em, tied up in the stage."

Porter shifted his gaze to Freeland. "What took so long? It's nearly an hour since the shooting stopped."

"Had to bury a couple," Freeland said.

Silas had lurched to his feet and stood eyeing the stagecoach with loathing. "I. . .don't know if I can stay in the saddle, but. . ."

"You can lie down on the roof," Freeland suggested. "You'd be in the sun the whole way, but I guess it's that or ride with the prisoners."

Silas limped over to the stagecoach and looked up at Benny. "Would you be so kind as to help me up, sir?"

Freeland wound up dismounting and going over to help. After three tries, they had boosted Silas to the driver's box. He looked at Eph, whose arm hung in a makeshift sling fashioned from two bandannas.

"I don't suppose. . ."

"You want me to give up my seat? No chance."

With a sigh, Silas crawled onto the roof and lay down between the rails designed to hold baggage. He stretched out and settled his bowler hat over his face.

"All right, two of you ride behind the stage," Duffield said. "I don't want to take any chances of those prisoners escaping.

Freeland fell in at the end of the line with Porter.

♥

Carmela, Deputy Marshal Orland, and six townsmen rode in silence. They passed a couple of ranches, and Carmela wondered how they found feed for their animals in the bleak country. Just four miles out of Prescott, they spotted a column of smoke. Butler, who had once more ridden a short way ahead, charged back toward them. He pulled his horse up short a few yards in front of Deputy Orland.

"It's the Howard place. The house and shed are burning. I didn't see any livestock. Likely the Apache got 'em."

"Forward," Orland called to the others, "but exercise caution."

They rode on until the burning structures came into view. To Carmela's horror, she saw a woman in full skirts hurrying toward the road. Was her family inside the blazing house?

Orland beckoned to them, and they all galloped toward the homestead, with Butler's bay horse outstripping the others. He reached the woman first, jumped down and was listening to her tale of woe when the others rode up.

"They shot Micah first," she sobbed. "Then they grabbed the children. I tried to stop them, but the one carrying Andy struck me. I must have been unconscious. I came to a few minutes ago, and the house was afire and the Indians were gone. I can't find a trace of the children."

"How many kids?" Butler asked.

"Two. Andy's four and Marjorie is six."

Carmela could tell that Mrs. Howard was expecting another child. If this trauma didn't send her into labor, she probably had a while to go before it was born. She had a welt on her cheek and a bruise on her brow. Carmela slid off her horse and ran to her side.

"I'm Carmela Wade. Is there anything I can do to help you?"

"I—I don't know what you could do," Mrs. Howard said uncertainly, looking back toward the fire and resting a hand over the mound of her stomach.

Orland had ridden up close, and he leaned down to speak to her.

"Ma'am, we're tracking those Apache. We think they stole a girl from a ranch on the south edge of Prescott."

Her eyes widened. "Yes. I saw that they had a white girl with them, but I couldn't do anything about it. I was trying to save my own children."

Orland nodded grimly and looked toward the fire. "We're too late to save your house, I'm afraid."

Butler nodded. "We couldn't haul water fast enough to save it. Do you have livestock?"

"They took our two horses," she said. "We have twenty cattle down in the canyon, but I don't know if they took them or not."

"They mighta missed 'em," Mr. Filmer said.

Carmela's heart pounded as she listened. This woman was living what to her had been only stories and nightmares of stories. Behind her was the tragic evidence of a home reduced to embers and a husband lying dead at his own corral gate.

"How many Apache?" Orland asked.

"I don't know. It seemed like a lot. Ten, anyway, down at the house, but I saw more passing up here by the road. Looked like maybe they were moving their whole village."

"They are," Orland said.

"No, they's not that many." Butler shook his head adamantly. "I was by there day before yesterday. There wasn't more'n twenty or thirty all told—counting the women and kids. It was just a small band come to trade."

"And up until now they've been peaceful," Orland said. "Mostly. They steal some, but they haven't given us much trouble."

"More could've joined them," said the burly man. "Butler said he saw tracks of another bunch coming in."

Mr. Filmer pushed his hat back. "We need more men, Orland."

The deputy frowned. "I know that."

"We can't go back now," Butler said. "They'll probably split up, and we'll lose 'em. They do that when they have captives."

"Well, we can't leave Mrs. Howard here alone. And we can't stop if we want to find out where they take those kids. There's three now, not just the Roote girl."

One of the men on the fringe of the group gave a shout. Three riders were loping toward them from the south. They barreled up to the group and pulled in the horses. Ranchmen, Carmela guessed.

A bearded blond man called, "Butler, what's going on? Injuns?"

"Yeah, Steger. They burnt the house and killed Howard. We think they've got three kids they grabbed—two here and one from Roote's place. Deputy Orland's in charge."

"The marshal ain't here?" one of the other ranchers asked, frowning.

"Gone back toward Tucson, chasing stage robbers," Orland said. "If you men want to join us, we'd appreciate it."

Steger said, "How about I take Mrs. Howard to my place? My wife can tend to her. Then I'll come back and bury her husband."

"Sounds reasonable." Orland turned to eye Carmela. "You want to stay, Miss Wade?"

Carmela didn't hesitate. She would be no comfort to these women, her face a constant reminder of the savages' deeds. "I'll go with you. For the children."

Orland nodded. "See to it then, Steger. Are you two in?"

The other two ranchers looked at each other.

"We got no supplies," said one, a young man with reddish hair.

"I don't expect we'll be days and days on the trail," Orland said.

"Our families," the older man said.

"I'll see they get word of what's happened," Steger said. "They can gather at my place if they want. Our house is the biggest, and my wife's got a shotgun and knows how to shoot."

"All right," said the red-haired man. "Tell Lena I'll be back and not to worry."

A lot of good that would do, Carmela thought. These men expected a lot, bringing their wives into an unsettled territory. And then to command them not to worry while they chased a band of thieving redskins—they really didn't understand women, did they?

"And get word back to Prescott if you can," Orland said. "Spread the word of what's happened and leave a message for the marshal to join us if he gets back before we do."

They rode out, now ten men strong besides Carmela, leaving Mr. Steger to boost Mrs. Howard up onto his mare and climb up behind her to ride the heavily laden horse back to his ranch a mile away.

Carmela only had to keep up, which wasn't hard. Mr. Roote stayed near her. He probably felt responsible for her, but she had made her own choice in this matter.

She turned her thoughts heavenward and prayed as they rode, for wisdom and peace with the Apache, and for the children's well-being. With three children now in the hands of the Indians, her concern shifted from her own troubles and the outrage people would feel when they learned of her deceit. Now she wished only to help the children survive and be returned to their families. She no longer cared what happened to herself.

The ride seemed endless, with the constant shock of pounding against the hard saddle. Carmela was certain she would have many bruises on her legs by evening. She reminded herself once more of the trek across the desert with Freeland McKay. If they were walking again, handcuffed or not, they would not have gone a third of the distance the improvised posse had traveled that morning, probably less. Had she ever thanked God for horses? She remedied that shortcoming at once.

They came to a creek that flowed toward the river, and before crossing, they stopped to water the horses.

"We'd better rest awhile," Mr. Butler advised Orland.

"No. We need to catch up to them," Mr. Roote said. "I want Lucy back before dark."

Deputy Orland threw him a sympathetic look. "That may not be possible. Our horses are tired. We don't want them played out when we confront the Apache."

Mr. Roote gave in. He sat by himself, brooding, until Carmela approached him.

"Will you have a biscuit and an apple, Mr. Roote? I'm sure Mrs. Finney intended for me to share, she packed so much."

He grunted and accepted the food she held out. Carmela sat beside him on the rocky ground and set down her water bottle. Some of the men had no provisions, and after a while, she decided to share from her supply with the ranchers who had joined them at the homestead fire. She learned that the young red-haired man was named Toole, and the older one, whose dark brown beard was streaked with gray, was Linnet. Both were fretting about the families they had left so precipitously.

"Steger will bring them up to his place," Mr. Roote said, but they didn't seem convinced, especially Toole.

"My wife's there with three little 'uns," he said.

Mr. Roote sighed. "Don't worry. The Injuns are all on the trail now. They know we'll come after 'em, so they won't be dallying. They're ahead of us, and your family's behind."

"There's more than one band of Apache," Toole said stubbornly.

Carmela finished her biscuit and cheese and brushed the crumbs from her dress. She started to rise and take the food bag and water bottle back to her horse. Mr. Linnet tossed his apple core over his shoulder, and she followed its track, ending where a horse suddenly came into view over a ridge. Astride it sat a fierce-visaged Indian. She gasped.

Mr. Roote looked around to see what had startled her and reached for his revolver. The other men stiffened and got to their feet, most of them holding their hands at shoulder height. In a quick glance around, Carmela counted eight armed warriors.

Chapter Eighteen

The numbers were fairly even, Apache versus whites. Carmela's chest squeezed so that she could hardly take in a breath. *This is it. We're all going to die, just like Mr. Howard.*

She thought of the derringer in her pocket, but pulling it out seemed like a bad idea when none of the men were going for their weapons. She would only ignite a battle if she produced it, and she would probably get some of them killed.

Her head whirled, and she felt as though she might pitch forward onto the rocks. The combination, she supposed, of the heat and the shock had caught up to her. Slowly she crumpled to her knees and sat down with her skirt billowing around her. Several of the Indian men eyed her curiously.

"You all right, miss?" Mr. Toole asked gruffly.

"I think so, yes. So far."

Orland was on his feet, and he looked around at the riders. One of them moved his horse forward a few steps, and Orland stood facing him.

Carmela studied the Apache's face. She couldn't guess his age. He had rubbed wide swaths of charcoal on his cheeks below his eyes, and his long, loose hair was dazzlingly black in the sun. His pinto pony snuffled, and Carmela's heart froze then pounded furiously.

She had last seen him by moonlight, but she was sure he was the man who had given her the water flask after the stagecoach holdup. Her lips trembled as his eyes swept over the group of white men and lingered on her. He made no sign of recognition but held her gaze for a long moment.

He spoke in his own language, and Orland looked helplessly to Butler, who stood beside him. "You savvy?"

"A little," Butler said. "Not much. Something about a horse."

The Apache man's expression did not change, but he cupped his hand at his chest and said distinctly, "Two Pony."

"You think that's his name?" Orland asked, "Or does he want horses?"

"Dunno." Butler cleared his throat and touched his own chest. "Butler." He gestured toward the deputy. "Orland. Law man." The badge on Orland's shirt front was obvious to all, and Carmela wondered if the regal Apache warrior thought they were simpleminded.

To everyone's surprise, he smoothly dismounted, dropped the rope by which he guided his horse, and walked toward Carmela. He looked into her face, and she could sense tension among the ranchers around her.

The warrior reached for her right hand, and then he held it up and examined her wrist.

"That's enough, Mr. Two Pony," Orland said, pulling out his revolver.

Carmela stopped breathing. Every Indian in the circle of horsemen trained his weapon on Orland.

The man before Carmela gave a low command, and they all lowered their guns and bows. He spoke to her in that odd language and traced a circle around her wrist with one finger.

"It's all right," Carmela said as loudly as she could manage. She could inhale now. "He's asking about the first time we met. He is a friend."

"You *know* this man?" Butler asked, stepping toward her. The Apaches' weapons now focused on him.

"We've met," she said.

"Was he part of the tribe that captured you?" Butler asked.

175

"No. He saved my life and Deputy McKay's after the stagecoach robbery." She looked up into Two Pony's dark eyes. "Thank you."

Two Pony's lips twitched.

"If you know how to say 'thank you' in Apache, please tell him," she called to Butler.

Butler swallowed hard and spoke a few words.

"Tell him 'friend,'" she instructed.

Butler spoke again, and Two Pony nodded, still looking at her.

He spoke once more, and Butler's eyebrows drew together.

"He said—I *think* he said—'Where is your man?'"

Carmela felt the blood rush to her cheeks. "He means the deputy," she said hastily. "Please tell him Mr. McKay lives. He is safe."

Butler spoke haltingly and added a couple of hand signals for good measure.

Two Pony looked back at Carmela. "Good." After a moment, he dropped her wrist and walked over to stand face-to-face with Butler.

He lapsed back into his native tongue, and this time Butler sighed in relief.

"He's asking what we want."

Carmela looked earnestly into the Apache's eyes. How much did he really understand?

"We're looking for a girl named Lucy Roote. This man's daughter." She placed a hand on Mr. Roote's shoulder.

Again the Apache spoke.

"He says we should sit down and speak," Butler said. "Wants to parley."

"Then we should do it," Orland said.

"No," Roote cried. "What if it's a trick? He could be stalling us so the others can get away with Lucy."

"I don't think so," Carmela said. "He helped me and Mr. McKay when he didn't have to. I trust this man." She turned to Butler. "Tell him."

Butler pointed at Carmela and spoke to Two Pony. "She says..." He paused for a moment then spoke Apache words and signed. He glanced apologetically at Carmela. "Sorry, I'm not real good at this.

176

I think I got that right."

Carmela sincerely hoped so.

Two Pony gazed at her impassively then nodded.

"Good," Orland said. "We'll parley."

Almost as weary as he'd been when he and Carmela staggered into Price's station, Freeland hauled himself up the steps to Mrs. Finney's boardinghouse. How had Carmela fared this past week? He wished he hadn't had to abandon her, but Mrs. Finney seemed like the sort who would take care of a destitute girl.

The landlady opened the door a few inches, and her dour face matched her somber dress.

"Deputy. It's about time."

"Mrs. Finney. Is Miss Wade in?"

"No. She's gone after the Apache with Deputy Orland."

"What?" McKay mistrusted his ears. "I heard a posse went after a band that burned a ranch near here, but why on earth would Miss Wade go with them?"

Tears gleamed in Mrs. Finney's eyes. "We didn't know about the Howard ranch when she left. Mr. Roote came and asked her to go with him to try to get his daughter back."

"Slow down," Freeland said. "Who's Mr. Roote?"

"You'd best come in. I expect you could stand a bowl of stew and a cup of coffee while I tell you what I know."

Freeland followed her through to her overly warm kitchen. He took off his hat and laid it on the table and sat down. A mug of coffee and a bowl of beef stew appeared almost magically before him. The landlady took a few steps and came back with a spoon and a pan of cornpone.

"She'd talked to the girl once before. Lucy was a recovered captive. The Apache had her six months, and she said things like how she wanted to go back to them. Her parents didn't know how to handle her. So when she ran off—at least, they think she ran off—Mr. Roote came here and asked Carmela to go along. He thought she could help persuade Lucy to come home."

"I see." Freeland ate while Mrs. Finney spilled the details of Carmela's departure.

"And then we heard they'd hit the Howards' ranch and killed Mr. Howard and stolen two more children."

"When?"

"Early this morning."

"So the posse hasn't been gone long?"

"Eight hours, maybe."

Freeland nodded. "The saloonkeeper pounced on the marshal as soon as we reached town. Duffield told us all to go get a meal and come back to ride with him. I thought I'd check on Miss Wade."

"Well, she's gone. I don't know if Lucy's with those savages or not, but the Howard children certainly are. But you and the marshal just got in. Are you really turning around and going after them?"

Freeland sighed. "We've got to."

Mrs. Finney was silent for a moment. She sat down next to him. "What about your other errand? Did you get those outlaws?"

"Yes, and we recaptured my prisoner."

"And Miss Wade's uncle?"

"He's alive but wounded. We brought him in and left him at the doctor's office on Gurley Street."

"Praise be," Mrs. Finney said. "Although I don't know how happy Miss Wade will be."

Freeland eyed her sharply. "She told you her story."

"She did. And she was about to make a public confession at church about the life that charlatan forced her to lead. Then this came up."

Freeland pursed his lips as though to whistle and let out a long breath.

"She means no harm," Mrs. Finney said. "But those Indians— they might see her and like the looks of her, too. Or the men in the posse might figure out she doesn't really know anything about their way of life."

"Oh, she knows a lot about it," Freeland said. "But it's book learnin' mostly. She could land in a fix, all right. I'd best get going. The marshal will head out soon, and I'll need to put my saddle on a fresh horse."

"You'll bring her back, won't you, Mr. McKay?"

He clapped on his hat as she stood. "I'll try my best, ma'am."

She smiled. "You've got a pretty good record so far this week."

❤

Butler frowned and stared off toward the distant mountains, his eyes vacant.

Carmela was certain that Two Pony's last remark had been directed at her, and she tried to be patient. Butler was doing the best he could.

Two Pony had insisted that Carmela sit on one side of him in the circle and Butler on the other. Beyond each of them sat an Apache man, and so it went around the circle, with alternate whites and Apache. Orland and two of the townsmen sat in on the parley, while the others stood back in a little knot, watching, their hands never far from their guns. Three more Apache stayed on their horses, watching everything, their stony faces revealing nothing.

Two Pony made hand signals to Carmela, and even before Butler gave his halting translation, she thought she understood his question.

"Do you want to go with them?" Butler asked. "That's what he's saying. He says go with your people."

"I believe he might be asking if I want to go back to the tribe. . . the other tribe he calls my people."

"Mojave," Two Pony said distinctly.

She caught her breath. Uncle Silas had tried to copy genuine tribal tattoos, using a photograph of Miss Oatman. Perhaps he had done a better job than she'd thought. But she had always believed the Yavapai had put the markings on Miss Oatman's face. It was true that the accounts she had read disagreed on what tribe the Oatman sisters had sojourned with, and they had been sold from one group to another after a winter with those who had killed the rest of the family.

"He wants to take you to the Mojave?" Butler frowned and looked at Orland.

"Is that who you were with before, Miss Wade?" Orland asked.

Carmela hesitated. "To be honest, I'm not certain. I was very young and had never been in the West before."

"Of course," Orland said. "Back East, they think all the Injuns out here are either Apache, Pueblo, or Comanche."

Two Pony spoke again.

Butler wore an expression of severe disapproval as he translated. "He says he will help his little sister."

Stunned, Carmela looked into the warrior's grave face. She reached a hand toward him but stopped short of touching his arm.

"Thank you. You have been very kind to me." She waited for Butler to translate. "But no," she continued, shaking her head. "I do not wish to go back. I will stay with my white people now."

After a moment, Butler informed her, "He says you would be treated well. I think. He seems to think you're family of his."

Carmela frowned. Perhaps this man had kinfolk in the Mojave tribe. She spoke with care, not wanting to disappoint him but also not wishing to give the impression that she preferred the Indian life.

"You gave me water when I needed it. You kept me alive. Kept my friend alive, too. I will never forget that. But I do not wish to go back to the people. I have come only to search for my friend Lucy Roote."

Butler stumbled to find the words to express her meaning, but Two Pony cut him off with a quick motion of his hand.

Carmela quaked inside as she waited. The Apache man gazed into her eyes for a long moment, making her want to shrink and hide. He and his friends might be able to overpower the posse of white men if they wanted to. He could force her to go with them.

Two Pony tipped his head back and gave a quick order. One of the Apache still on horseback turned his gray mount and loped off, soon out of sight in the rugged terrain.

"What?" Orland asked Butler softly. "What's happening?"

"Not sure," Butler murmured.

They sat in uneasy silence. The Apache in the circle did not seem worried, but Carmela's skin prickled and she felt she might faint. Was Two Pony truly her friend?

A few minutes later, she heard the muted thud of unshod hooves on the rocks. The gray horse hove into view, its black mane tossing as it jogged toward them. Around the Apache man's waist, slender hands gripped him. He brought the horse close to the circle, and a girl in a moss-green dress slid down the horse's flank.

Mr. Roote sprang up and bolted to her, enfolding her in his arms before Lucy could even turn around. She gave a little scream but fell silent as she turned and gazed into her father's face.

"You're safe, my love," Mr. Roote said. "We've come to take you home."

Lucy's lips trembled. She looked up at the Apache who had brought her to the circle and spoke to him in Apache.

Carmela and the others who had sat for the parley stood and moved toward the horses. They paused when Two Pony approached Lucy and Mr. Roote. He looked down at the girl and spoke to her in Apache. Lucy answered him earnestly, seemingly comfortable with the language.

"What'd she say?" Orland asked Butler.

"I'm not sure."

Lucy looked up at her father. "These people know the band I was with."

"Then they're not the ones who took you the first time?"

"No, but they are friends. Relatives. They can take me to them."

Mr. Roote's jaw clenched. "Lucy, dearest, you cannot go back to them. We need you at home. Your mother's heart is breaking, child. You *must* come home."

Tears welled in Carmela's eyes, and her throat constricted. Silently she pleaded with God for right to be done. She blinked against the burning tears. When she focused again on Lucy, the girl was looking at her.

"Carmela!" Lucy left her father's side and hurried forward. She seized Carmela's hand. "Can you help me?"

"Help you?" Carmela asked. "I don't know what you want of me. I came to help your father plead his cause. Lucy, surely you don't mean to go back to the tribe?"

Lucy looked toward the Apache and back to Carmela. "I. . .I don't know what to do."

"Do you not love your parents and your brother and sisters?"

"I. . .suppose I do. But with the tribe I am a woman."

"Yes," Carmela said. "No doubt they will marry you off soon. Do you think you can choose a man among them who will be kind to you? One who will keep you fed and warm in winter? One who will treat you with respect? Your father would never give you to a man who would mistreat you."

Lucy's mouth quivered as she looked at her father and Two Pony, standing close to each other, waiting for her decision.

"I know it is hard in the winter, but they haven't starved."

"Haven't they?" Carmela asked. "A week ago, I sat at the governor's table. I heard stories about the Pima and the other tribes in this area. They are in dire circumstances. The Indian agent had to feed them all winter, and it wasn't enough food. Lucy, why do you think the Apache steal the white men's cattle? Because they are hungry. Look at them. Do you see any fat people among the tribes?"

"But. . ." Lucy pulled in a shaky breath.

"And the people who stole you. Did you love them so much? Did you make closer friends than your own sisters? Did they truly treat you with love? Or were they just keeping you alive to help with the work of gathering food? Did you dig roots all day? Did you help dry meat the men killed? I can't believe you had a soft life with the tribe. Maybe as a child, but as you say, you're a woman now in their eyes. You will do the women's work. And I know—it's not a lark. You will work hard. And yes, you will be hungry. Perhaps not this summer but soon. I don't say the white people are always right in the way they treat the Indians, but the tribes' day is waning. They cannot prevail or drive the whites out of their land."

Lucy lowered her gaze.

"Lucy." Carmela stooped and touched the girl's wrist until Lucy looked her in the eyes. "Stay with the people who truly love you, my dear. Your father risked his life to come after you. He would do anything for you. Come home and give yourself a chance to grow up before you're shoved into womanhood. Give yourself time to learn and grow. Time to decide what is really freedom."

Lucy looked toward the two men who waited. Carmela held her breath. Had what she said made sense? Was she even correct in her views? How did she know what life was really like with the Indian tribes? She didn't. Uncle Silas thought she did. He thought they had delved into every facet of the Southwest tribes' lives through their studies. But she knew now that they had only skimmed the surface.

"Those children—from the ranch—"

"You saw them?" Carmela asked. "You saw the Howard children? And what these men did to their home? They killed Mr. Howard, you know. They murdered him."

Lucy pulled in a shaky breath. "If I don't go with them, who will look out for those children?"

Carmela studied her face. "You think you can keep those two children safe? Keep the Apache from abusing them? I think you're very optimistic. The only way to keep them from harm is to make sure they are returned to their mother now. They've had enough trauma. Can't you remember what it was like the day they stole you?"

Lucy bowed her head. A tear escaped from beneath her closed eyelid.

Carmela touched her shoulder. "Lucy, you can help them now. You can refuse to go with these people. You can ask them to return the Howard children. Don't let them commit more crimes."

"Orland, how long are we gonna wait?" Mr. Toole asked.

The deputy held up a hand, signaling him to be quiet.

"Those kids are nearby," Mr. Filmer said in a low tone. "We can't let 'em just ride off with 'em."

"We can take 'em," Toole said. "This bunch, anyway." He turned steely eyes on Two Pony and his men.

Two Pony spoke to Butler, who said, "He claims his people didn't steal the Roote girl. He says they were going to join another band when she came to them and asked to go with them."

Orland cleared his throat. "Miss Wade, what does the girl say?"

Carmela put her arm around Lucy and walked toward Two Pony. Lucy moved with her, for which Carmela was thankful. If the girl hadn't budged, she probably would have lost this round. Now she had hope.

She stopped before the warrior and made the hand sign for *friend*. "Please, Two Pony. Send Lucy back with her father today. Now."

Before Butler could speak, Lucy said, "I don't want to go back." She looked up at Carmela. "You must understand how I feel."

"No, I don't understand at all, Lucy. But I am concerned about the Howard children."

Two Pony eyed Carmela with what she felt was a less than friendly air. He turned that gaze on Lucy then on Orland and the other whites.

He spoke vehemently. When he paused, Butler, his face sober, reported, "He says they can kill us all if they want."

Mr. Roote stepped forward. "Well, you just tell him he's wrong. There's a detachment of soldiers behind us. They'll be here any minute."

So far as Carmela knew, they hadn't even dispatched the news to Fort Whipple. But she was also pretty sure Two Pony understood what Roote said.

The Apache men began talking among themselves. Butler eased over closer to Orland.

"They're telling him they should go on and stop wasting time here. One of 'em said something like they can make it to their rendezvous before the soldiers come, but if not and the army catches up to them, they'll kill those children."

Carmela felt faint, but she knew she needed to remain strong now. She reached out to Lucy, and the girl let her lean on her shoulder.

Two Pony studied Carmela's face, frowning. He reached out and took her chin in his hand and turned her head slightly. Carmela's heart hammered. He was looking at the ink on her face.

He spoke, and Butler's brow furrowed. "I don't savvy. Sorry." ·

Two Pony looked directly into Carmela's eyes. "How long? When Mojave do this to you?"

Carmela's throat felt squeezed. Could she stand here and lie to the man who had spared Freeland and saved her life?

"I . . ." She pulled in a shallow breath. "Not Mojave."

Creases formed between Two Pony's eyebrows. "Who? What tribe?"

She shook her head. "I have to speak truth to you. You are my friend." She tried not to think about the eight white men and half a dozen Apache warriors who stood close by, staring at her. Now was the moment when she must speak the truth before God and these witnesses.

"No tribe," she said. "I was not captured."

Slowly, Two Pony lowered his hand. The other men gaped and then began to look at each other and murmur.

"What on earth?" Mr. Roote took a step toward her, and Carmela shrank back. "You lied to us."

Two Pony held up a hand, and Butler said, "Quiet!"

"Who do this to you?" Two Pony asked.

Carmela couldn't get enough air. She stared up into the dark eyes, fearing she would fold up at his feet. "My uncle. My mother's brother."

Two Pony turned to Butler and spoke rapidly in Apache, accompanied by hand signs.

After a moment, Butler turned to Carmela. "He wants to know why anyone in your family would do this to you. And frankly, so do we all."

Carmela felt herself sway. Deputy Orland jumped forward and caught her.

Chapter Nineteen

*S*he came to her senses to find Orland, Two Pony, and Butler hovering over her, and Lucy grasping her hand painfully tight.

"Carmela, can you hear me?" Lucy had tears in her eyes.

Carmela focused on her and tried to speak, but her mouth was dry and her throat still felt as though a boulder had crushed it.

Butler looked around at the throng and shouted, "Get back and give her some air, would you?"

Orland continued dabbing at her brow, and she realized he was using a damp bandanna.

Two Pony leaned back a little but didn't rise.

"Water." He held up a leather water bag, similar to the one he had given her.

Carmela struggled to sit up, and Lucy and Orland supported her. She drank warm water from the skin and looked up at Two Pony.

"Thank you. Twice you have given me water when I needed it."

"You wait." He turned to Butler for help and spoke his rapid-fire Apache.

"You rest," Butler said. "Then you speak."

"The children," Carmela whispered.

"All in good time," Orland said. "I think right now we all want an

186

explanation of your circumstances. Let us know when you're ready."

They sat in a haphazard crowd around her, waiting for her to speak, not in the formal parleying circle they had formed earlier. This time all the men were part of the audience. It was almost like one of her performances, Carmela thought, but this time she wouldn't be acting. She wouldn't be lying.

She took another drink of water and thanked Orland and Lucy for their ministrations.

"I think I can talk now." With her hearers so close, she still felt penned in tightly, but she knew she couldn't put it off. She hauled in a breath, deeper this time.

"When I was twelve years old, my parents died on the trail. They were not killed by Indians. I was kept at Fort Yuma until my uncle made the journey to fetch me. He conceived a plan at that time for me to say I had been captured and my parents massacred. He saw it as a way to make a living to support the two of us."

No one said a word, but every eye was on her, waiting for her to continue. She searched their faces for anger and hatred, but so far most seemed to reserve judgment.

"I hated this life, and I wanted to stop it, but my uncle insisted I had to go on. He said my father owed him money. I saw no way out, and so I did it. I...I think I became good at it. Convincing, you might say. I knew I was lying, but I felt I had no choice."

Now a few murmurs started, from the townsmen. Two Pony glared at them, and they quieted.

"My uncle was shot in a stagecoach holdup last week," Carmela said. Butler did his best to carry on a choppy translation as she continued. "I do not know if he is dead or alive. The marshal has gone to try to catch the outlaws who did it and discover what became of my uncle. But I knew that I was done lying to the public."

"You lied to me and my family," Mr. Roote said.

"I let you think it was all true." She looked at the girl beside her. "I'm sorry, Lucy. After I met you, I talked to the minister, Reverend Bardwell." Several of the white men nodded. "He agreed with me that it was time to end the lying. He was going to help me this Sunday."

"Help you what?" Mr. Linnet asked.

"I planned to tell his congregation the truth. He and his wife and my landlady, Mrs. Finney, said they would support me. When Mr. Roote came to me with the news that Lucy was gone, I didn't know what to do. I couldn't refuse to help, and yet. . ."

"And yet, your so-called help is all based on lies," Mr. Linnet said bitterly.

Carmela sighed and looked down at her skirt. An ant had crawled up one of the folds, and she brushed it away.

"Why did you even come?" Mr. Roote demanded. "Doesn't sound to me like you wanted to quit lying."

She raised her chin and met his angry gaze. "I care about Lucy. I hoped I could help her because it was the right thing to do. It wasn't my intention to ply her with lies."

Lucy looked at her then turned to her father. "She always told me she didn't understand, Pa. She never really said she was with Indians. She always urged me to stay home and—and let you and Mama love me. . . ." Her plaintive voice trailed off. Mr. Roote couldn't hold his daughter's gaze.

Mr. Butler did his best, trying to keep Two Pony informed. Carmela had picked up enough of the sign language to show Two Pony the sign for friend and point to Lucy.

"I cared about her. And I wanted to speak the truth, to you and to everyone else. I want to start over, and I hope people will forgive me." She included Two Pony in her gaze then looked around at all of the others.

Two Pony nodded.

"Carmela," Lucy said in her high-pitched voice, "I think you are very brave."

Butler translated that with no problem.

Carmela pressed her lips together and shook her head. "No. I'm a coward, or I would have told you sooner."

"You were younger than me when it started," Lucy said. "I think you were afraid."

Carmela drew in a deep breath. "Yes, I was. I'm still afraid, but. . ."

Lucy reached over and squeezed her hand. "If you can do that, tell all these people you've been lying for years and that you want to stop, then I can be brave, too." She stood and looked straight at Two Pony. "Mr. Butler, tell him I'm going to try to sort out living with my parents."

Butler obliged, and a moment later, he told Lucy, "He says you have a true friend in Miss Wade. But he also says you must decide for all time which world you will live in."

Lucy frowned and stood still for a moment. Carmela held her breath. At last, Lucy walked over to her father.

"I'm sorry, Pa. I'm ready to go home."

Mr. Roote pulled her into his arms. His eyes shone with tears as he held her. "All right, Lucy. We'll go home."

Two Pony turned and spoke to his men. The warriors immediately mounted and turned their horses away.

"Wait!" Carmela ran after the leader. She wasn't sure why she dared, but she caught Two Pony as he was about to swing up onto his paint horse and laid her hand on his arm. "Please! You can't take those children. The Howard girl and boy. Please don't do this."

Two Pony surveyed her, his dark eyes cool and distant. "I did not take them."

"But they are with your people. Their father was killed, and their mother weeps for them."

He looked down at her for a long moment. If only she hadn't told him about the lie behind her inked markings. She might have a better chance of getting those children back if he still believed her falsehood.

No, she told herself. *I will speak only truth to him now.*

"Be at peace with what you have done today." Two Pony leaped onto the horse. He and his followers rode off. As they reached a rise in the trail, two more riders emerged from a ravine, riding up a steep slope to join them.

Carmela gasped. Each of the two riders joining them had a white youngster in front of him on his horse. *"Andy's four and Marjorie is six."* Carmela's saw Mrs. Howard's grief-stricken face clearly in her mind.

"Marjorie," she screamed.

The two children strained to look for her. Their captors restrained them, but Marjorie and Andy flailed and kicked against them. Andy especially put up a violent struggle.

Lucy had run to stand beside Carmela.

"Oh! That's them, isn't it? Pa, you've got to do something."

The man holding Andy drew back his hand and struck the boy across the face. Marjorie apparently saw it, because her shrieks increased until her captor clamped a hand over her mouth and forced his horse into a gallop.

Mr. Roote, Orland, and several of the other men had reached where Carmela and Lucy stood, watching the party flee.

"Pa, please!" Tears streamed down Lucy's face. "They're hitting them."

"We would all be killed if we pursued them now," Mr. Roote said. "Two Pony made that clear."

"No!" Lucy fell against him, sobbing.

Carmela watched helplessly as Two Pony raced his horse alongside the other Indians until he was at the front. He led the band of Apache westward.

A shout from Butler reached her from behind, and she turned to see what caused it. Mr. Linnet stood near him, pointing back toward Prescott. Butler put his hands to his face to form a trumpet.

"The marshal's coming!"

Freeland spotted the ragged band ahead of them and spurred his horse. They hadn't expected to catch up to Orland this soon. Something had delayed the civilian posse.

His anxiety over Carmela had begun when Mrs. Finney told him she had joined Orland's expedition to bring Lucy Roote back, and it had festered while he found a fresh horse and rode out here with Duffield. They had seen the smoking ruin of the Howards' house but hadn't stopped there. Minutes lost could mean lives. Now they were close.

Scanning the figures in the distance, he could make out the skirts of at least two females, but all of the people stood on the ground. Where were their horses? As he came closer, he spotted their mounts, tethered down over an outcropping, where a few clumps of grass grew beside the stream. Eight men, two women, he counted.

It didn't take him long to pick out Carmela. Her hair glinted in the sunlight. Why wasn't she wearing a bonnet, or even that ridiculous hat she'd worn on the stagecoach? Soon he could see the discoloration on the lower part of her face, though it was considerably lighter than when he'd last seen her. From this distance, she almost looked like a bearded lady from the circus. He clenched his teeth and fought the natural repulsion the idea caused. He'd seen the true woman beneath the ugly markings. More important, he knew her spirit.

"Something's happened," Marshal Duffield said, riding alongside him.

"I thought the same," Freeland said. "But they don't look to be in distress."

"Come on."

They pushed forward, with ten more men following them. Freeland found a rough trail down to where the horses were and steered his gelding down it. The buckskin picked his way carefully, not missing his footing once. At least the liveryman had found him a decent horse. Freeland jumped off, letting the reins trail, and hurried toward where Deputy Orland and the others stood.

He sought out Carmela, and her eyes widened as their gazes met. She surprised him by running to him and seizing his hand.

"Freeland, I'm so glad you came! Two Pony and the others stole two children. They wouldn't give them back to us, but we have Lucy."

"Slow down." Freeland patted her hand. "Tell the marshal everything."

By this time, Duffield and the others had joined them, and Orland's party gathered around.

"Orland, what's happening?" Duffield asked the older deputy.

Orland quickly filled him in about how they had started out hoping to recover Lucy but then discovered Howard's murder and the abduction of the children. "Miss Wade and Miss Roote saw the two kids as they rode off."

"One of the men hit the little boy," Lucy said.

"But Two Pony seemed trustworthy," Carmela said quickly.

"Who's Two Pony?" Freeland asked.

"He's the man who saved us in the desert. He's not the one who kidnapped those children."

"But he wouldn't make them give them back to us either," Orland noted. "They must have been hiding them until they knew what would happen."

"All right," Duffield said. "I've got a dozen men, counting myself, but I'd appreciate any of you who'll go along with us. A couple of you will need to take charge of these two young ladies and see them safely back to town."

"I want to stay with my daughter," Mr. Roote said.

"I'll go back with him, unless you need a translator," Butler said. "I'm not very good at it."

"Several of my men speak the lingo," Duffield said. "All right, all those who can, mount up and let's go."

Freeland had time only to squeeze Carmela's hands.

"Take care," she said, her brown eyes anxiously searching his face.

"I will. And I'll come to you at Mrs. Finney's as soon as we return."

He left her and ran for his horse. The marshal's men, Orland, and the townsmen joining them mounted and urged their horses up the slope to the trail and tore off across the desert. Tracking the Apache was easy today. The party was a large one, but the knowledge that they were moving women and children with them meant they had to travel more slowly than a raiding party could on its own. They would catch up quickly.

His only regret was having to leave Carmela behind so soon after he'd found her. He couldn't wait to hear her story. Amazing that she had met up with the warrior who had given her the water flask. It occurred to him that he hadn't told her about Holden. She would have taken comfort in knowing he was alive.

"There they are."

Duffield's words interrupted Freeland's reverie.

"I see them." The Apache band moved slowly, and although they had probably sent the villagers on ahead while Two Pony and the others talked to Orland's party, they hadn't gotten far. The riders bringing up the rear were all men, fiercely painted and armed to the teeth.

"Ease up." Duffield held up a hand so the men behind him wouldn't run them over as they slowed.

Half a dozen warriors stopped and turned their horses to face them. Orland pushed his bay up close to the marshal. "They wanted to parley with us before."

"Well, that posture doesn't look like parleying to me." Duffield didn't take his eyes off the waiting warriors.

"I dunno," said Benny, who crowded his horse up close. "Could be worse. They could be charging at us full tilt."

"You want us to go forward?" Freeland asked.

"I don't like it." Duffield grimaced. "All right, might as well get it over with. You all stay alert." He nudged his horse forward. "Give me a bunch of outlaws any day. At least with them, I'd have some idea what they were thinking."

Chapter Twenty

Carmela ached all over by the time they got back to Prescott. Her dress was damp with perspiration, and the folds of the skirt clung to her legs.

Mrs. Roote was waiting with the family's farm wagon on Gurley Street, keeping watch over the road that led westward out of town. She had found a bit of shade in front of a hotel, and the plow horse hitched to the wagon stood dozing with his head drooping. She stood when she saw them approach and peered toward them. After a moment, she waved her handkerchief and scurried to climb down from the wagon.

"Lucy, my darling!"

Lucy had taken the other big workhorse from her father's corral when she ran away that morning. She stopped him, slid down to the ground, and ran into her mother's arms.

Mrs. Roote gathered her close. Tears streamed down her cheeks as she scolded. "You bad, bad girl! You scared us so. You mustn't ever do that again. You hear?"

"I hear," Lucy choked. "I'm sorry, Mama."

"There now." Mrs. Roote stroked her hair and her shoulders. "Praise be, we've got you back."

A group of people had made their way down the street and gathered about them now.

"We heard you'd gone after your daughter," one man said to Mr. Roote. "This be her?"

"Yes, praise God," Mr. Roote said.

"What about the family those Indians massacred?" a woman asked.

"Marshal Duffield's trying to get the kids back. The missus went to a neighbor's ranch to wait."

"So we heard right?" the first man said. "They really killed that Howard fella?"

"I'm afraid so. Let us pass, folks. We're all tired, and we'd like to get home 'fore suppertime."

Carmela realized she hadn't eaten anything for hours. She and Mr. Butler left the Roote family and rode on down the street.

"You're that captive girl, ain't you?" someone in the crowd called.

Carmela was too tired to respond. They made their way through the streets until they came to the livery stable, where she dismounted and turned the horse over to the owner.

"Thank you, sir. Do I owe you anything?"

The man ran a hand through his beard. "Did you get the Roote girl back?"

"Yes, we did."

"Where's Orland and the marshal?"

"They're still out there," Carmela said. "Did you hear about the attack on the Howard ranch?"

"I did."

"Well, the men are following the Apache, in hopes of recovering the Howard children."

"*Humph.* Well, I lend out horses for posses when they're needed. I don't expect any recompense for that unless the horses get shot or the Injuns take 'em. Then I send the governor a bill."

"That's very good of you," Carmela said. "This one's a good horse. She didn't give me any trouble today." She gave the mare a last pat and turned her weary steps in the direction she vaguely knew Mrs. Finney's boardinghouse lay.

The streets seemed more crowded than usual as Carmela plodded along. The people who passed her on the street stared without fail at her chin. Carmela's legs dragged but she stumbled on until she was sure she had taken a wrong turn. She looked up at a sign that said Assay Office.

A bearded man leading a donkey walked up to the hitching rail and tied his pack animal. He looked at Carmela and grinned, exposing a gap where he'd lost a tooth.

"Lost?"

"Yes sir."

"Well now, you don't want to 'sir' me. I might be able to help you out. Where you headed, missy?"

"Mrs. Finney's boardinghouse. It's on—"

"I know it," the prospector said. "Fine woman, the widder Finney. You just want to turn left at the corner." He pointed. "Go two blocks and turn right. I expect you'll be in familiar territory."

"Thank you," Carmela said and hurried on.

"Tell the widder to expect Zeke Ferris later."

Carmela turned and looked him over carefully. "I will."

He nodded and winked. "I hope she's got a room for me. 'Bye, now."

When she at last found the boardinghouse and stumbled over the doorstep, Mrs. Finney emerged from the kitchen, moving faster than Carmela had ever seen her go.

"At last! I was afraid you'd be all night in the desert. You don't need that, not after all you've been through."

She put a strong arm around Carmela and supported her, guiding her into the dining room. As they passed the parlor door, Carmela could hear the murmur of voices. Some of the other boarders were socializing this evening.

"You sit right there and I'll bring you some supper. Did Mr. McKay find you and the children?"

"Yes. You heard about the Howard children?"

Mrs. Finney brushed a hand through the air. "It's all over town. Those savages! The ranchers are all coming in to fort up in town, or else barricading themselves with their weapons, ready to defend their property. But what about Lucy Roote?"

"She's with her family now."

"God be praised. And the Howards?"

"I don't know," Carmela said. "The mother is with a neighbor. The marshal and the others went after the Apache to try to recover the two children."

"Well now, we've more praying to do. Don't move. I'll get your plate."

Carmela leaned back in the chair and closed her eyes, ashamed that she had not prayed on her way here from the stable. She was just so tired. *Lord, help them.* It was all she could muster.

"Here we go." Mrs. Finney bustled cheerfully about, setting a plate of chicken and biscuits, smothered in gravy, before her. This was followed by her cutlery, a glass of milk, a bowl of custard, and a cup of strong tea.

Carmela looked up at her wearily. "Thank you so much. Would you ask the blessing for me?"

"Of course. Poor child, you're exhausted." Mrs. Finney sat down beside her and offered a brief but heartfelt prayer.

Carmela began to eat and felt her strength returning. She was halfway through the chicken and biscuits when she remembered the prospector.

"Oh! I nearly forgot to tell you. Someone named Zeke Ferris is coming by and wants a room."

Mrs. Finney sighed and shook her head. "Good old Zeke."

"A friend of yours?" Carmela's interest piqued.

"More a friend of Mr. Finney's in the old days, but he comes here now and then and stays a night or two. Then he goes back out to his claim. Did you see your uncle yet?"

"What?" Carmela was suddenly wide awake, but she had the

heart-pounding, confused feeling she got when a loud noise wakened her in the middle of the night. "Uncle Silas?"

"Did Mr. McKay not tell you?"

"No. We hardly had a minute before they dashed off after the Apache."

"Marshal Duffield brought him in, along with the outlaws. Had them all handcuffed and bound in that stagecoach you were on."

"But Uncle Silas—?"

"Him, too. Not handcuffed, but they brought him and left him at Doc Greenwood's."

"How badly hurt is he?"

"Very serious, so I hear tell."

Carmela shoved her chair back. "I must go to him."

"You eat your supper."

"But—"

"Eat." Mrs. Finney's stern eyes allowed no room for argument. "I'll take you there after you finish, but you need sustenance."

"Yes ma'am." Carmela shoved down the rest of the meal as quickly as she could. When she had finished the milk, she set down her glass.

"Eat the custard, too," Mrs. Finney said. "I had to save it from Clark Shifton when he tried to sneak seconds."

"Mr. Shifton? I thought he was gone."

Mrs. Finney shook her head. "Decided to stay another night, until he's sure the Apache are taken care of. Doesn't want to risk his freight wagons being attacked when he leaves here."

Carmela was nothing if not obedient. She picked up the spoon and took a bite. The smooth custard flooded her mouth with a sweet and spicy taste.

"*Mmm.* If I'm here long enough, will you teach me how to make it?"

"Goodness, yes. Custard's not hard."

Carmela hurried to finish it and carried her dishes to the kitchen. "May we go now?" she asked.

Mrs. Finney looked her up and down. "Best go and arrange your hair, dear. Your uncle hasn't seen you for a while, and he'll want assurance that you're safe and secure."

Carmela hadn't considered that showing up at the doctor's office with tousled hair might reflect badly on Mrs. Finney. She wouldn't want that. She hurried to her room, washed her face and hands, put on the dress Mrs. McCormick had given her, brushed out her hair, and pulled it back into a knot at the back of her head. She nodded at herself in the mirror. At last she looked presentable, not like some half-wild hoyden, which was probably Mrs. Finney's opinion of her appearance when she arrived home half an hour ago.

Mrs. Finney came out of the parlor.

"There. Don't you look nice? I told the boarders you're returned safe and that we're going out for the evening."

"Aren't you afraid they'll raid your pantry?"

Mrs. Finney smiled indulgently. "I left the cookie tin out, and I told them they'd better not eat anything else. All right, to Dr. Greenwood's."

They stepped out into twilight. Although the saloons were blocks away, Carmela could hear faint music and an occasional gunshot in the distance.

"This way." Mrs. Finney led her quickly along the street and around a corner. They made three more turns, and Carmela was glad she hadn't tried to find the place on her own. At last they approached the front door of a white clapboard house with green trim. Near the street, a small sign hung, proclaiming, R. L. GREENWOOD, M.D.

Mrs. Finney knocked briskly on the door and then opened it without waiting for an invitation. They stepped into a small, homey room with half a dozen chairs, a bench under a window, and a bushel basket full of newspapers.

"He leaves the old newspapers out here so people can catch up on the news while they wait," Mrs. Finney said. She stepped to an open doorway that led into a hallway. A small bell hung on a bracket on the doorjamb, and she reached up and pushed it, causing it to ring.

"Coming," called a male voice from the depths of the house.

No other clients were waiting, and Carmela supposed the doctor had cleared out the sitting room so he could have his supper.

He appeared in the hall doorway suddenly, a tall man with bushy brown hair, a mustache to match, and crinkles at the corners of his eyes.

"Well, Mrs. Finney. Is the niece returned, then?"

"Yes, this is her." Mrs. Finney drew Carmela over to him.

"Hello." She stuck out her hand. "I'm Carmela Wade. You have my uncle here?"

"Indeed I do, and he's been inquiring after you ever since the marshal brought him in."

"He's awake, then?"

"Well, he may have dosed off, but he was very much awake and alert when I first treated him."

"How is he?"

The doctor moved his head to one side. "He has a serious wound and some infection, but I think I can keep him alive."

Carmela caught her breath. "I'm sorry. When I heard he'd ridden all the way here with the marshal, I assumed he wasn't so badly injured as I first thought."

Dr. Greenwood sighed. "If I could have treated him in the first hour after he was shot, he would be near to recovery now. Unfortunately, he was hauled about the desert for days. At least this climate is a healthy one, not so friendly to germs as some. And your uncle is a fastidious man. I believe he did all he could to keep his wound clean."

"I'm thankful for that," Carmela said. "At least our luggage went with him, so he had some clean clothing and supplies." As much as she had regretted losing her own bags when the stagecoach left her behind, if she'd had a choice between the baggage going with her or with Uncle Silas, she would have sent it with him.

"Well, I've cleaned it out and dosed him pretty heavily. He was also dehydrated, so I made him drink a quart of water before I gave him anything that would put him to sleep. If we can keep ahead of the infection, I think he can make a full recovery. Only time will tell."

Carmela nodded. "Thank you. How long will it take?"

"Several weeks, but he may be able to get up in a few days. We'll have to see how it goes."

She nodded. "May I see him now?"

"Of course. Oh, and just so you know, I was able to send the two outlaws I treated over to the jail, so none of them are in the house now."

"Thank you. That does ease my mind," Carmela said.

Mrs. Finney walked over to one of the cushioned chairs. "I'll wait out here."

Carmela nodded and followed Dr. Greenwood down the hall, past a couple of open doors, to a small bedchamber. The curtains were pulled, and a lamp burned low on a small bedside table.

Carmela would not have recognized the thin form that lay under the blanket on the iron cot. The skin of Uncle Silas's face was drawn tight and sunburned a bright red. Blisters had formed on his forehead, nose, and cheeks. Some had broken and the skin peeled away. His eyes were closed, and his meager shock of brown hair lay plastered against his skull. His breathing was shallow and fitful. The hand lying outside the covers looked almost skeletal.

She drew in a determined breath and reached for his hand. "Uncle Silas? It's me, Carmela."

His eyelids fluttered open, and he peered up at her. "Is it really you?"

"Yes, Uncle Silas. I'm here."

He exhaled deeply and focused on her face. His words came out slow and breathy. "I was afraid they'd really got you this time."

"Who?"

"The—" He stopped and looked past her.

She realized he didn't want to speak of their deception in front of the doctor.

"I'm fine." She patted his hand and let go of it. "I'm staying at a nice boardinghouse. You get some rest, and I'll come back to see you in the morning when you're more awake."

"Yes. We'll be on the road soon." His eyelids fluttered closed.

"The laudanum is taking over," Dr. Greenwood said. "He'll

probably sleep for hours."

"How early may I return in the morning?"

"Eight o'clock," the doctor said. "That will give me time to see to his needs. I usually open my doors at nine for patients, but you may come before then."

"Thank you."

Carmela walked with him out to the waiting room. Mrs. Finney folded the newspaper she had been reading and laid it in the basket. "Well? How is he?"

"Sleepy," Carmela said. "He knew me though. I'll come back tomorrow, and perhaps he'll be more alert."

"Good." Mrs. Finney rose, and Dr. Greenwood escorted them to the front door.

"Thank you, Doctor," Carmela said.

The two women headed along the sidewalks toward the boardinghouse. The noise from the saloon district had, if anything, increased. Quite a few people, mostly men, were out in the streets, some on their way to a destination and others seeming to wander aimlessly about. Mrs. Finney took Carmela's arm and hurried her along.

When they entered the boardinghouse, Mr. Ralley came out of the parlor.

"Well, I'm glad to see you're back, ladies. I was afraid you might have had some trouble downtown."

"We only went to Dr. Greenwood's house." Mrs. Finney untied the strings of her bonnet.

Ralley nodded. "That's good. I ran into Joe Butler at the Horseshoe. He was telling anyone who would listen how Miss Wade bunked everyone into thinking she was an Indian captive. Some folks were quite riled up about it."

Carmela caught her breath.

"Nonsense," Mrs. Finney said. "There's nothing for folks to be upset about. This girl was made to tell lies, but she's stopped now. The way I hear it, they should be praising her for having the courage to stand up and tell the truth in front of an Apache chief and his tribe."

Ralley shook his head. "That's not the way Butler's telling it."

Carmela felt her cheeks flush. After the time he had spent translating for her to get Lucy Roote back, Butler had come home and begun spreading tales about her. But she supposed he had a right. She walked over to the dining table, pulled out a chair, and plunked down into it.

"There now," Mrs. Finney said, patting her shoulder. "He's nothing but a gossiping old woman, that man. There's no use getting in a dither about it."

Carmela looked up at her. "But he's telling the whole town what I did. That I'm a fraud and that I took people's money for telling lies."

"So you really did?" Ralley asked. "You're such a quiet young thing, I figured Butler was making it up."

Carmela pulled back her shoulders and managed to meet his critical gaze. "Mr. Butler is correct. My uncle and I have traveled for more than seven years performing, and in the course of our programs, falsehoods were told."

"So the Apache never stole you? Did they kill your parents?"

Carmela held back a sob. It wasn't worth explaining that she'd never claimed it was the Apache who kidnapped her but the Yavapai or possibly the Mojave. But the rest of it had to be laid bare.

"No. My parents died of illness, probably cholera, on the trail. No Indians were involved. And I was not kidnapped." Unless, she thought, some might construe Uncle Silas's taking control of her life as an abduction, but she kept that thought to herself.

"And what's more," Mrs. Finney said firmly, "if you can force yourself to attend church this Sunday, sir, you will hear Miss Wade confess the entire truth to the congregation and beg their forgiveness."

Oh dear, Carmela thought. Would she still be able to get up in front of everyone, now that Uncle Silas had returned, and tell her entire story? If her uncle was able to rise from his bed, she was certain he would try to stop her.

She let out a little moan, and Mrs. Finney took hold of her arm. "There now, child, you should be in bed. Mr. Ralley, I'd thank you to stop spreading dissension. Miss Wade has not done anything wrong, or if she has, she did it under duress. Excuse us."

She tugged Carmela toward the hallway, and Carmela didn't have the energy to protest. She let the landlady guide her along to the door of her own room, her sanctuary.

"You get right into bed," Mrs. Finney said. "Don't give a thought to what that no-good half-wit said. Come morning, we'll see what your uncle has to say for himself by light of day."

Her words vaguely disturbed Carmela, but she was too fatigued to think about it. She mumbled a thank you, closed the door, and collapsed on her bed.

Morning came sooner than she was ready for it, but the sound of raised voices from the other end of the house roused her. She dressed quickly and opened her door with caution. It sounded as though the boarders were arguing over the breakfast table.

"I say you should throw her out in the street," came one harsh voice. Carmela thought she recognized it as belonging to Mr. Hoffman, a miner who had joined the household two days before her excursion with Deputy Orland.

"Gentlemen, you're taking this far harder than is warranted," Mrs. Finney said loudly, to drown out the other voices.

"How can you defend her?" Surely that was Mr. Ralley. "She's taken money from hundreds of people—thousands, even—under false pretenses."

"I say we don't talk to her when she comes to the table," said Mr. Shifton.

Carmela shrank back down the hallway and into her room. She closed the door and sat down on the edge of the bed. The tears came unbidden, and she sat for a long time, gasping a breath every few seconds.

Perhaps half an hour passed before a gentle tapping at her door roused her. She got up and walked stiffly across the room to open it.

"Oh my dear," Mrs. Finney said. "What's got you down?"

"I heard them talking," Carmela managed to get out.

Mrs. Finney put her arms around her. "You mustn't let what other people say cripple you. You need to think about what is right. You're going to do that now. You're never going to give anyone reason to say nasty things about you."

Carmela sniffed. "I suppose."

"Come, now. Wash your face. They're all gone but Zeke Ferris. He came in late last night, and he's just having breakfast. I saved you some porridge."

"That was kind of you."

Mrs. Finney pushed her gently toward the wash stand. "Your uncle is probably awake by now. We'll go and see him straightaway."

Before long, the two women were out the door.

"You don't have to go with me." Carmela was still subdued, and Mrs. Finney eyed her sidelong.

"We shan't stay long, or if you want to, I'll go back and start dinner preparations."

They walked on another block, and Carmela said softly, "Thank you."

She had scrubbed with new fury at the ink marks that morning, and though her face was red, the ink had faded even more. People didn't stare so much. Of course, Uncle Silas would be livid.

A pretty woman of about thirty stood in Dr. Greenwood's waiting room, which was filled to capacity with miners, ranchers, and a woman who sat with a crying baby and a toddler who alternately hid in her skirts and pulled newspapers from their basket.

"Mr. James," the standing woman said, scanning the people on the benches and chairs.

A man shuffled to his feet.

"Dr. Greenwood will see you." Her gaze lit on Mrs. Finney and Carmela. "Ah, Mrs. Finney, as you see, we are quite busy this morning. You know the way, so you may go through. Forgive me for leaving you on your own."

"It's no matter," Mrs. Finney said. "We'll be fine."

As Mr. James walked over to follow the woman into the hallway, Carmela caught a foul odor. He was holding his left hand with his right, and the bandage around the injured limb was encrusted in dirt and dried blood. She couldn't help flinching.

Mrs. Finney put a firm hand on her elbow and guided her to the small bedroom at the end of the hall, where Uncle Silas lay ensconced in his cot, seemingly asleep. A bowl and spoon sat on his bedside table, the bowl containing what looked like the remains of a serving of gruel.

Uncle Silas looked cadaverous in Carmela's eyes. She swallowed hard and stepped to the edge of the bed.

"Good morning, Uncle," she said.

His eyes opened, and he stared up at her. For a few seconds, she wondered if he recognized her. Then his lips twisted. "What have you done to your face?"

Chapter Twenty-One

"Nothing," Carmela said. She remembered Uncle Silas's orders for when she was to address a paying crowd and straightened her shoulders. "I let nature take its course."

He struggled to sit up. Mrs. Finney leaned over, grabbed an extra pillow from the far edge of the bed, and slipped it behind his shoulders. Uncle Silas ignored her but continued to scowl at Carmela.

"How many people have seen you like this?"

"Quite a lot, actually. I told Two Pony, who seems to be a man of substance in the Apache tribe, and all of the men who were in the posse with Deputy Orland heard me say it."

"Told him what?" Uncle Silas spoke slowly, and his words held an ominous tone.

Carmela blinked back tears at the memory of the angry voices she had heard that morning. "I told him that I was never with any of the tribes and that the story of my captivity was false."

"Why would you do such a foolish thing?"

Carmela sniffed, knowing she had lost the battle with the tears. "Because he knew my story couldn't be true. I've met two girls who have really been captured, Uncle. One of them wanted to go back and live with the Indians. I couldn't stand there beg-

207

ging her to come back to her family and let them all think I'd been through that ordeal. Two Pony had saved my life, probably because he thought I'd been living with the Mojave, or whoever makes these kind of marks. I was trading on his good will based on a lie. I couldn't stand it."

"You couldn't stand it." His voice was deadly cold now. "We'll have to leave town as soon as possible. Find out when the next stagecoach leaves."

"Here, sir." Mrs. Finney stepped forward, her face lined with concern. "The doctor says you'll be several weeks recovering. You can't set out again on a stagecoach in this state."

"We'll see about that." He moved as if to fling aside the bedclothes and sank back on his pillows with a moan.

"Now, now," Mrs. Finney said. "That's enough of that. I think it may be time for some more pain medicine for you."

Uncle Silas's eyes opened and focused on her. "Who is this woman?"

"Uh, that's—she's Mrs. Finney," Carmela said. "She's my landlady at the boardinghouse."

"You were in here yesterday," he said, his voice fading a little.

"Yes sir," Mrs. Finney said. "I came in after I heard the marshal had brought you here. I knew Miss Wade would want word of you the minute she got home."

Uncle Silas's eyes narrowed. "Did you tell her she had to do all this nonsense?"

"What nonsense?" Mrs. Finney gazed down at him with all innocence.

"Recanting the story she's been telling for years, that's what."

Mrs. Finney frowned. "Well, sir, if it's a lie, then it ought to be recanted, hadn't it?"

"Who says it's a lie?" What started out as a roar ended as a whimper, with Uncle Silas flopping back on the pillow exhausted. Beads of sweat stood on his brow, and he closed his eyes, drawing each shallow breath with a painful jerk.

Carmela looked at Mrs. Finney, torn over what to do. "Perhaps you should leave."

"You come with me, child. Don't let him bully you."

She shook her head. "I need to talk this out with him, if he's able." She dredged up a wobbly smile. "Don't worry. He's so weak he can't hurt me. But I must make him understand I'm serious about this and that I can't go back on my course now."

Mrs. Finney's hazel eyes still looked troubled, but she patted Carmela's shoulder. "All right, if you're sure. But if you don't feel safe walking home alone, you tell Mrs. Greenwood. She can fetch someone to walk with you."

"The lady who brought us in?"

"Yes, she's the doctor's wife."

Carmela nodded. "I will do so. Thank you."

Mrs. Finney left the room, and Carmela pulled over a stool and sat down beside her uncle. She half wished he would drift off into sleep again, but she knew she had to discuss things with him sooner or later, and it might as well be sooner.

Before she could begin, Dr. Greenwood entered the room quietly.

"Everything all right in here?"

"Yes, thank you," Carmela said.

"I was in the room next door, and I thought I heard raised voices." The doctor eyed her keenly.

"So you did," she replied. "My uncle was not happy with my recent actions."

"Oh?"

"She wants to ruin me," Uncle Silas said suddenly, making Carmela flinch.

"Beg pardon, I thought he was sleeping." Dr. Greenwood moved in to take Uncle Silas's pulse. "So, Holden, got yourself worked up, have you? I shouldn't wonder if you'll exhaust yourself."

"This girl has done a reckless thing."

Dr. Greenwood said evenly, "Well, she looks like a woman to

me, not a girl, and a levelheaded one at that. She can't have done anything too rash."

"If you knew," Uncle Silas said with menace in his voice, "you would know she doesn't care a whit for my well-being, my reputation, or my fortune."

The doctor arched his eyebrows at Carmela. "*Hmm.* Sounds rather extreme. But Mrs. Finney told me she's a respectable young lady."

"And that she is, or always has been, until now."

"I tell you what." Dr. Greenwood turned to the nearby table that held medicine bottles, glasses, and spoons. "I think you should sleep for a while and let your wound heal. When you're feeling better, perhaps you and Miss Wade can discuss this matter calmly. Does that sound reasonable?"

"It does to me," Carmela dared to say.

"Well, not to me." Uncle Silas's roar faded again as he grimaced and put a hand feebly to his side. "I tell you this, girl: If you cannot carry out your duty to me and to your father, who owed me a king's ransom when he died, then you can just not bother to come back here again. You can find your own way in this godforsaken wilderness. What do you say to that?"

Carmela clapped her hands to her burning cheeks.

"Surely you don't mean that," Dr. Greenwood said affably. "Here now. Take this." He held a spoonful of liquid up to Uncle Silas's lips.

"I do mean it." He opened his mouth and accepted the medicine then slumped back with a sigh. "I've cared for her all this time, met her every need. I've put the food in her mouth and the clothes on her back. And now she wants to denounce me in public." His voice trailed off, and his eyes closed.

"There," Dr. Greenwood whispered. "Shall we let him sleep?"

Carmela nodded, unable to speak, and followed him out of the room.

"I'm sorry," she said, unable to stop tears from flowing down her cheeks.

When he had closed the door, the doctor beckoned her into the room across the hall, a small office with a cluttered desk in the center. He shut that door also.

"I just want to say, Miss Wade, that I've heard bits and pieces, both from Mr. Holden and outside this house. I want you to know that I think you are doing the right thing, or trying to. Now, it's none of my business, but it seems to me you got into rather a bum situation when you were only a child. Now you're grown, you want to get out of it. Am I right?"

"Yes sir. He says we'll have to leave town, now that I've told people I wasn't a captive."

Dr. Greenwood shook his head. "He's in no condition to travel. I'll keep him confined to bed as long as I can. Perhaps he'll cool off as he heals."

"Thank you," Carmela said. "I'd better go back to Mrs. Finney's and help her. Shall I come back this afternoon to see Uncle Silas?"

"You may if you wish, but it might be better for you if you stayed away."

"I couldn't do that."

Dr. Greenwood studied her for a moment. "No, I don't suppose you could. Come back around five if Mrs. Finney doesn't need you then. You can help him with his supper."

Mrs. Greenwood, true to her word, found a lad to escort Carmela home, but she didn't feel the menace she'd felt earlier. Maybe it was because she kept her chin down and avoided making eye contact, or perhaps there weren't as many people milling about the streets now.

When they got to the house, Mrs. Finney gave the boy a penny and sent him on his way.

"I'm glad you're here," she said. "I've had three more miners come in today and a ranching couple. All my rooms will be full tonight."

"What can I do to help you?" Carmela asked.

"If we could get the beds made, that would take a load off my mind. Then I'll let you bake a cake while I fix the chicken and vegetables for supper."

"Put me to work," Carmela said sincerely. She actually enjoyed the hard work she put in that day, from changing beds and laundering the vast array of sheets that came off the dirty ones to filling the water pitchers and baking.

At four o'clock, she was tired but felt a great satisfaction. Mrs. Finney insisted she stop work and eat an early supper so that she could get off to Dr. Greenwood's before the other boarders came to the dining room.

At the doctor's house, Mrs. Greenwood met her at the door and ushered her into the empty waiting room.

"The doctor was called out to one of the mines, but I expect him back soon. Your uncle is awake. You may go right in."

"Thank you," Carmela said. "Has he had his meal?"

"He ate a small amount," Mrs. Greenwood replied. "The doctor is trying to get him to take more liquids, so perhaps you can encourage him to drink some water. I left a pitcher on the bedside table."

Carmela walked down the hall and into Uncle Silas's small room. The late sunshine slanted in through the small window, and much of the room was thrown into shadow. She let her eyes adjust and saw that he was resting against several pillows, probably in the elevated position so that he could eat and drink more easily. He watched her in silence.

Carmela walked to the bedside and sat down.

"Are you feeling better?"

"Not really, but I forced myself to eat the broth they brought me. The doctor seems to think I won't be able to travel for some time, but we must. I shall try to get out of this bed tomorrow. If I can walk, we'll leave."

"We can't leave unless there's a stagecoach to take us, Uncle Silas."

He frowned. "You must find out what the schedule is."

"I think I can do that," Carmela said. "Now, will you drink something?"

She held the glass for him, and he swallowed an ounce or two of water. Her best course was not to argue with him, she decided. If he got too agitated, it would only slow his healing. Instead, she tried to introduce other topics. He was very interested in her dinner at the governor's mansion.

"Perhaps you can meet Mr. McCormick in a few days," she suggested. "When you're up to it."

"If I hadn't been shot, I'd probably be sitting at his dinner table tonight." Uncle Silas scowled. "We were to be the toast of Prescott this week. How could you—"

The door opened, and Mrs. Greenwood came in carrying a medicine bottle. "There now, Mr. Holden, Doctor left orders for me to give you your next dose if he wasn't back, and it's time."

"I don't want that stuff." Uncle Silas waved an impatient hand. His face reddened, and Carmela knew he wanted to vent his wrath about her confession again.

"You need to rest, so that you'll heal up," Mrs. Greenwood said calmly. "I know you want to heal as quickly as possible. You told me so yourself."

Uncle Silas submitted to her ministrations and swallowed the laudanum. Carmela sat with him a few minutes longer, until he drifted once more into slumber. She tiptoed out into the hallway and listened. Sounds of clattering dishes came from the rear of the house, and she followed them hesitantly until she came to an open doorway that led into the family's kitchen.

"Hello," she called.

Mrs. Greenwood looked up from her supper preparations.

"I'm leaving now," Carmela said. "He's gone to sleep."

Mrs. Greenwood nodded. "Thank you. We'll see you tomorrow."

Carmela nodded and showed herself out. On the way home, she mulled over the situation. She wanted Uncle Silas to get better, but she didn't want him to rant about what she had done. Even worse would be his insistence that she leave with him on the next stagecoach. Her ultimate nightmare was that he would somehow force her back into performing. She would not allow it. Even as she had the thought, she wondered if she had the power to stop him.

Chapter Twenty-Two

$\mathcal{C}$armela didn't get away from the boardinghouse the next day until late morning. Dr. Greenwood was talking to a man in the waiting room when she got to the office, but the merchant left almost immediately and the doctor greeted her.

"That was Mr. Timmons, the haberdasher," he said. "I asked him if there was any news of Marshal Duffield and the posse."

"What did he say?" Carmela asked eagerly.

Dr. Greenwood shook his head. "Nothing yet. I'm usually among the first to know if there's trouble, but so far we've heard nothing here."

"They've been out another night, then."

"So it appears." The doctor frowned. "I'm sure the marshal and his men can take care of themselves, and with the combined posses, they must have more than a dozen men."

"Yes." Carmela had seen only half a dozen Apache men, but there must have been more out of sight. They knew a large band had left its camp near Prescott the morning Lucy left home, but Carmela wasn't sure how many were women and children. Still, Rilla had said Apache women were known to fight alongside their men.

"Mr. Holden is having a bad time of it this morning," Dr.

Greenwood said. "His infection just doesn't want to give up. I'm watching him closely."

"Can I see him?"

"Of course. I'm hoping he'll respond to the treatment I'm giving, but if he's worse tomorrow. . .well, we'll see about that. He's not out of danger."

When she saw him, she could tell at once that Uncle Silas was subdued and in pain. She stayed only a short while, watching him doze fitfully. She concluded that she might as well go back to Mrs. Finney's, where she could work and pray at the same time.

When she emerged into the waiting room, Marshal Duffield and several other men were talking to the doctor. In their midst stood Mrs. Howard, her arms about a child on either side.

"I'd like you just to check 'em over, Doc," Duffield said. "Mrs. Howard has burns on her hands and arm, and we don't know about the kids. The boy jumped off a horse when they were trying to get away, and he says he got stepped on. The girl seems to be all right, but Mrs. Howard would like to be sure."

"Of course," Dr. Greenwood said. He looked around and spotted his wife. "Dora, would you please take Mrs. Howard and the children to the examination room? I'll be right in."

"How are the wounded men I left here the other day?" Duffield asked.

"They've been moved to the jail and are doing fine. I go over once a day to examine them and dress their wounds."

The crowd in the room thinned out, and Carmela noticed Freeland, leaning against the wall by the front door. She couldn't help a smile as she hurried toward him, and yet she wondered how he would receive her.

His smile started in his eyes and spread to his lips. By the time she reached him, he was grinning.

"Miss Wade."

"Please—Carmela. I'm glad you're safe. And the Howards. Mrs. Finney and I have been praying for them."

He nodded. "It took us a while to convince the Apache, but they finally relinquished the kids. Then we had to ride out to the Steger ranch to take them to their mother. We slept there last night, and the Stegers insisted on feeding us all."

"That was very generous of them." Carmela now knew how much food and hard work it took to feed more than a dozen men, from her hours with Mrs. Finney in the boardinghouse kitchen. "I admit we were worried about you."

"We're fine," Freeland said.

"There's so much I'd like to discuss with you. Do you know all about it? About what I told Two Pony? Everyone heard it."

"Yeah, Orland told us on the way back."

"McKay," the marshal called, and Freeland looked toward him.

"Yes sir?"

"I'll need you to help me make a report on the wounded prisoners and arrange payment for the doctor. And I'll have to write up my report for the governor and probably several letters as well. We need to take statements from as many of the outlaw gang as will give them and find out when they can appear before a judge."

"I'm happy to help you any way I can, Marshal." Freeland looked down at Carmela and nodded. "We'll have to speak later. I'll come to the boardinghouse when I can."

Duffield and his men trooped out of the doctor's office, and the room suddenly seemed large and quiet. Carmela realized she was alone, except for a miner in ragged clothes who huddled on a chair in the corner.

She went outside and turned toward Mrs. Finney's house. As she walked, she tried to sort out what had changed. Mrs. Finney would want a full report. Freeland was back. She couldn't help smiling. *Thank You for that, Lord.* All of the marshal's men had returned safe, bringing Mrs. Howard and her children, who were now under the doctor's care. But as far as her own situation, nothing had changed. Uncle Silas was worse off than when he had arrived. If he started to recover, he would be in a fouler mood than ever. He wouldn't just disown her.

Even if she separated from him, he would hound her for a debt that, so far as Carmela could determine, was purely imaginary.

And Freeland—he had smiled when he saw her, but how much did that mean? Surely he wouldn't stay in Prescott long. His work and his home were in Tucson. He had recaptured Dix and delivered him, with the other outlaws, to jail. What would keep him here now? And what would she do after he was gone? She couldn't make plans that included him.

She supposed she should wait until Uncle Silas was well enough to travel. Would the marshal really arrest them? If so, she wouldn't have to worry about her immediate future. If they remained free, she decided, when she knew which way Uncle Silas was going to travel, she would set out in the opposite direction.

Freeland took great satisfaction in arranging the prisoners' hearings for the marshal. Duffield had received word that the judge would hold court in less than a week. While he questioned each man and arranged legal counsel for those who could not afford it—meaning all of them—Freeland made up the schedule.

Dix would be first. Freeland would have to stay in Prescott until the man's hearing, and perhaps return to testify at his trial, unless Dix's lawyer could convince the judge to push his case through quickly.

Lawyers. Were they always among the first in a new territory? Wherever miners flocked, lawyers must follow, because there was bound to be legal trouble over claims and such. For this reason, at least three attorneys now made their livings in Prescott. Each was assigned to a couple of the outlaws.

Dix got a fellow named Carson. When he arrived to consult his new client, Duffield advised him that Dix would answer to his old charges from Tucson, as well as escape, assaulting a law officer, and whatever other charges he could tack on from Dix's time with the outlaws.

The more the better, Freeland thought. He'd like to see Dix put away for a good long time. He just hoped he didn't have to stick around for weeks, waiting for the trial. He'd already sent his mother a letter by way of a freighter headed for Tucson, telling her he was all right and had been delayed for a while. He hoped the deputy left in charge while he was gone was keeping a lid on things there.

Marshal Duffield came out of the inner hallway that led to the cells shaking his head. "What a mess. I'll be glad when we move that bunch out of here."

"I hear you," Freeland said, looking up from the paperwork.

Duffield poured himself a cup of coffee and sat down in the extra chair beside the desk. "What do you think about Holden? Should we ask for charges to be filed against him?"

Freeland felt as though he'd been kicked in the chest. "What kind of charges?"

"Fraud, I guess. Three people have asked me since we got back if I'm going to arrest him and that girl."

Freeland dropped the pen he'd been working with on the desktop. "Wait a second, Marshal. You don't think Miss Wade is a criminal?"

"The way I hear it, she took part in fleecing a whole lot of people."

"But her uncle forced her to do that. She was twelve years old when he got hold of her and made her start pretending. He treated her like she was some kind of actress and he was her promoter, I guess you'd call it. He set up all her engagements. And he told her what to say and everything."

"That so?"

"Yeah. You can ask Miss Wade. She'll tell you. She was a child. Wouldn't that fall under child endangerment? There's some kind of law against that."

"Yes." Duffield rubbed his whiskery chin. "I guess I'll have to interview her. If it's like you say. . ."

"Oh, it is," Freeland said.

"What about the uncle though?"

"Now there I think you'd have a better case. He thought up the whole scheme. Over the past seven or eight years, he's taken thousands of dollars for Carmela's performances, and you can bet he's the one who pocketed the cash, not Carmela."

"*Hmm.* That money he kept yapping about. . ."

Freeland nodded. "From his precious money belt."

"Yeah. I guess we should hold onto that as evidence."

At that moment, a clanging sounded from the hallway.

"One of the lawyers is done." Duffield held out a large key on an iron ring. "Go let him out, would you, McKay?"

"Sure. And I finished copying your report." Freeland pushed the paper toward him as he rose. He took the key and went down to the cells thinking about Carmela. He was proud of her. Even though she was in turmoil over her own situation, she had gone to help others. This whole ordeal must have been horrible for her, from the stagecoach robbery to confronting the Apache. Even before that, she had struggled with her circumstances and longed to do what was ethical. He couldn't help caring for her, and he realized how deep his feelings went.

Three outlaws shared the cell where the lawyer was waiting by the barred door. "All set, Mr. Carson?"

"For now. They need a place where attorneys can talk privately with their clients though."

"You'll have to speak to the marshal about that."

"Oh, I have," Carson said.

Freeland unlocked the door, let him out, and relocked it. They walked toward the front office together.

"You a pretty good lawyer, are you?" Freeland asked.

"I do all right."

"Maybe you can tell me what you think of a case I know about. A young woman who was forced to do things for the benefit of a relative."

Carson paused and eyed him sharply. "Slavery?"

"Of a sort." They stopped in the hallway.

Carson's brow wrinkled. "Are we talking prostitution?"

"No, no!" Freeland shook his head vehemently. "She was made to tell lies. For money. Sort of an entertainment, but people thought it was true."

"Oh, you're talking about the tattooed girl. I heard about it."

"You did?"

"Sure. Everyone in town is talking about her."

"Then you know she didn't intend to deceive people."

Carson shrugged. "She stood up and told them a pack of lies in return for money."

"But her uncle forced her to do it." Quickly Freeland passed on to him everything Carmela had told him about the situation and his own suspicions that Holden had mistreated her. "He threatened her for sure. She was only twelve years old when it started. Now she's twenty, and she wants out."

Carson cocked his head to one side. "Tell her I might be able to help her. My office is on Montezuma."

"She doesn't have any money," Freeland said, watching his eyes.

Carson sighed. "What else is new? Seems no one around here has money, or if they do, they don't need a lawyer."

Freeland grimaced. "Well, maybe I could stake her ten dollars or so, if I get paid."

Carson stuck out his hand. "We have a deal."

They stepped out into the office.

"Hey Carson," Marshal Duffield said, rising from his chair. "Mrs. Greenwood just brought a message around from the doctor's office. Mr. Holden, the one who was shot and abducted by the outlaw gang, wants a lawyer, but he says he can't pay unless we return the money that was in his money belt."

Carson laughed. "That's a new one on me. Is he likely to get it back?"

"Maybe. I'm not sure yet. Might depend on what he tells you."

"Hey, wait a minute," Freeland said. "Carson, that's Miss Wade's uncle. You just told me you'd help her. You can't represent her uncle, too, can you?"

"Oh, I see." Carson shook his head. "Sorry, Marshal. You'll have to get another lawyer for Mr. Holden."

"He seems to be progressing," Dr. Greenwood told Carmela on Saturday. "His inflammation is greatly reduced, and he's more alert and has regained some appetite. But he seems bent on travel, and I strongly advise against it for another two weeks. I didn't medicate him so heavily this morning, since he insisted he wanted to be awake when you came in. Do you want my wife to go in with you?"

Carmela swallowed against the lump in her throat. "I'll be all right." But she wondered about that as she walked with trepidation down the hall. If Uncle Silas was feeling stronger, he would also be more insistent on putting his plans in motion.

"There you are! It's about time."

His harsh words told her she was right. He had gotten past the sharp edge of pain and was ready to work toward his own best interest.

She walked over to the stool beside the bed and sat down just out of his reach.

"Did you check on the stagecoach schedule? You'll need to make the arrangements." His cheeks were flushed, but his eyes seemed brighter and more focused than on any of her previous visits.

Carmela sent up a silent prayer for strength and drew in a deep breath.

"Dr. Greenwood says you can't travel for some time yet, and the only arrangements I am making are for your continued care and for my announcement at church tomorrow."

"You can't do that! It will be worse than ever."

"No, Uncle Silas, it's the only way to begin righting all the wrongs we have done."

"Wrongs? What wrongs?"

"I think you know what wrongs. The lies and all the money we took from people who wanted to hear about my experiences. Experiences that never happened."

His face blanched beneath his sunburn. "You can't."

"Yes, I can."

"Carmela, I am your only living relative."

He groped for her hand, but she pulled away.

"Don't you understand?" he cried. "I spoke to a lawyer. We could both be arrested. Do you want to be thrown into jail with drunkards and murderers?"

She drew in a shaky breath. "If that is what God wills for us, I'll trust Him to see us through it." She stood.

"Where are you going?" His brown eyes darted from her to the door and back again, filled with panic.

"I think we've said all we need to say. I will not change my mind."

She walked resolutely to the door. Inside, she wasn't sure she could hold out against his demands. For so long, she had listened and obeyed his every command. Part of her felt it was wrong to disobey him now.

"You still owe me thousands of dollars, and I don't know yet if the marshal recovered what was in my money belt!"

She stopped but did not turn around. All he cared about was the money. She had earned enough to more than repay him what he claimed was owed, and still he wouldn't let her go.

She raised her chin. "I owe you nothing. Do not speak of it again."

As she walked out into the hallway, she could still hear him.

"If you don't buy the tickets, I shall have to punish you, girl. Have you no decency? I am helpless, and you must—"

Chapter Twenty-Three

Carmela dressed carefully on Sunday morning. Her stomach roiled at the thought of standing before the congregation, but she knew Mrs. Finney wouldn't let her out of it. She wanted to do it, but at the same time she would give anything not to have to face the people of Prescott.

Would Freeland be there?

When he returned, he had seemed glad to see her and sympathetic to her cause. But they hadn't had a chance to talk out everything, and she couldn't know how he really felt about her. After she made a public statement about what she and Uncle Silas had done, she couldn't unsay it. She wished she knew whether Freeland thought this was the best way to go about changing her course. Maybe she should do it more quietly, more gradually. Go to another town until all traces of ink were gone from her face, then go back to New England and blend into the culture where she was born. But that would mean never seeing Freeland again.

What had she hoped for from Freeland? She hadn't been able to help imagining a life with him. But if he didn't see things that way, she wouldn't blame him. Her steps toward the future depended on him.

She paused in brushing her long, glossy hair as she remembered

223

that moment when they were alone in the desert and she had explained to him about her tattoos. He had touched her cheek gently, and her heart had pounded. She had thought for a moment he might kiss her. He had assured her that she could make her own decisions now and not obey Uncle Silas. *"You don't have to do it again if you don't want to. Ever."* She could still hear his words, clear as day. And she still felt the excitement of anticipating his kiss. The kiss that never came.

She had to face reality now. Freeing herself from Uncle Silas was not connected to Freeland, although she had made up her mind in the moment when Freeland was closest to her. She could go on with this alone. She had to, because there was no going back to her life of lies. A pang of regret hit her as she resumed brushing her hair. She would never meet another man like Freeland McKay.

As she slid the last pin into her hair, Mrs. Finney tapped on her door.

"Ready, dear?"

"Coming." Carmela picked up her hat. She had no Bible and no handbag. It was too hot to wear a shawl. She felt underdressed as she walked the quiet streets to the church beside her landlady.

"I thought some of the boarders would come out this morning," Mrs. Finney said. "I guess it takes a lot to get them into a church."

Carmela remembered many times she had spoken in churches, and the rooms were packed, but she didn't say anything.

The church had three walls closed in now and a pine pulpit at the front. When they entered, Reverend Bardwell came down the aisle to greet them. Only a few people had arrived before them, families from outlying ranches who had driven into town for the service.

"Good morning, Reverend," Mrs. Finney said.

The minister shook their hands. "Thank you for coming early. I'd like to seat you near the front so that you don't have far to walk when I introduce you, Miss Wade."

"Thank you," she whispered, though sitting up front would enable everyone to stare at her all through the sermon. He led them to the first row, where Mrs. Bardwell stood to greet them with a warm smile.

Carmela sat down between her and Mrs. Finney, her stomach aflutter.

Other people began to trickle in, and as the hour for the service drew nearer, they came in clusters and droves, until the unfinished building was filled. Carmela looked around only once, and the stares kept her facing forward after that, but she could feel them crowding in and hear the shuffle of feet, the low chatter, and the protesting creaks of the benches.

"Land sakes, we never have this many people," Mrs. Finney whispered. "Word must have gotten around."

To Carmela's surprise, the Reverend Mr. Bardwell didn't wait until after his sermon to present her. They sang one hymn, and he opened in prayer. Then he looked out over the congregation and said, "I know you all didn't come here this morning to listen to me. You came to hear what Miss Carmela Wade has to say. I remind you that she is a sister in Christ, and she is striving to obey the Lord's commands. In the past, she was made to bear false witness under duress. But today, she is here to tell the truth."

A murmur ran through the crowd, and Carmela shuddered. She wasn't used to this type of reception, where people came inclined to doubt and condemn her.

"So, Miss Wade, if you'll come up here now, I'll turn it over to you."

Carmela stood with difficulty. Her legs were like sticks of dried firewood. She managed the few steps to the front. Reverend Bardwell smiled at her, but she took no encouragement from him. Slowly, she turned and faced the people.

She began her story much as she did when she told the captive version, telling how she had set out with her parents for a new life in California. But the part where their wagon journey was interrupted was much different this time from her usual tale. Her parents became ill, and their wagon and two others were left behind by the train. She told of the deaths in her family and the Jessups' and the Basfords'. One by one, their loved ones slipped away. She told of arriving weak and hungry at Fort Yuma with Mr. Basford and his one surviving son, and of how the kind Captain Owen and his wife had cared for her for several months, until her new guardian, Uncle Silas, had arrived to claim her.

She felt numb as she told what happened after that, and yet her heart felt lighter than it had when she'd given a performance. Instead of glancing to the side and seeing Uncle Silas's grim face as he listened to every word, alert for inconsistencies, she saw Mrs. Finney and Mrs. Bardwell in the front row, nodding with sorrowful eyes.

Carmela found that she was able to look beyond them, at other faces in the congregation. Most held the rugged features of miners and ranchers, but a few families were sprinkled throughout the room, and here and there a couple sat together. She found the Roote family, with Lucy and her siblings sitting between their parents. The sister next to Lucy listened wide-eyed, and tears streamed down Lucy's cheeks.

Then she spotted Rilla, sitting next to a careworn woman in a gray dress. Carmela didn't recognize Rilla at first. Her hair was combed and pinned up, and she wore a dress made from soft coral-colored calico. The woman beside her must be her mother. The man beyond her was no doubt the father. He nodded as though drifting off to sleep and jerked away, meeting her eyes for a moment.

Carmela caught a breath and went on, telling how her journey of deceit had ended when the stagecoach was robbed. She didn't tell of her time in the desert with Freeland but simply said that when her uncle was shot and carried off by the outlaws, she knew she had reached a crossroads in her life. Now was the time to start over, to live the truth.

She stopped and looked toward the minister. He stepped up beside her and cleared his throat.

"I'm sure you're all touched by this account."

"What happened to the uncle?" called a man in the back of the congregation.

Reverend Bardwell looked at Carmela. "Do you wish to address that?"

Carmela swallowed hard. "My uncle was rescued by Marshal Duffield and his men. He is seriously injured, and he's now under the care of a physician here in Prescott."

"So, are you going to stay with him?" Mrs. Roote asked.

Carmela felt faint. "He is very ill. We haven't been able to reach an agreement yet on what to do next."

"But you won't keep telling them lies," said one of men she recognized from Lucy's rescue party.

"No. I won't." She almost went on but decided it was better to say less for now. She knew what she wanted, but she couldn't ensure that cutting ties with the past would be easy or that her story would have a happy ending. If Uncle Silas insisted she continued performing, she would part ways with him.

"What about all that money you stole? You gonna pay it back?" This question was hurled by Buck Chard, the boarder who claimed to have heard her speak in Albuquerque. She had sat at the table with him several times this week at Mrs. Finney's, but he had never spoken to her directly. Instead, he had thrown her baleful glances and chosen to bring up his questions here, in a public forum.

Carmela felt as though the air had been squeezed from her lungs. A quick look at Mrs. Finney showed her that the loyal woman sat with her hands folded in her lap and her lips moving. *She's praying for me*, Carmela thought.

She breathed as deeply as she could and straightened. "If you mean the receipts my uncle collected, I don't know much about that. As I told you, he insisted I owed him money—that is, my father did, and I was obligated to repay it. Everything I did for him was to that end. I never received more than small amounts of money from him— enough to buy a meal or purchase sundries when we traveled. I don't know if Mr. Holden spent it all, or if he still has some of it. I do know that the money he had collected at our most recent appearances was stolen from him when the stagecoach was robbed."

"Who's payin' for your board now?" Chard yelled.

Carmela's head felt like it floated above her body. Reverend

Bardwell touched her arm lightly, and she looked up at him, pleading with her eyes for him to stop this.

"It's my understanding," the minister said firmly, "that Miss Wade is working for her keep now. The matter of whether or not crimes were committed and restitution should be made is up to the marshal and the court system."

"Is she gonna be arrested?" another man called.

Reverend Bardwell looked at Carmela, his eyebrows raised. She couldn't speak. Her lips trembled, and she reached for his arm for support.

"I don't know anything about that," Reverend Bardwell said. "Mrs. Finney, could you please come and help Miss Wade? I think that's enough for now."

Mrs. Finney leaped up and came to Carmela. She put an arm around her. "Come on, dearie. You did fine, but you need to sit."

"Thank you." Carmela managed to get to the bench, but the air seemed close, and scores of people stared at her, their eyes boring into her. Tears welled in Carmela's eyes as the people began to talk among themselves.

"Please," she whispered. "Can we go home?"

"Soon," Mrs. Finney said. "Calm yourself if you can."

Mrs. Bardwell reached across Mrs. Finney with a small vial in her hand, and Mrs. Finney took it.

"Smelling salts."

Carmela waved it away. "No, but thank you."

"Let us pray," Reverend Bardwell intoned, and the room grew quiet.

Carmela didn't hear the words of the prayer. She only heard the roar of her pulse in her ears and a vague, rushing sound that she knew was his voice.

When he finished, people began to stand and shuffle. Skirts rustled, and men's boots thumped on the board floor. Mrs. Finney sat with her arm about Carmela's shoulders.

"Might be best to wait here a few minutes," Mrs. Bardwell said.

"Some folks are lingering."

Carmela nodded and took the handkerchief Mrs. Finney held out. No use going down the aisle now and running a gauntlet of harsh comments.

"God is pleased with you," Mrs. Finney whispered.

Carmela gulped and swabbed at a new rush of tears.

About ten minutes later, the church had emptied. Reverend Bardwell came in from where he had stood outside the door to greet people.

"Well, Miss Wade, I think that went rather well," he said.

"Really?" Carmela croaked.

"Oh, yes. Could have been worse. Much worse."

A wave of anger washed over her for just an instant. If he'd thought they might tear her apart, why had he encouraged her to do this?

Mrs. Finney must have read her expression. "You did the right thing." She patted Carmela's shoulder. "Shall we go home and put dinner on?"

Carmela could barely breathe. "What about Mr. Chard?"

"He'd better not cause trouble, or I'll toss him out. Let him find other lodgings if he wants to fuss about you telling the truth."

Mrs. Bardwell nodded and patted her hand. "That's right, dear. Some of these people don't understand. They're used to being lied to and cheated."

The reverend lifted his gaze toward the ceiling and quoted, " 'O, full of all subtilty and all mischief, thou child of the devil, thou enemy of all righteousness, wilt thou not cease to pervert the right ways of the Lord?' "

Carmela blinked at him, wondering if he was in some kind of trance.

"That's from Acts," his wife said. "My husband knows the most obscure passages. But he's right. Some of the people in this territory will turn the purest things into mischief. When a body wants to change, they have no idea what's going on, and they're not sure they can believe it. Time will be the proof."

"That's it," the minister said. "You'll live an honest life now, and after a while they'll see."

"Thank you." Carmela rose and walked slowly to the door with Mrs. Finney. It sort of made sense to her now. Would she be able to go on living in Prescott, or would the hatred of some be too divisive?

As they headed toward the boardinghouse, she realized that didn't really matter. She would be bothered if some of the townspeople misunderstood or rejected her, but her biggest disappointment was Freeland. He'd known this would be an ordeal for her, but he hadn't even bothered to come.

Chapter Twenty-Four

fter lunch, Carmela helped do the dishes and then retired to her room. She lay on her bed thinking about the condescending looks Buck Chard had sent her way during the meal and the disapproving sniff from Mrs. Tuttle, one of the newcomers. She supposed she ought to go and see Uncle Silas, but she needed to gather her courage first.

A soft knock came on her door, and she sat up.

"Yes?"

"You've a visitor in the parlor, dear," Mrs. Finney said.

Carmela bounded to her feet and shoved her shoes on. Freeland? She hoped so. She hurried down the hall but slowed as she reached the empty dining room. What if it was someone who wanted to rail at her? Or worse, what if Marshal Duffield had come to arrest her?

Her legs shook as she stepped to the open parlor door. Rilla waited for her, sitting primly on the settee in her becoming Sunday dress. She jumped up when she saw Carmela and came to her smiling. Carmela couldn't help but notice she wore black leather shoes, not the worn moccasins.

"Carmela! Dear friend, are you all right? I wanted to stay after church and talk to you, but Pa insisted we leave right away. His mare is going to foal any minute, and he had to be there. But he let me take the wagon this afternoon. Tell me! How are you?" Her bright brown eyes and eager questions chased away Carmela's dread.

"Aren't you angry with me?"

"Angry? I think you're wonderful." Rilla seized her hands and drew her to the settee. "Tell me how you dared to do it."

"To. . .tell the truth?"

"Yes. After so long, it must have been hard."

Carmela gulped. "It was. I'd been telling that story since I was twelve." She blinked against tears. "I'm sorry I let you believe the lie. I didn't dare tell you the truth when I first met you. I was very frightened of what might happen if people found out. Can you forgive me?"

"I already have." Rilla sobered. "When I first heard the rumor, that you had lied about your captivity, I didn't believe it. But then I thought, if that's so, why then were you taking a bold step to correct things?"

"I never wanted to lie." Carmela fumbled for her handkerchief as her tears began to fall.

"He forced you to, didn't he? That awful man! At least the Apache were honest about what they did to me."

Carmela wiped her face and eyed her friend for a long moment. "How can you not hate them?"

Rilla sighed. "I still feel all mixed up inside, and it's hard not to be angry with my parents. My pa wasn't there when the Indians came, and he should have been. He could have protected us. Ma and I were out in the garden. When we saw them, instead of running to the house, Ma pulled me down the path to the river to hide. She hoped they wouldn't find us there, but they did. And do you know what Ma did when the warriors found us?"

Carmela shook her head.

"She shoved me into the river."

"She was trying to save you from them," Carmela said.

Rilla gave a bitter laugh. "She tried to hold me underwater. She said it was better to drown me than to let me be captured."

Carmela's breath left her in a puff. How could a mother think that? And yet, after all that Rilla had endured, perhaps her mother had some logic.

"They took you."

"Yes. Pulled me right out of the water."

"What about your mother?"

"They killed her."

"What?" Carmela stared at the girl. "But. . .your ma and pa were in church this morning."

"She's my stepmother. They hatcheted my real ma."

Carmela couldn't breathe. She wanted to say something comforting, or at least offer a sympathetic pat, as Mrs. Finney would, but she couldn't move.

"By the time the army brought me back, my pa had got married again," Rilla said.

Speechless, Carmela felt tears sting her eyes.

"But I survived," Rilla said softly.

"I'm so, so sorry." Carmela sought her hand, and Rilla squeezed hers.

"What you had to do was awful, too, but in a different way."

"No," Carmela said. "I wasn't injured or made to live with a savage man."

Rilla shook her head. "At least I don't have to lie about it. I think. . .I think we could be friends. If you want."

"Oh, yes." Carmela's tears flowed freely now.

Rilla took a folded handkerchief from her pocket and handed it to her. "I've started praying again."

"That's wonderful," Carmela choked. "Might we pray together?"

Rilla smiled and took her hand again. "I'd like that. We can pray for each other, and maybe the two of us can help Lucy Roote."

Carmela's heart leaped. "Do you want to go visit her?"

"Yes, if you'll go with me. And if her parents will let me in the door. They don't think much of me."

"They have no reason for that."

Rilla shrugged. "I suppose I was rude to them. I probably said some hurtful things when Lucy was taken. At that time, I was acting more like an Apache."

❤

Carmela approached Dr. Greenwood's house reluctantly that evening. Her uncle would probably scream at her and demand that she make travel arrangements. She had floundered among her options and decided that if the doctor gave Uncle Silas leave to travel, she would buy him a stagecoach ticket, but she was staying here. Mrs. Finney had assured her that she could stay as long as she liked, and her work at the boardinghouse would more than pay for her room and meals.

Mrs. Greenwood opened the door. Her eyes flickered when she saw Carmela.

"Come in, please. The doctor is with Marshal Duffield. He asked me to bring you in if you came."

"With the marshal?" Carmela's stomach fell. The specter of arrest hung over her once more.

Mrs. Greenwood opened the door to the doctor's cramped office. To Carmela's surprise, Freeland was in the room with the doctor and Duffield. He stood back, leaning against the wall. When Carmela entered, he straightened and nodded soberly to her.

"Oh, good, Miss Wade is here," Dr. Greenwood said. He stepped from behind his desk and touched her sleeve. "Please sit down, my dear. I have news."

"What is it?" Carmela sank onto the chair he indicated.

Marshal Duffield cleared his throat. "It's about your uncle. I'm afraid he's gone."

Carmela's mouth went dry. They all looked so somber. Could Uncle Silas have passed away since last night? He was very much alive then, and getting better, the doctor had said. He was well enough to be very angry.

"But—he was improving. You said so, Dr. Greenwood." She looked up at him anxiously.

"No," said the marshal. "I mean, he is missing."

"Missing? How could he—"

"Apparently he slipped out this afternoon, while I was making house calls," Dr. Greenwood said.

The marshal nodded. "Since there's no stagecoach outbound until tomorrow, I've put several of my deputies out, trying to determine whether he left here alone, and if he's checked into a hotel."

"But. . .how would he pay for that?"

The marshal gave a little cough. "I, uh, returned five hundred dollars to him this morning. He claimed he had more in his money belt, but he couldn't prove it, and there are other people who need to be recompensed as well. Notably, the stagecoach company. They were carrying a payroll, and we didn't recover as much as they said they lost. I'm sure the gang spent some of it on liquor and such, and they may have hidden part of it. Anyway, I gave Mr. Holden five hundred, and apparently he took that as license to leave town."

"I see."

"He hasn't contacted you at the boardinghouse?"

She shook her head. "I've heard nothing, and I'm sure Mrs. Finney would have told me if he came there. I had one visitor this afternoon, Rilla Landis. She stayed about a half hour and then left. After that, I helped Mrs. Finney prepare the evening meal for the boarders." Carmela looked up at Duffield. "Were you going to press charges against Uncle Silas? Is that why you're here?"

"No. In fact, I'd decided not to. So far as I can see, most of what he did took place outside my jurisdiction, except for Tucson, and after talking to McKay, I figure the people of Tucson got at least some of what they paid for—an evening's entertainment."

Carmela let out a deep sigh. "Thank you, Marshal. I promise you, I won't be giving lectures anymore. I'm done with my public speaking career."

He nodded. "I thought as much."

"So Mr. Holden isn't wanted," Dr. Greenwood said slowly.

"That's right. He hasn't been charged with any crimes," Duffield

235

said. "Unless he owes you for his care?"

"No, actually, he gave my wife twenty dollars after you gave him the money. That more than covers what we've done for him here."

"I see. Well, I guess there's no point in looking for him, then. Miss Wade, perhaps he will contact you when he's ready."

"Perhaps."

"I'll be going. Thank you, folks. Just keep me posted if he shows up here again."

"I guess he might, since he's a long way from being healed," Dr. Greenwood said. "I hope he'll realize the folly of leaving here too soon."

The marshal nodded and headed for the door.

"There are a few things in his room," the doctor said to Carmela. "My wife can help you gather up what you want to take."

"Thank you," she said.

Freeland stepped away from the wall. "May I walk you back to the boardinghouse when you're finished?"

Carmela hardly knew what to say. Ten minutes ago, she would have been ecstatic at his offer. Now she just felt numb. "Y–yes, thank you. And thank you, Dr. Greenwood."

She walked out into the front room with Freeland. The doctor's wife was sitting in one of the chairs, and she rose as they entered. Carmela walked over to her.

"Mrs. Greenwood, thank you for all you did for my uncle. I'm sorry he left in such an abrupt manner."

Mrs. Greenwood took her hand. "Your courtesy makes up for his lack of it. What will you do now, Miss Wade?"

"Mrs. Finney has invited me to stay on with her as an employee. That suits me for now."

Mrs. Greenwood smiled. "Then we shall be neighbors awhile longer. You're welcome to visit anytime, though we're often busy here."

"You must visit us," Carmela said. "Come see Mrs. Finney and me if you'd like to relax for an hour."

"Thank you. Perhaps I shall."

"Dr. Greenwood says my uncle left some things?" Carmela asked.

"Oh of course. Come with me."

Carmela followed her to the room where Uncle Silas had lain for the past few days. The rumpled bed brought the calamity home to her. He had seemed so helpless, and yet he had gotten himself out of bed, presumably dressed without assistance, and left the house without Dr. Greenwood or his wife realizing it.

"His satchel is gone, but these were on the dresser." Mrs. Greenwood handed her a tortoiseshell comb and a shaving mug and brush.

"Thank you. I'll keep them at Mrs. Finney's in case he returns."

"I hope he will," Mrs. Greenwood said. "He's far from mended."

"I know. I do hope he'll be sensible and come back, either here or to the boardinghouse." Carmela put the comb in her pocket and carried the mug out to the front room.

Freeland laid aside the newspaper he'd picked up to read and stood, putting his hat on. "Ready?"

"I guess so." Carmela couldn't think straight. She had been abandoned, and once more she was alone.

Freeland went to the door and reached for the knob, but before he could open it, the door was flung open. Freeland stepped back, and Mrs. Finney bustled in.

"Oh, thank heaven you're here, Deputy."

"Is something wrong?" Freeland asked.

"See for yourself." Mrs. Finney looked over her shoulder.

Freeland stepped into the doorway and stood still. Carmela could hear wheels rattling, footsteps, and the murmur of voices outside— the usual street sounds in town, but it seemed louder than usual for this neighborhood. She walked to the door, where Freeland stood with one arm braced against the jamb.

She peered out beneath it. A crowd had gathered in the street outside Dr. Greenwood's house.

"You still got that thief inside there?" a man called.

Chapter Twenty-Five

$\mathcal{F}$reeland's first instinct was to protect Carmela. He reached for her, but Mrs. Finney had already pulled her from the doorway. He stepped back and closed the door.

"What do they want?" Carmela's face looked stricken, her skin tight across her cheekbones and her mouth a thin slash.

Mrs. Greenwood and Mrs. Finney gathered her to them, a couple of comforting mother hens.

"We need to get the marshal back here," Freeland said.

"He hasn't been gone long," Mrs. Greenwood said. "Didn't he say he was headed back to the jail?"

"I think so. Can someone go out a back way and fetch him?"

"My husband can go out the kitchen door, or I'll go if you think he should stay here."

"I'd hate to send you out alone right now, ma'am," Freeland said.

"I'll tell John." Mrs. Greenwood strode down the hallway to the doctor's office.

Freeland turned to Carmela and Mrs. Finney. "I'm going out there and talk to them. You ladies stay out of sight."

Mrs. Finney drew Carmela to the side of the room, away from the doorway and the front window.

This was the last thing Freeland wanted to deal with now. He'd hoped for a time in private with Carmela, when he could speak to her about her circumstances and her future. Seeing her face when she learned her uncle had slipped away without her had wrenched his heart. He wanted her to know that there were still people who cared about her—deeply. He wasn't about to leave her alone and bereft. And now the town seemed to conspire to prove the opposite—no one cared about her feelings or her well-being.

He sent up a quick prayer for wisdom, opened the door, and stepped outside. He recognized a few people, but most were strangers to him.

"Hey Deputy! Has that charlatan been arrested?" yelled a man wearing a barkeeper's apron.

"Are they going to give back money to people they cheated?" called another.

"Folks, calm down," Freeland said. "I've sent for the marshal, and he'll be here soon to answer your questions. So far as I know, Mr. Holden never cheated anybody here in Prescott."

"Some of us has seen him and his niece—if she really is his niece—other places," said a man Freeland thought might be one of Mrs. Finney's boarders.

"Yeah, that little gal oughta be arrested, too," said the first man.

Near the edge of the crowd, a tall, middle-aged man with shaggy, light-brown hair pushed forward.

"Excuse me, folks. Pardon me." He worked his way to the front of the throng and paused below the steps. "Deputy?"

"Yes?"

"I'm Reverend Bardwell, a friend of Miss Wade's." The preacher climbed up to stand beside Freeland on the doctor's stoop. "Miss Wade has done nothing wrong. I don't know about her uncle. I never met the man. But I think we should let the law sort it out."

"If he's in Doc Greenwood's house, I say we get him out and over to the jail," a man on the fringe of the rabble called.

"What if he ain't?" asked the man in the apron. He frowned at

Freeland. "We heard he's disappeared. We want to make sure he don't get away and that somebody pays for the fraud those two perpetrated. Ain't that the word, Deputy?"

Freeland opened his mouth, and someone else yelled, "Yeah, restitution!"

"It's a disgrace," said the man Freeland was certain he'd seen at the boardinghouse. "They ought to pay every cent they have to people who've had family stolen or kilt by the Indians."

To Freeland's relief, the door opened behind him and Marshal Duffield stepped out of the house. He held up both hands.

"All right, settle down."

"You going to arrest them two?" a man shouted.

Another added, "You ought to string up that feller!"

"Hold it now," Duffield said firmly. "In the first place, everything is going to be done according to the law. We'll have no talk about lynching. You hear?" He glared at the man who had suggested it. "Some might interpret what you just said as inciting a riot, so sober up and simmer down!"

Nobody moved.

"Go on," he said, louder. "Go home and have your supper."

The crowd began to fragment as people turned away. Duffield looked at Freeland and the preacher.

"Well. Thanks."

"Have you heard anything about Holden yet?" Freeland asked.

"Nope," the marshal said. "I sent a man to check all the livery stables. It seems maybe Miss Wade needs protection. At least until I'm sure those troublemakers won't try to stir things up again."

"Go to jail?" Carmela's heart hammered and she felt lightheaded. "You want to put me in a cell?"

"Only for your own safety," the marshal said. "Just tonight."

"You wouldn't be under arrest," Freeland explained. "The marshal just thought you'd be safer at the jail, and it would keep the crowds from the saloons from drifting over to the boardinghouse or back here."

"We certainly don't want a bunch of drunks bothering the doc or Mrs. Finney," Duffield said.

"I should say not," Mrs. Finney said, her eyes snapping. "And if that Buck Chard says one word to me about Carmela, I'll throw him out in the street. He can find other lodgings."

"I can't do my work if there's a mob outside my house yelling," Dr. Greenwood said, looking anxiously out the window.

Carmela hesitated. "I'd need some things from my room—"

"I'll see Mrs. Finney home and bring them back for you," the marshal said. "You go on with McKay to the jail."

"But don't you have the outlaws locked up in the jail?" Carmela asked.

"Well, yes, but I also have a cot in the back room where I stay sometimes, if I have prisoners overnight. You can go in there, and the gang members won't see you. The townsfolk will hear you're in the jail, and I hope that will be enough to keep them away."

She agreed reluctantly. Mrs. Greenwood took them through the family quarters and out the kitchen door. Carmela and Freeland set out for the marshal's office, while Duffield and Mrs. Finney headed for the boardinghouse.

Carmela walked in silence for a few minutes. They paused to let a wagon pass before they crossed a side street.

"Are you all right?" Freeland asked.

Carmela sighed. "I know it's senseless, but I feel abandoned, almost as much as when my parents died."

"Mr. Holden is the last of your family?"

"There are some more distant relatives, but I don't know them, really." The sun had gone down, and she eyed Freeland closely in the twilight. "Did the marshal tell Uncle Silas he was free to go?"

"I'm not sure. I wasn't there when he gave him the money."

"So he might still think he'll be arrested."

"I doubt it. Why would the marshal give him back the money if he thought it was ill-gotten gains?"

"True. So I guess the truth is, he simply felt I was no longer of use to him."

Freeland said nothing to dispute that. After a moment, he touched her sleeve briefly. "I'm sorry."

She nodded. They were approaching the center of town, and the noise from the saloons could be heard from blocks away.

"There're a lot of miners in town tonight." Freeland spoke loudly so she could hear over the racket. "Word got around about the Apache being on the rampage, and a lot of folks came in for safety."

"And now I need to be protected from them." Carmela heard the bitterness in her own voice. They reached the marshal's office, and Freeland opened the door for her. Before she went inside, she looked over her shoulder, toward Whiskey Row. "I wonder where Uncle Silas is tonight."

As soon as they stepped inside, a clamor began from deeper within the building. A deputy had been sitting behind the desk dozing, and he rose and nodded to them. "McKay."

"Hey Marshal," men called from inside.

"The prisoners want to know when Duffield's gonna let 'em out or when they'll have their trials or when their lawyers will come see 'em again." The deputy ran a hand over his short-cropped beard. "I'm telling you, I'll be glad to get home and get some peace and quiet."

"They all been fed?" Freeland asked.

"Yes, and the cook came from the tavern to get the dishes."

"You might as well go along," Freeland told him. "The boss will be here soon."

The deputy lost no time in vacating the premises. Freeland took Carmela into the small chamber where Duffield kept a cot, a rocker, and a couple of crates for storage. A lantern sat on a rough bedside table.

"It's not a cell," Freeland said, "but you can lock the door from inside if you don't feel safe."

She nodded. "I think I'll be fine. If those men will quiet down."

Freeland huffed out a breath. "Bunch of hooligans. Want coffee? The marshal keeps a pot on the stove yonder."

That explained why the office was so warm. Carmela accepted the offer, and Freeland let her sit behind the desk while he took a stool nearby.

"You'll be all right," he said.

She wasn't completely sure, but she said, "I think so."

"Not scared, are you?"

She shook her head. "Those men can't get out."

"And the marshal won't let anyone else in."

"Right."

The rowdy prisoners had quieted down again. She sipped the strong coffee.

"I expect folks will forget about all of this in a day or two," Freeland said. "Something else will happen. There'll be a big gold strike, or the Indians will act up again, or somebody's store will burn, and everyone will forget about you and your uncle."

"I hope so." She jerked her head up. "Not that I want anyone else to have misfortune."

"I know what you mean." Freeland's crooked smile brought back those feelings of longing, and she made herself not look into his eyes too long.

"Uncle Silas decided to go on without me," she said after a moment. "Decided I wasn't profitable anymore."

Freeland's lips twitched. He turned his coffee cup carefully, watching the liquid in it. "That doesn't mean you're not useful to other people. God has other things for you; that's all."

"I hope so." She set down her cup.

"Mrs. Finney seems to want you."

Carmela nodded. "I'm grateful to her."

"It could be a new start for you."

"I don't know." Carmela just didn't feel easy about that plan. What if the people in Prescott didn't forget what she had done?

The marshal came along in a few minutes, bringing her a bundle of comforts from Mrs. Finney's house. Freeland drained his cup and promised Duffield he would return first thing in the morning. When he turned back at the door and gazed at Carmela, she wished he would stay. But that was silly. The marshal would be out here behind his desk. She couldn't ask Freeland to sit up all night just so he'd be near her.

"Good night," he said.

" 'Night." She watched him go and took a deep breath.

"I'll be out here," the marshal said. " 'Course, I might get called out if things get too wild on Whiskey Row. I suggest you lock your door. I'll leave a deputy here all the time if I can, but you never know."

Carmela went into the little room and threw the bolt on the door. She turned the lantern low and started to unbutton the basque of her dress, but she stopped when a burst of gunfire sounded from down the street. She decided to lie down in her clothes.

The streets were much noisier here than in Mrs. Finney's neighborhood. If anything happened in the night, she didn't want to be caught in her nightclothes.

Reluctantly she turned out the lantern and eased onto the cot. She knew the door was locked, but even so, she didn't feel secure.

"God is my refuge," she whispered, but she still felt utterly alone.

Chapter Twenty-Six

reeland rose early and went down to Mrs. Finney's kitchen. She was there already, packing a basket with biscuits, slices of ham, boiled eggs, and a jar of jelly.

"I'd go with you if I could," she said mournfully.

"No, you've got to fix breakfast for the other boarders," Freeland said. "I'll take this to Carmela for you."

"Mind you keep it steady." She put in a small corked jug. "Miss Wade likes tea in the morning, not coffee."

He smiled. "I don't think she's been getting it very often the last few weeks, except when she was at your house."

"Well, she deserves it," Mrs. Finney said. "She's a good girl."

"That she is." Freeland's throat felt a bit prickly, and he swallowed hard. He hadn't known Carmela long, but he'd seen strength in her, as well as a compassionate side that drew him. He longed to ask her to return to Tucson with him, but he feared it was too soon for that. He didn't suppose she cared about him the same way he had come to care for her. That would take some time, and he couldn't just stay here in the capital, hoping she'd fall in love with him.

"There." Mrs. Finney tucked a checked dish towel over the top of the basket. "She can bring those things back when she's ready to come home."

Home. This would be a good home for her, Freeland thought. Even so, he wished she wouldn't stay here. He would hardly ever see her if she did. Only once or twice a year, when he brought prisoners in for trial.

"Go on with you," Mrs. Finney said. "I've got to start my flapjack batter."

"Yes ma'am. Thank you." He took the basket and hustled out the back door.

Early risers were opening their shops or harnessing their teams for the day's work, but overall, the town seemed much quieter than it had the day before. Freeland hurried to the marshal's office and found Benny Lassiter sitting at Duffield's desk, leaning back in the chair with his booted feet on the desktop.

"Morning," Freeland said. "All quiet?"

"Yup." Benny lowered his feet to the floor with a thud. "The marshal went home a couple hours ago to get some sleep."

"I brought breakfast for Miss Wade," Freeland said. "Is she up?"

"Haven't seen her." Benny reached out and tweaked the checked napkin that covered the basket. "Smells good."

"Keep out of that!" Freeland held the basket away from Benny, though he knew it held enough provisions for at least four people.

"Oh, don't wake the snakes," Benny said. "She's yonder." He jerked his head toward the closed door to Duffield's room.

Freeland went over to the door and tapped lightly then listened.

"Yes?" came Carmela's wary voice.

"It's me. Freeland. I brought you something to eat."

A moment later, the bolt slid and the door opened. Carmela, a bit puffy-eyed but looking fit to go calling, peered out at him. "You brought breakfast?"

He nodded. "From Mrs. Finney. I spent the night there, and she insisted."

"How kind of her." She opened the door wider. "There's a little table in here, or do you want to eat on the marshal's desk?"

"In here's fine," Freeland said. "There's enough for Benny, too, if you don't mind."

Carmela smiled, as though relieved they would have a chaperone. "Please invite him."

Freeland turned and nodded to the deputy. "Come on in, Benny. If you're quick, you can eat some real food before they bring that slop over from the tavern for the prisoners."

"Their food ain't that bad," Benny said, but he rose and entered the now cramped room.

"Fetch the stool," Freeland said.

Soon the three of them were seated, and Carmela unpacked Mrs. Finney's bounty on the cleared nightstand. Benny went to the main room to pour coffee for himself and Freeland.

"Oh, she sent tea." Carmela face softened as she sniffed the brew. "She's such a thoughtful woman."

Freeland had barely offered a blessing when the prisoners' breakfast arrived. Benny sighed and went to help distribute the rations.

"So, the crowd didn't come back," Carmela said.

"No, and I don't think anyone bothered the doc either." Freeland opened the jar of jelly and fished a spoon from the basket. "Want some?"

"Yes, please. Mrs. Finney makes the best apple jelly I've ever tasted."

"Good morning!" Marshal Duffield's large form nearly filled the doorway. His eyes were shadowed underneath, but that was the only sign he gave of not getting enough rest.

Freeland jumped up. "Howdy, Marshal. Have you had breakfast?"

"No, I haven't."

"Well, have a seat," Freeland said, giving him Benny's plate.

"Thank you. Miss Wade, I trust your night was tolerable?"

"Yes, reasonably peaceful."

Duffield nodded. "I don't see any reason to keep you here, unless you feel unsafe."

"I think I'd like to go back to the boardinghouse." She threw Freeland an anxious glance. "Unless Buck Chard is going to make a fuss."

"Mrs. Finney sent him packing last night," Freeland said. "I think you're safe there."

Benny came to the doorway. "Oh Marshal, I'm glad you're here. One of them outlaws says he feels poorly and needs to see the doctor again."

Duffield sighed, took a bite of his biscuit, sipped the coffee from Benny's cup, and pushed to his feet. "Always something," he muttered as he left the room.

In the quiet, Freeland and Carmela looked at each other. Freeland wanted to smile, but the thought of him leaving for Tucson and her staying behind made him feel all droopy inside.

She opened her mouth as if to speak when the outer door of the office opened and a feminine voice called, "Hello?"

Freeland rose and hurried into the main room. A young woman stood uncertainly on the threshold, a basket over her arm.

"Hello, ma'am," Freeland said.

"I'm Rilla Landis. I heard Miss Wade spent the night here for safety, and I brought her breakfast."

Carmela came to the door of the small room and smiled broadly. "Rilla! How kind of you. Please come in." She gave her friend a quick hug and led her to the chamber where they had their breakfast set out.

"Oh my, you've got aplenty," Rilla said.

"Never too much with all the men who come and go here," Carmela said. "Won't you join us? I guess you know Deputy McKay."

"Not really," Rilla said, eyeing him cautiously.

Carmela soon made the introductions, and they decided to move the meal out to the marshal's desk after all, so they would have more room. Carmela gathered plates and Freeland's basket, while he moved the stool and chairs, and he settled once more to eat with Rilla and Carmela about the desk. The two women pushed more food on him until soon Freeland had so much bacon, biscuits, eggs, ham, and cornpone on his plate that he doubted he could eat it all.

"So, you think you'll stay on with Mrs. Finney?" Rilla asked Carmela.

"I. . .don't really know what else to do."

"You can come live with me." Rilla grasped her arm. "If you don't want to live at my pa's place, we could rent a room together. I could get a job in town."

"Thank you. That might be nice. But Mrs. Finney wishes me to stay with her." Carmela hesitated. "I'm still not sure about staying in this town. Some of the people are very bitter against me. I keep wondering if I should just leave. But I don't know where I'd go."

"Your uncle. . ." Rilla raised her eyebrows.

"He's gone," Carmela said. "I'm on my own now."

Rilla nodded.

"I think I'll stay with Mrs. Finney, at least for a few days, and ask the Lord what I should do." Carmela's smile seemed more determined than happy. "If only I knew a place where I could go and live peacefully, without folks getting all upset."

"Well, you think on it," Rilla said.

When they had eaten, Rilla extracted a promise from Carmela to keep her advised of her plans and then left for home. After the chaos of collecting the prisoners' breakfast dishes was done, Freeland told the marshal he would escort Miss Wade back to the boardinghouse.

"All right," Duffield said, "but I may need you later. We're going to transfer a couple of these hoodlums out of here."

"I'll be back in an hour," Freeland promised.

Duffield nodded. "Good day, Miss Wade. If you have any trouble, you send for me and my men, you hear?"

"Thank you. I will."

They went outside and began the walk to Mrs. Finney's. Freeland realized that between the two of them, they now knew quite a few people in town. It seemed every other passerby had a word for one of them or at least a tip of the hat.

He wanted to know if she truly wished to stay here in Prescott. She hadn't sounded that way, really. But she might want to be on her own, be independent. She'd said other times that she'd never had a chance to do that. So far as Freeland knew, most women didn't want to live on their own. Men did, sure, but. . .but what did he know about women, anyway?

"People seem friendlier today," Carmela said.

"Yes." Freeland wondered how he was ever going to find a chance to talk to her. The people they encountered on the way made the walk too distracting for a conversation. But if he waited until they reached Mrs. Finney's, the landlady would want a full account of Carmela's stay at the jail. Finally, he drew her aside, where a sizable oak tree had somehow escaped being chopped down for firewood or lumber and now shadowed a vacant lot.

"Carmela, stop here a minute," he said. "I want to talk to you."

She complied and stood beneath the oak's branches, looking up at him expectantly. "What is it?"

"What you said to Rilla a while ago—about wanting a place where you could go and live peacefully. . ."

Carmela nodded.

"Well, I don't know if Tucson could be considered a peaceful place. In fact, since the war, it's been kind of a mess. A lot of Southern sympathizers and more than our share of army deserters seem to think it's a good place to settle."

Carmela frowned at him, and he realized he wasn't making a very good case for his town.

"What I mean is, it might not be the ideal place, but it's where I live, and it's where I work, and. . .well, I wondered if you'd consider coming back to Tucson and staying there with me and my ma. She'd love to have you, and—"

Carmela cocked her head to one side. "Do you think I could get a job there? I couldn't just board with you and your mother without paying something."

"Oh, I—that's not exactly what I meant." He hauled in a deep breath. This wasn't going the way he had hoped. "I was thinking. . . Well, that is. . ."

Her dark eyes took on a troubled cast, but otherwise she was beautiful, and that in itself made it hard for Freeland to concentrate. He gathered his courage in both hands and opened his mouth again. "I was hoping you'd marry me."

♥

Carmela's heart leaped at Freeland's words. It was what she had hoped for these last few days, but she had decided it was too much to expect. Her heart pounded. He wouldn't say something like that if he didn't mean it, would he?

"I. . ." She caught her breath and tried again. "Are you sure?"

His face softened, and his anxiety seemed to melt. "Of course I'm sure."

"But what about. . ."

"The people who wanted you arrested?"

Carmela shook her head. "I meant the ink on my face. And what I did with Uncle Silas. All of it."

Freeland's eyes widened, and slowly he smiled. "This may sound strange, but for a little while I forgot all about the tattoos."

She put a hand up to her chin. "They're still there, aren't they? I haven't seen a mirror today. . ."

"Oh, they're still there. But I guess I don't notice them anymore. And they are getting faint. I bet they'd be gone by the time we got to Tucson. . .if you want to, that is."

"Maybe people won't recognize me when they're gone." Her voice quivered, and she looked to him for assurance.

"If they do, I'll be right there with you to help you explain things."

Such love and joy welled up inside Carmela that she could barely contain it. She reached out to touch his arm, below the basket handle, and realized she was trembling.

"Thank you. That sounds truly wonderful. But I'm not sure it's enough, Freeland."

He swallowed hard. "I know you don't want to have to do what someone else tells you all the time. I get that. You spent a lot of years at your uncle's beck and call. But I wouldn't make you do anything like speaking or—or anything you didn't like doing. I promise."

Carmela pressed her lips together and looked deep into his eyes. He was such a good man. And right now, she had him scared to death. She didn't like having that power over him.

"That's not what I meant. Not at all."

"Well, what is it, then?"

"Respect and kindness are good things, Freeland. I appreciate those. But I want to marry a man who truly. . .loves me. I thought before that I could do without it, but no one's truly loved me since my parents died. I want. . .I want a man I love, who will love me in return for the rest of my life."

Freeland's fretful expression faded, and his smile grew. He set down Mrs. Finney's basket and put his hands on her shoulders. "I do, Carmela. It's not something that's easy for a man to say the first time, but I do love you."

Her joy spilled over in a little laugh. "Then I say yes, because I love you, too. Yes, I'll marry you."

His grasp on her shoulders tightened. "You won't regret it." She wondered if he would lean down and kiss her at last.

"Hey Deppity," a man called from the street. "Whatcha up to?"

Freeland's face flushed. "Come on. Let's get back to Mrs. Finney's. She might let us use her parlor, where there aren't any clodheads."

Carmela smiled. That sounded like a good idea to her. Freeland picked up the basket, and she slipped her hand through his other arm. "Mrs. Finney likes you. I believe she'll allow you to call on me."

Epilogue

Three months later

*C*armela walked the short distance from the McKay house to Freeland's tiny office. The sun beat mercilessly, causing her cotton dress and chemise to stick to her. She had known it would be hot, but August in Tucson exceeded her imaginings when it came to discomfort. The month was nearly over, but Freeland had warned her that September might not be much cooler.

Her mother-in-law had taught her to use an outdoor oven and to do her baking early, before the sun rose high. Even so, Carmela found the afternoons nearly unbearable.

And yet, in spite of the searing heat, this summer had been the happiest of her life. Mrs. McKay had welcomed her as the daughter she'd never had, and the people of the town seemed to like Freeland and respect him. They didn't hesitate to extend their friendship to Carmela, and no one had ever brought up the subject of her feigned captivity.

She stepped inside the marshal's office, but the shade of the building didn't do much to relieve the heat. Freeland sat at the battered desk, his top two shirt buttons undone and his sleeves rolled up beyond his elbows.

"Hi. I brought your dinner."

Freeland smiled and stood. "Let's take it down to the river. We might get a breeze there."

"That sounds good. You don't have any prisoners today?"

"Nope. Had two drunks last night, but I turned 'em loose this morning." Freeland reached for his hat.

The door opened before they could reach it, and a dusty, trail-weary man with a gleaming badge on his chest stood in the doorway.

"Benny!" Freeland hurried forward to shake his hand. "You remember Benny Lassiter, Carmela?"

"Of course." She smiled. "How nice to see you again."

"What brings you down here?" Freeland asked.

Benny grimaced and shook his head. "You know they're talking again about moving the capital down here?"

"Oh yes, there's nothing else to talk about, seems." Freeland frowned.

Carmela knew his feelings, and she also wasn't sure that moving the capital would be the best thing for Arizona. And while it would make some things handier for her and Freeland, she wasn't sure about setting up the territorial government so close to the Mexican border.

"So the marshal sent me down to scout out locations for his office if we have to move it." Benny looked around. "This one sure ain't big enough."

"No, it's not," Freeland said, "and we've only got one cell. I reckon we'll have to build a new jail."

Benny nodded. "That's what he's afeared of. Well, I've got a bunch of papers to deliver, but the marshal told me to be sure and let you know what he heard about Miss Wade—that is, Mrs. McKay's—uncle."

Carmela caught her breath. "You've had word of Uncle Silas in Prescott?"

Benny nodded. "The marshal had a letter from an old friend of his in Missouri. The man's a congressman now. Well, he said Silas Holden is the sensation of St. Louis, or he was a month or so ago."

"But—" Carmela stared at him. How could he carry on without her? As much as she hated to bring up the subject of her past, she was curious.

"What's he up to?" Freeland asked, with a quick glance at her. He stepped closer to her and rested a comforting hand on her back.

"Well, he's apparently filling some speaking engagements he had set up for you, ma'am," Benny said.

"Yes," she said slowly. "We were supposed to go back by train after we went to California, and I know he had scheduled events in Jefferson and St. Louis, then on into Illinois."

"Well, he's talking to the crowds instead of you," Benny said.

Carmela felt faint. "Surely not about me!"

"No ma'am. The way the marshal heard it, Holden's doing lectures on his 'Ordeal with an Outlaw Gang'."

Speechless, Carmela turned to her husband.

Freeland's lips twitched. "Doggone if he's not creative. I'll give him that. Benny, if you don't have other plans, why don't you stop at our house for supper tonight?"

"I'd like that," Benny said. "Thanks. I'll catch you up on the doings with the Pima and the Apache."

"You do that." Freeland smiled down at Carmela. "Now, sweetheart, let's get our picnic. I'm about to starve."

Carmela let out her breath and found she was able to smile back. "That sounds like a fine idea, Mr. McKay." She took his free hand and walked out with him into the harsh sun.

Susan Page Davis is the author of more than sixty Christian novels and novellas, which have sold more than 1.5 million copies. Her historical novels have won numerous awards, including the Carol Award, the Will Rogers Medallion for Western Fiction, and the Inspirational Readers' Choice Contest. She has also been a finalist in the More than Magic Contest and Willa Literary Awards. She lives in western Kentucky with her husband. She's the mother of six and grandmother of ten. Visit her website at: www.susanpagedavis.com.